THE TURBULENT TRAIL

THE TURBULENT TRAIL

MIKE THOMPSON

THORNDIKE PRESS

A part of Gale, Cengage Learning

GALE
CENGAGE Learning·

Farmington Hills, Mich • San Francisco • New York • Waterville, Maine
Meriden, Conn • Mason, Ohio • Chicago

GALE
CENGAGE Learning·

LIBRARY OF CONGRESS CATALOGING-IN-PUBLICATION DATA

Names: Thompson, Mike, approximately 1942– author.
Title: The turbulent trail / by Mike Thompson.
Description: Large print edition. | Waterville, Maine : Thorndike Press, a part of Gale, Cengage Learning, 2017. | Series: Thorndike Press large print western
Identifiers: LCCN 2017007709| ISBN 9781432839369 (hardcover) | ISBN 1432839365 (hardcover)
Subjects: LCSH: Cowboys—Fiction. | Cattle drives—Fiction. | Large type books. | BISAC: FICTION / Historical. | FICTION / Action & Adventure. | GSAFD: Western stories. | Adventure fiction.
Classification: LCC PS3620.H6839 T87 2017 | DDC 813/.6—dc23
LC record available at https://lccn.loc.gov/2017007709

Published in 2017 by arrangement with Mike Thompson

Printed in the United States of America
1 2 3 4 5 6 7 21 20 19 18 17

To my dear, departed mother, Wanda Thompson, who gave me my first cap gun, signed my rotten report cards and figured this cowboy thing would pay off someday. To my friend Orv Mayer, who laughs at my bad jokes and appreciates my writing; Greg Holverson, my old horse-trading partner, who refrained from laughing, most of the time, when I got thrown off a horse; and Doctor Larry Wilson, who gives me medical advice for my writing. To all the good folks who dance at The House of Fifi DuBois on Wednesday nights here in San Angelo. To Tiffany Schofield, Hazel Rumney, the greatest editor in the world, Tracey Matthews, and Nivette Jackaway, the ladies from Five Star who have been such a great help with another of my literary endeavors. Most of all to my wife and best friend, Ruthie, the woman who is patient and understanding, puts up with all my cowboy art and gear, does a super job of in-house editing, is a tough critic who speaks her mind, a great cook and the finest dance partner in Texas. With Ruthie, life is a constant adventure!

CHAPTER ONE

Charlie Deegan looked out across the darkened yard of the Yuma Territorial Prison and then leaned his head to the far side of the door so he could see the dimly lit corner guard tower. Just before sunrise was the coolest part of the day and the strap-iron slats that made up the cell door were soothing against his cheek. He lived in a cell across from the portal opening into the west yard. He knew that by mid-afternoon these same metal slats would be warm and exposed metal in the courtyard hot to the touch, even with his blacksmith shop-calloused hands. The adobe-plastered walls were twenty-two feet high, eight feet thick at the base and tapered to a five-foot-wide walk on the top for the wandering guards. By ten o'clock, the far wall was heated from the sun and by noon, the dirt and sand that made up the floor on this side of the prison yard came into the direct overhead light of the blistering Arizona sun. The yard would fill with shimmering heat waves that danced off the walls and drifted upward into the cloudless sky. When six o'clock rolled around and all the prisoners lined up to go into the mess hall for supper, the sun would slowly slip down behind the west wall and the yard would be covered with a maze of shadows. It would still be hotter than hell, but the dancing heat waves were harder to see. He knew this scenario by heart because he had been in the Yuma Territorial Prison for one year.

Before coming to the door, he had knelt on his bunk and used a pencil stub to make a diagonal slash across six vertical lines. *Another week.* He looked down the sets of lines on the whitewashed wall. He knew the number and there was no reason to count them. In front of the first group of lines was a date: *13 July 1890.* After the line he had just drawn, he wrote another number: *13 July 1891. Today I've been in here one year. Why in the hell did I ever do this to myself?* How many times during the past year, had he asked himself the same question?

He ran a finger around the inside of a small square between the metal slats of the cell door. "I can't take this for another nine years. Dead or alive, I'm gonna get outta here. I'll escape or be carried out in a bag to be buried down on Cemetery Hill. One way or another, today's the day," he said softly.

Three years earlier, at the age of nineteen, Charlie Deegan had joined the army to escape the dull life of his family's grocery business in Chicago. He trained as an infantry soldier and was sent to Fort Yuma, Arizona Territory, as his assignment. The fort was situated on a hill across the Colorado River from the Fort Yuma Quartermaster Depot that consisted of offices, docks and warehouses where the riverboats loaded supplies for the trip westward. On the hill above the docks was the Yuma Territorial Prison and behind and below that was the town of Yuma.

Yuma was a typical Mexican border town. It contained a courthouse and jail, churches, several stores, saloons and blacksmith shops. It had a railroad bridge over the Colorado River that could be opened by turning to allow the riverboats to pass. Most of the homes were made of adobe or sticks and mud. Many of them had ramadas, gardens, stables and corrals. Cottonwood and mesquite trees grew along the river.

The insufferable heat, along with poor

military living conditions and boredom brought on by long periods of seemingly senseless, mundane military routines, led the soldiers to spend most of their off-duty time in the saloons and whorehouses of Yuma and other small communities in the area. The tequila and mescal were much cheaper than the *gringo* whiskey and the flashing eyes of the *señoritas* would melt the heart of any man, especially one who had a pocket full of coins and a belly full of Mexican liquor.

Deegan began hiding bottles of tequila and mescal in the stables and storehouses so he could steal an occasional drink to help him forget how miserable his life had become. Liquor on the post was illegal and he knew better than to hide any in his personal area.

The one thing he enjoyed and seemed to maintain through all of his problems was his ability to shoot a rifle. He had been on marksmanship teams ever since he joined the army.

"Your shooting won me twenty dollars yesterday, Deegan," the first sergeant told him. "If I'd had more I'd a bet it. You must've been born with that ability to shoot a rifle. I've been in this man's army a helluva long time and you're one a the best shots I ever seen."

"The boys are putting together a little kitty to bet on ya at the range tomorrow," Corporal Murphy stated, with his thick Irish brogue. "I'd be a thinkin' a little extra rest might be a good thing, wouldn't it, First Sergeant? That, and a little extra practice time?"

"I was thinking the same thing, Corporal. Put Private Deegan on early guard duty. No, better yet, take him off guard duty tonight. He can make it up later."

"Maybe if he wins us enough tomorrow, he can be left off guard duty for a while," Murphy added with a laugh. "I heard the captain braggin' him up to some of the other officers this morning. I'd not be a bit surprised if the good captain wasn't laying down a wager or two himself on the shooting abilities of Private Deegan here."

As good as Deegan was with a rifle, he was as bad with a pistol. For some unknown reason he could not seem to hit anything over twenty feet away with a pistol.

Over time, the shaking of his hands, caused by the amount of cheap liquor he was drinking, seemed to be taking away his ability to shoot well and he was forced to quit doing the one thing he had always enjoyed about the army. He found he wasn't as popular as he had been when he was making a little extra money for the other troopers. This became another excuse for him to drink. There were days he actually wished he were home in Chicago working in the family grocery. He started drinking earlier in the day to help the hours pass and most afternoons were nothing but a drunken blur. When all of his hidden bottles were empty, or he couldn't find any of them, he would sneak down for a drink or two at the little adobe shack in the high bushes along the river that served as a soldier's bar.

The mescal made him ornery and mean and he would fight with anyone over the slightest provocation. In the beginning, Deegan won most of his fights, but he quickly began to lose more than he won and the ravages of the fights began to show on his face. An army doctor had removed most of the bone from his flattened nose, making it soft and pliable as a slice of cucumber. Scar tissue carved lines through his eyebrows and little ridges and valleys around his eyes and on his lips and chin. His right eye developed a permanent squint from an improperly set broken cheekbone and his hands and fingers were scarred and bent. From a single look, a person got the immediate impression Charlie Deegan was a brawler and not a man to mess with.

Even after nights of drinking, whoring and fighting, and no matter how bad he felt, he somehow always managed to appear at the morning formations. Standing there, he inevitably heard comments from the other soldiers as to how bad he looked, how much they had seen him drink or detailed descriptions of the fights he had been in the night before. This attention was like a badge of honor and gave him inner satisfaction. These formations became his personal award ceremonies and he was proud to attend them.

". . . shoulda seen Deegan last night. He put away a big corporal from C Troop . . ."

". . . Deegan musta drunk three bottles a that stuff."

". . . there's three of them on the floor before Deegan was through."

". . . and Deegan just kept getting up for more. Yes sirree, he's a brawler, he is."

The evening retreat formations were a sign that it was time to fall back into another alcoholic oblivion. Eventually, the retreat formations weren't a sign of anything to Deegan because the whole day was an alcoholic blur.

Deegan hid more bottles of Mexican liquor and slipped off to the adobe shack by the river earlier and earlier. The pain from the hangovers and fights would eventually fade with enough booze, but the pain in his mind from knowing what he was becoming wouldn't leave his thoughts. He tried to work out solutions to the problem, but was usually drunk before he came up with any answers.

One afternoon he broke a last remaining cardinal rule and didn't bother to return to the fort for retreat. Instead, he caught the ferry across the river to Yuma and wandered from bar to bar, getting drunker and drunker. He passed out with his head and shoulders lying on a table and was groggily awakened by a whore's hand in his pants pocket. His besotted brain soon realized the whore was looking for money, not his manhood, and he grabbed her wrist and twisted. "What'n hell ya lookin' for?" he demanded in a slurred voice and twisted harder.

She screamed and several of the men at the bar turned to watch and then laugh as she tried to pull her wrist free of his grip. Still struggling, she managed to scratch his face with her other hand.

Deegan let go of her wrist, wiped his hand across the scratches, looked at the blood and backhanded her across the face.

She dropped to her knees on the dirt floor,

her hand came from under her dress with a small knife and her eyes narrowed with anger. "You *gringo peeg!*" she screamed and began cursing him in Spanish. She slashed out with the knife and cut a neat slit across the thigh of his pants that quickly darkened with blood running out and down onto his boot. She leaped to her feet, swinging the knife in wide arcs in front of her.

Deegan leaned down and put his hand over the cut as if trying to stop the blood. "Bitch," he muttered as he glanced down at the redness running from between his fingers.

She slashed again, cutting his shirtsleeve, and blood ran down his arm and mixed with the blood on his leg.

Deegan became amazingly sober as he backed away from the woman and her waving knife. The back of his legs hit a chair and he reached around without looking and swung it up in front of him.

The woman thrust the knife in a short arc and a small curl of wood flew from the leg of the chair. *"Peeg, gringo peeg, peeg, gringo peeg,"* she chanted, slashing with the knife.

Deegan poked the legs of the chair to keep her at a distance as she swung the blade and another curl of wood flipped from the chair leg. He retreated and when the woman

15

lunged forward, he spun the chair, hitting the back of her knife hand sharply with one of the legs.

She screamed from pain and the knife dropped to the hard dirt floor between them. She rubbed her hand, glanced down at the knife and quickly back up at him, the hatred in her eyes changing to fear.

He smiled wickedly as he advanced, poking the chair legs at her. "You shouldn't a cut me, s*eñorita*. I don't like being cut, especially by a damned Mexican *whore*!" he shouted as he stooped and grabbed the knife from the floor.

One of the men at the bar laughed and, almost nonchalantly, swung a bottle to smash down on the top of Deegan's head. Glass and tequila formed a quick, lopsided halo above him and immediately became a shower of liquor and glass as his knees buckled; he folded over the chair and crashed to the floor.

The man who hit Deegan stepped forward, kicked the chair away and slammed a boot into his ribs, lifting his body slightly from the floor. He leaned down, grabbed the back of Deegan's collar, hoisted him up and, as he lifted, brought the jagged neck of the broken bottle down toward his face.

Deegan grabbed the man's wrist above the

bottle and the blade of the knife reflected briefly in the dim light as Deegan drove it up into the man's groin, twisted and pulled it free.

The man screamed as he released Deegan's collar, dropped to his knees and grabbed the bloody knife wound below the buckle of his gun belt.

Deegan managed to get to his knees and, with both hands, drive the knife into the man's chest.

The man's eyes widened with pain as he clutched at Deegan's hands.

Deegan shook the knife free of the man's hands and sat back on his heels as he watched him sag and flop backwards onto the floor.

The man's eyes rolled upward, he coughed and blood bubbled from his lips as he died, clutching a wad of his bloody shirt.

The bar was hushed, then pandemonium broke loose as the whore screamed and threw herself on the body of the dead man.

All the men at the bar charged and Deegan managed to slash three of them before he was beaten unconscious.

The sheriff saw the commotion as they carried Deegan out onto the street in search of a place to dispense quick justice and hang him. He ran toward the crowd, firing his pistol in the air.

When Deegan regained consciousness and managed to see something through his badly swollen eyelids, it was his own purple hand hanging above him from a chain pulled through a rusty metal ring in the adobe wall. His fingers looked like little fat colored sausages bunched on top of the chain. His arm was pale and dirty with the remnants of a shirtsleeve stuck to it with dried blood. He tried to move his fingers and a jolt of pain shot down the length of his arm. He groaned as he grasped the chain with his free hand and pulled himself up on the wall until his shoulder was even with his hand. He slowly lifted his hand and eased the pressure of it in the chain. The blood in his arm and hand began to circulate again and he felt a rush of pain in his hand from every beat of his heart.

As Deegan waited for the agony in his hand and arm to subside, the fingers of his free hand gingerly explored the damage to his face. He felt the hard, puckered edges and scabs of fresh cuts on his forehead, nose, cheeks and chin where he had been kicked and punched on the floor in the cantina. Three front teeth were loose behind his puffy lips and an assortment of walnut-sized lumps covered his face and head. He peered through his swollen eyes and saw his fingers were getting closer to their natural size and color. His ribs hurt with every breath and the pounding pain in his head grew as he tried to remember the events of the afternoon and evening.

I'd probably be better off if they'd killed me, he thought. *God! I killed a man back in the cantina! They'll hang me!*

CHAPTER TWO

Charlie Deegan had been wrong; they did not hang him. Two weeks later, he was given a bad-conduct discharge from the army and sentenced to ten years in the Yuma Territorial Prison for involuntary manslaughter.

"He's lucky the judge didn't string him up by the neck" was heard in the courtroom immediately after Deegan's sentence was pronounced.

Even before he was transferred up from the Yuma City Jail to the prison, the underground rumor mill had magnified Deegan's ability with his fists and a knife. He was one bad *hombre* and it was better to be his friend or stay out of his way.

The day Deegan processed into the prison, they questioned him, filled out the papers, shaved his head and face and took his photograph using a mirror on the side to get both the front and side of his face in the photo. The final step was to give him his number; Charlie Deegan became Yuma Territorial Prison prisoner number 1207. He changed into his new coarse black-and-gray-striped prison uniform and pulled on his socks and rough leather boots. In addition, he was issued a straw hat, an extra pair of trousers, two pairs of underwear, two pairs of socks, two handkerchiefs and two towels. He was also given a toothbrush, comb and tobacco. He carried these items in a canvas sack and draped an old gray military blanket and a thin straw-ticking mattress over his shoulder. A surly trustee prodded him from time to time with a large billy club as he walked him along the open, metal-slatted doors to his assigned cell. The cell doors were left open during the day to give the guards freedom for contraband inspection. An occasional face could be seen in the dark interior of a cell with a closed, locked door.

"Sonsabitches should be out on a work party," the trustee muttered and swung the club over Deegan's shoulder pointing toward the next open door.

Deegan stopped and looked back at the trustee, who nodded and jabbed his shoulder with the end of the club. He took a deep breath and stepped through the narrow doorway into the cell that was to be his home for the next ten years.

The trustee muttered again, rapped his club on the door slats, turned and sauntered away, whistling and swinging his club in a short arc from the wrist thong.

Deegan looked around the empty cell with the stack of three bunks on each side and the strap iron wall separating it from the cell behind it that allowed air to pass through both rooms. Clothing and other items were stacked on the bunks or hung from the rails on the ends. He had been told during processing that he had to get along with his cellmates to maintain his health and his sanity and each small room had a pecking order. There were ticking mattresses on all six bunks, so he folded his on the bottom bunk, sat on it and slid the rest of his meager possessions into a corner. *I guess someone'll be along to tell me what to do.* He stared down at his new boots, then leaned back against the wall, closed his eyes and asked himself again, *How'd I do this to myself? This is gonna be a long ten years.*

Charlie Deegan was roused from a light sleep by a voice roaring in Spanish and a hard kick to the side of his leg. He swung himself upright and was knocked to the dirt

22

floor by a solid fist to the side of his head. He was kicked in the ribs twice before he managed to grab the ankle of the foot that was kicking him and roll under a bunk. He lifted and yanked the foot up to grind the shin onto the metal edge of the bunk and the kicker cried out and flopped backward to land on the bunk across the narrow aisle.

Deegan rolled out from under the bunk, leaped to his feet, growling with rage. His hands were a blur as he bent down and punched the man's face hard and fast several times.

The big man covered his bloody face and rolled to the wall at the back of the bunk.

One of the other men in the cell leaped forward and waved his arms in front of Deegan.

"No more, señor. You have beat him. Let him be."

"No man kicks me like a damned cur dog!" Deegan shouted as he leaned down and hit the man again. "No man, you hear, you bastard? No man kicks me."

Two of the other men in the cell grabbed him from behind and managed to pin his arms to his sides.

"It is finished, señor," the first man said. "You have beat him. Now you are *El Jeffe* of this cell. You are the chief."

Deegan relaxed and shook off the arms of the men behind him. "What do you mean, chief?"

"He was the boss of this cell until you beat him. Now you are *El Jeffe.* You are the boss, the headman. You make the rules now," one of the men answered.

"He's the rooster that ruled the roost," a skinny *gringo* chimed in. "We's all afraid a him so we done what he told us to do. You beat him so that makes you the rooster now."

Deegan took a deep breath and let it out slowly as he glared down at the man curled up at the back of the bunk. *Calm down,* he told himself as he looked at the three men staring at him. *Now's the time to let them know how bad I can be.* "How'd he get to be headman in this cell?" he asked. "Because of his size?"

"Diego has many friends in the prison, s*eñor.* He took our tobacco and money. If we did not do what he wanted, he said he would have us beaten or killed," one of the men answered.

"He has beaten all of us one time or more," a short Mexican added. "He is very big and strong, s*eñor.*"

"Do you know these other men who're supposed to be his friends?" Deegan asked.

24

"We seen him with some bad *hombres,*" the skinny gringo replied. "And we wasn't gonna take a chance on havin' any a them meetin' us in the shadows. Hell, it's bad enough him beating us when he wants. He's mean enough by hisself."

Deegan looked carefully at the faces of the three men, reached down, grabbed the big man's arm and roughly pulled him to the edge of the bunk. "Diego, you got friends in here, but I doubt if you could beat all of us by yourself. From now on you ain't gonna beat me or any of these men. You understand?"

The big Mexican glared up at him in hatred. "You will know who my friends are when they cut your throat, *gringo.* I will beat these little mice when I want and you will soon be just like them. You too will just be another little mouse."

Deegan was over six feet tall, but had to stare up into the man's eyes when he stood. He understood the main reason this Mexican controlled the cell . . . his size and his weight. He outweighed Deegan by at least forty pounds. Deegan nodded and hit the big man as hard as he could in the stomach.

The air exploded from Diego's mouth as he folded over, clutched his gut and moaned.

Deegan grabbed the big man's long greasy hair and smashed his knee up into his face.

Diego flipped back onto the edge of the bunk and slid to an unconscious heap on the floor.

"This's one damned mouse you're gonna have a hell of a time beating," he hissed and prodded Diego with his foot for emphasis. He stepped back and looked at the others. "This his bunk?" he asked, pointing to the bunk where Diego first attacked him.

"*Si, señor,*" one man answered. "The bottom bunks are best because hot air goes up to the top and sometimes there is a breeze through the door and the back wall. The mattress on that top bunk is his extra one. He takes it down and sleeps on both of them."

"Then, this is my bunk now," Deegan declared as he unfolded his mattress on top of the one already in place, smoothed it with his hands, straightened and motioned to the man on the floor. "Put him on the top bunk."

As two of the men lifted Diego from the floor, he began to stir and shook off their hands. "You are dead man, s*eñor!*" he shouted, wiping the back of his hand across the blood running into his mustache. "*A dead man.*"

Deegan stepped forward to stand toe-to-toe with him. "You won't be the first man who's tried to bury me," he said, his voice almost a whisper. "I'm in here for ten years because another pig like you tried to kill me and I cut his guts out. I ain't afraid of you or any of your friends. I don't die easy. Now, you pile a shit, you wanna try me again?"

The Mexican looked down into Deegan's eyes and at his scarred fighter's face. He slowly shook his head, wiped his dirty shirtsleeve across his bloody face, turned and walked out the open cell door muttering to himself.

Three of the men crowded around Deegan again.

"You an' me an' Bob, over there, are the *gringos* in this here cell," the thin white man told him pointing to a man standing by the door, staring blankly out into the corridor. "Bob ain't right in the head an' they's gonna put him someplace else one of these days." He stuck out his hand. "I'm Jim Warren. Folks call me Skinny Jim."

Deegan gave his hand a firm shake. "Charlie Deegan, but I guess you already knew that."

"Yup, you been talked about for a couple days now. Word is you're a scrapper and you just showed you can handle yourself, but

27

that big sumbitch's gonna come back in here and try to kill ya for sure."

Deegan took a deep breath and shook his head. "I don't think so. He had all you buffaloed, but now that someone's put him in his place, he won't do anything. I've known his kind before."

"What about his friends, s*eñor*?" a man asked.

"You think he'll bring a bunch of others over here to fight? You said they're bad *hombres,* but do you think they'll fight all of us? He called you mice. You gonna be mice?"

"I would rather be a live mouse, s*eñor,* rather than a dead *man,"* one of the Mexicans stated.

"After this show, you're gonna have to spend all yer time in here watching yer back," Skinny Jim stated. "How about you an' me step out into the yard an' talk a spell?" He put his hand on the shoulder of the man looking out into the corridor. "You come too, Bob."

They walked down the corridor, into the yard, and Skinny Jim led them over into a shaded corner.

Skinny Jim nodded at Bob. "When he got here a couple a months ago he was a bit foggy in the head, but he told me what'd happened to him. About six months ago, he and a friend robbed a bank down in Somerton and hid out for a while. They needed supplies, so they went into a town up north of here where the sheriff recognized them from the posters. There was a shoot-out, and his partner was killed. Bob gave up. The sheriff questioned Bob and, for no reason, smashed him in the face with the stock of a shotgun. When Bob came to he had some broken teeth, his eyes's swelled almost shut, a busted nose and he was sure some of the bones in his face was broke. His mind keeps gettin' further and further away. The prison doc is gettin' him transferred to a hospital."

"A lawman did that to him?"

"Yeah, I'll think of his name in a minute. I speak good Mexican, but I pretend I don't *hablar* any of it. Helps me hear 'bout things I ain't supposed to know 'bout. I'll be watchin' your back."

Deegan looked at the man and smiled. "I appreciate that, Jim."

"Since you an' me are the only two *gringos* got our wits about us, I guess we'd best be covering for each other. Bob, here, don't really know what's going on anymore."

"Agreed."

"You been assigned a place to work yet?"

"No."

"Me an' Bob work in the adobe brickyard. It ain't a bad place to work. We make adobe bricks they use on the new wall over there an' some of them is sold to the people in town. We gits to keep a bit of that money for ourselves. Hope you get to work with us."

"Sounds good to me."

"Baca."

"What?"

"Baca . . . that's the name of the sheriff hit Bob with the shotgun."

"Do you know where it was?"

"No, Bob wasn't sure. He just knew it was north of here someplace."

"What're you in here for?"

"Too many cattle."

"What?"

"Seems I had an assortment of brands wasn't mine. I'm lucky they didn't string me up."

Deegan nodded and chuckled.

"I'll be in here for another two years."

"I'm doing ten. What time do they lock us down for the night?"

"Nine o'clock."

"I'd best stay out here until nine, then."

"An' sleep with one eye open. Diego'll try again."

CHAPTER THREE

Just before nine o'clock Charlie Deegan returned to his cell, dimly lit by a lone electric bulb in the corridor and light filtering in through the portal to the west yard. The others were already in their bunks, all facing the wall. It was as if they didn't want to see what would happen in the cell once the door was locked. Deegan quickly studied Diego's back, sat down on his bunk, put his face in his hands and thought about his first day in prison. *I gotta lot to learn.* He looked up when a guard rested a lantern on one of the crossbars of the cell door.

"Hands," the guard called.

Deegan saw each of the men hold up a hand without turning over.

"When he don't see faces," Skinny Jim said, "he calls for hands to make sure they ain't nobody put a dummy in his bunk an' hid out someplace. He don't do it most nights."

There was a loud clang as the bar dropped across the door and a lock snapped in place. Minutes later a whistle gave a long mournful blast that echoed off the walls signaling that the day was officially over.

"How many times a day they blow that damned thing?" Deegan asked Skinny Jim in the bunk above him.

"It blows at six in the morning to git us up an' head us to chow," Jim answered. "Blows again at seven for us to go to work. Noon to go eat an' one o'clock to git back to work. Six it tell us to go eat an' nine it lets us know lockdown's done an' so's the day. Three short blasts over an' over's a signal someone's broke out or someone's missin'."

Deegan found a small rock on the floor, turned and made a short vertical line on the whitewashed wall behind his bunk. "One," he said softly. "One day."

Hours later, Deegan lay on his back with his hands behind his head and listened to the men snoring as he waited for the big man on the top bunk to make his move. He knew the man would have to do something to try to regain control of the cell. There was the sound of weight shifting above and then silence.

There was a soft thud as Diego's feet hit

the cell floor and he dropped to his knees and began to flail wildly at Deegan.

A fist smashed onto Deegan's forehead and stars burst before his eyes. He rolled off the bunk, landed a punch on Diego's mashed nose and watched him sag back against the door.

Diego pushed off the door and his arm was a blur when it whirled up from his side.

Deegan staggered back from a hard impact on his shoulder and brought his hands up to protect his face. *Bastard's got something in a sock.* He swayed back and forth looking for an opening to throw a punch.

Diego's arm swung again.

Deegan dodged back and threw his arm up to deflect the swinging sock, but it glanced off his head above his ear and he saw stars again.

"Fight!" someone shouted.

Deegan tried to clear his head. His blinking eyes made out the shape of the big man settled back against the steel-slatted door. He glanced around, saw all the men sitting on their bunks, but knew that no one was going to help him. If they helped the wrong man and the other man won, their life in the cell would be miserable.

"Fight, fight!" reverberated in the cell block.

Diego pushed off the door and his arm moved forward.

Deegan's hand shot out, grabbed the sock, yanked it toward him and landed a sharp jab on Diego's cheek.

The corridor brightened by lighting of more electric bulbs; the air filled with the sounds of whistles, shouts and banging of guards' clubs on the doors as they ran to the fight.

Diego shook his head and sagged back against the door.

Deegan landed another fist on Diego's bloody face, wrenched the sock from his hand and drew it back to swing. *You'll kill him.* He dropped the sock and sat back onto a bunk as a group of guards gathered outside the door. He tentatively touched a finger to the lump growing under his eye and then put a finger into the trickle of blood running down the side of his head and dripping from his chin. He stared at his bloody hands, flexed his fingers, wiped them on his shirt and looked up to see Diego slide down the door and settle onto the floor. "I beat you, you bastard," he muttered as he waited for the guards.

Captain Grant Knotts, the head guard, signaled to raise the locking bar, the door swung open and Diego flopped back into the corridor. Knotts squatted, looked quickly at the groggy convict, stood and pointed his club at Deegan. "Seems to me your name's Deegan and this's your first day in here and you already got problems. Maybe a little time in the snake den'll learn you a thing or two about prison life."

Skinny Jim jumped down from his bunk and raised his hands. "Hold on a minute, Cap'n, the big fella laying out in the hall started this ruckus. That's his sock there on the floor."

Knotts gave him a curious look, stepped into the cell, picked up the dirty sock by the toe and a fist-sized rock plopped to the floor. "Damn, that coulda killed a man."

Skinny Jim nodded. "I'd say that was his plan, Cap'n."

Everyone was silent as Knotts looked at the men sitting on their bunks and the men looking through the barred wall at the back of the cell. "Anybody got anything to say?"

Several of the men shook their heads, but no one spoke.

"All right, both of these men go to the snake den for the night. Chain the man out in the hall inside the cage and chain Deegan, here, to the outside on the far side. I don't want them to be able to reach each other. Superintendent Ingalls can decide what to do with them in the morning. Get the man in the hall on his feet and take him over there first."

When the escort guards returned, Knotts pointed his club. "All right, Deegan, let's go."

They crossed the yard, passed a heavy steel door and stepped into a short tunnel blasted out of solid caliche. Light at the far end of the tunnel was from a lantern hanging on the small strap-steel cage in the center of a fifteen-by-fifteen rock room that smelled strongly of urine.

Diego sat on the floor leaning against the steel wall inside the cage. A rusty chain ran through the wall to a large steel cuff locked on his ankle. He held a bloody rag under his nose, glared at them with hateful, swollen eyes and muttered as they approached.

Knotts pointed to the far side with his club. "Over there, Deegan."

Deegan sat down on the cold stone and was quickly chained and cuffed.

"I'll be back in the morning," Knotts said as he lifted the lantern from the hook and handed it to a guard. "Let's go. These boys need to get a little sleep." Their footsteps and the light faded down the tunnel. The outside steel door made a loud clang and it was silent in the room.

"You are a dead man, *pendejo,*" Diego shouted, followed by a long string of Spanish cursing.

Deegan laughed, "Be sure to bring your sock, asshole."

Chapter Four

The hinges of the steel door screeched open and a shaft of light filled the short tunnel to the outside. "Time to get up, boys," Grant Knotts shouted and his shadow blocked most of the light in the tunnel. Knotts, dressed in his gray uniform, was a man of medium height, with a deeply lined face, narrow eyes, brown-and-gray hair and a heavy mustache that covered his bad teeth. He was a man who never smiled.

Deegan and Diego blinked at the soft light filtering into the room.

"Deegan, you'll be seeing the superintendent first." Knotts bent down and opened the lock on Deegan's leg cuff. "Let's go."

Deegan rose slowly to his feet and stretched. "Bed's a bit hard," he joked.

Knotts prodded him with his club. "Save your damned humor for the superintendent. He could use a laugh."

They crossed the yard and Knotts pointed

to the bathhouse door. "Go in there and get cleaned up. You look damned rough this morning. I'll get you a clean uniform and a towel. I don't want the super to see you looking like that. There's soap in there. We got an hour. Go."

I think he's covering his ass with the super-intendent. Deegan walked into the bath-house, shrugged out of his dirty shirt, looked at it, tossed it onto a bench, sat down and pulled off his boots and socks. He stood, walked to the urinal trough, relieved himself and continued on to a metal mirror mounted on the wall. He leaned forward, examined his face and chuckled weakly, "Damn, you look like your old drinking days." His jaw and head had a shadow of brown hair, the welt under his eye looked like a small plum and a trail of dried blood from the scabbed, walnut-sized lump above his ear wandered down the side of his cheek to his chin. He gingerly touched the welt, felt the lump, looked at the large bruise on his shoulder and sighed, "I guess it coulda been worse . . ." He pulled the suspenders off his shoulders, stepped out of his pants, kicked them onto the bench and walked into the shower.

When he came out, he found a uniform and a towel draped on the bench. He shook out the shirt and saw 1207 stenciled in black on a white stripe on the shirt. The same number was on the pants and the towel. He dried himself, wrapped his first uniform in the towel, glanced at himself in the mirror, smiled and walked to the door.

Knotts stepped out of the shadows and motioned toward the chow hall. "We got time, so git yourself something to eat. You look considerably better now that you've cleaned up."

The mess hall was empty except for the kitchen crew cleaning up. One of them looked at Deegan. "Next chow call is noon."

"Find something for him," Knotts said from behind him.

The man looked at the guard, shrugged and motioned for Deegan to follow him. He disappeared into the kitchen and returned with a tin cup in his hand. "Ain't a lot left."

Deegan took the cup and looked down into it. "Gruel?"

The man nodded. "Told ya there ain't a lot left." He pointed to a cloth-covered bundle on the counter. "Biscuits."

Deegan lifted a corner, pulled out a biscuit and rapped it on the rim of the cup. "Damn, how old are these?"

The man shrugged. "A day or two, I guess. Dunk it in yer gruel. It'll soften it up some."

Deegan shook his head, sat down at a table, pushed the biscuit down into the liquid, took a bite and grimaced. "People actually eat this crap?"

Knotts, with two steaming cups of coffee, slipped onto the bench across the table and pushed one across to Deegan. "Maybe it'll burn your tongue enough so you can't taste that."

"Why're you being easy on me?" Deegan asked.

Knotts looked at him with narrowed eyes and took a sip of coffee. "I don't like Diego. I don't trust the big bastard. We know he's taking tobacco and money from the other cons and he hangs out with the incorrigibles. I've got a few things on him, but I want to make sure I've got enough on him to let Superintendent Ingalls have me put him back in the snake den for a few more days. I wanna make his life in here miserable as possible."

"So going easy on me'll make his life miserable?" Deegan took a bite from his dripping biscuit.

Knotts shrugged. "You're off to a bad start here, you know. Your second day inside the walls and the super is gonna have a talk with you. That ain't good. You wanna keep a low profile. Be a small target. Understand?"

41

Deegan nodded, finished his biscuit, pushed the gruel away and lifted the cup of coffee. "What about my talk with the superintendent?"

"Be respectful and give short answers." Knotts pulled a watch out his pocket and glanced at it. "Time to go."

Superintendent Frank Ingalls was a nattily dressed, short fireplug of a man with a halo of gray hair and a matching mustache. He only needed his round, steel-rimmed glasses for reading, so they always rode down on his nose. He looked up from the papers on his desk at the sound of a loud knock on his office door, wiped his long, constantly sweating forehead and cleared his throat. "Enter."

The door opened and Knotts stepped into the room. "I have inmate Charles Deegan to meet with you, sir."

"Come in, Captain."

Knotts reached back through the doorway and pulled Deegan, in handcuffs and leg chains, into the room.

"I won't need you in here for this, Captain Knotts. I have your report," Ingalls said. "So will you please wait in the outer office? I'll call you when I've finished or if I need you."

42

"Yessir."

The door closed and Ingalls pointed to a chair across from his desk. "Sit."

Deegan shuffled to the chair and sat down.

Ingalls squared a small stack of papers in front of him. "So, inmate Deegan, I read Knott's report, now give me your version of last night."

Deegan quickly recounted the previous night's events and sat back in his chair.

Ingalls nodded. "Your story matches what I've been told in the report. Diego will be spending a few more days in the dark cell and then he'll be moved. I won't take a chance on having the two of you sleeping in the same cell." He rose to his feet, walked to the window and stood with his hands clasped behind his back as he gazed out on the prison yard.

Deegan nervously watched the man until he returned, sat down and tapped the stack of papers. "I have your official records here, inmate Deegan. Your problems all seem to be related to alcohol." He sat back, steepled his fingers and gazed over them at Deegan. "Liquor, booze, beer, demon rum, hooch, firewater, John Barleycorn . . ." His voice trailed off. "Do you like the taste of liquor, inmate Deegan?"

Deegan shrugged. "I guess so."

Ingalls smiled. "Well, inmate Deegan, you've got ten years to get over it. Do you have a work assignment yet?"

"No, sir, but I'd like to work at the adobe yard making bricks."

Ingalls clapped his hands. "So be it, inmate Deegan, the blacksmith shop it is. Now get out of here and remember that I know who you are."

"That's not what I . . ."

"Knotts," Ingalls shouted.

The door opened immediately. "Take inmate Deegan to the blacksmith shop and introduce him to Fred. Bring inmate Diego here at one o'clock."

"Yessir."

When the superintendent's door closed, Knotts unlocked Deegan's handcuffs and handed him the key ring. "You take off the leg irons."

Deegan squatted, unlocked the chains, pulled them free, stood, draped the chains over his shoulders and handed Knotts the keys. "What now?"

"You heard the super, let's go meet Fred. He's been here since the second year the place was open. Eighteen seventy-seven. He's inmate number one-oh-five."

"Damn."

"Oh yeah, one more thing, the super is

gonna give Diego another six days in the snake den and sixty days of solitary confinement. He ain't gonna be your friend when he gets out."

"I didn't know he was my friend now."

The clanging of the hammers grew louder as they approached the prison blacksmith shop. The front half was open and the back had a low roof over the smoke-blackened adobe walls. Sparks and noise flew around the three shirtless, sweaty men as they beat sledgehammers on glowing strips of steel. The glow in a hearth grew brighter as a small man, with wide shoulders, pumped the handle of the bellows beside it. He lifted a pair of tongs out revealing a bright, glowing horseshoe that he laid on an anvil and slammed a hammer down on. A shower of sparks filled the air from the impact.

They approached the small man. "Fred," Knotts shouted. "Fred!" He called out several times before reaching out and tapping him on the shoulder.

Startled, the little man spun, raising the hammer toward them. His face was craggy and darkened from years of forge smoke. His squinty eyes peered through dirty, steel-rimmed glasses. He lowered the hammer and broke into a toothless grin. "Why, howdy, Mister Knotts, ya shouldn't be sneakin' up on a man like that."

Knotts motioned toward the yard. "Let's go out there so we can talk, Fred."

"Fred, this is Charlie Deegan, Charlie, this is Fred."

The men shook hands and Deegan felt the strength of the man's hand.

"Charlie's gonna be working for you," Knotts said. "Tell him what he'll be doing here."

"You got any smithy experience, Charlie?" Fred asked.

"None."

"That's all right. It don't take a man long to understand what he's a gonna be doin'. We's building metal bunks for all the cells and we got 'bout ten to do. That's 'bout sixty more bunks. We're gittin' rid a the old wooden ones because a bedbugs and roaches."

Deegan gave him a questioning look.

"You haven't been here long enough to know 'bout the bugs," he said. "The bedbugs hide in the cracks and joints in the wooden bunks and there's no way to get rid of 'em. Metal bunks is the only answer an' 'sides that, it gives men something to work on. Lemme tell ya 'bout the bugs in here, Charlie. We got bedbugs, roaches, ants an' skeeters. They all got a bite that'll make ya

46

itch. A little axle grease helps that some. Them roaches is so big the guards tell they seen 'em sneaking out in the desert an' mating with the javelinas." Fred slapped his thighs and doubled over with roars of laughter.

Knotts shook his head. "Ol' Fred just loves to tell that story."

Over the years, the hair regulations at Yuma Territorial Prison had varied, but mustaches were allowed as long as the hair on the man's head was a reasonable length.

As the days went by Deegan decided a large mustache would help to keep his *bad hombre* reputation alive. The story of his fight with Diego and the night attack on his first day broadened with each telling and his stature among the inmates grew. Also, he had met with the superintendent and been given no further punishment. Maybe he had an in with *the man.* He was no longer worried about Diego or anyone who might pose a threat to his health or safety. He now had men watching his back and they reported anything to him to gain his favor.

As time went on Deegan's face lost its alcohol puffiness and the skin on his face, hands and arms darkened from his work in the blacksmith shop. The scars on his face were less noticeably colored. His blue eyes bunched with wrinkles from squinting in the smoke of the forge and his brown hair and mustache were neatly trimmed. Deegan was becoming a model prisoner.

CHAPTER FIVE

Skinny Jim sidled up to Charlie Deegan in the main yard. "I missed chow because I's helpin' pack up Bob's stuff in the cell."

"They really gonna move him at last?"

"Yeah, some kinda hospital over in Phoenix."

"Probably for the best."

"Yeah. When I's in the yard a while ago I heard Diego talkin' mex to one a his bean-eater *amigos* out in the hall. He told that fella he's gonna git ya in the yard at night. He said he's gonna do it by hisself 'cause a what you done to his reputation as a bad-ass. The generators went down last night an' they ain't sure how long it'll be before they gits the parts needed to fix them. There ain't no moon for the next few nights so that means it'll be darker'n the devil's heart in the yard at night."

"Well, we both know the big sumbitch has waited a long time for a chance like this."

Skinny Jim nodded. "He said he knows yer in the library every night an' ya gits back to the cell before the nine o'clock lockdown."

"Studying law books, trying to find a way outta here, but I ain't found anything yet."

He was also studying maps and making plans for his escape.

"You want I should come over an' walk back with ya?"

Deegan chuckled. "No, Skinny, I appreciate the offer, but this is between me and Diego. It's gotta happen one of these days. I guess this is as good a time as any. Thank you, my friend."

Charlie Deegan glanced up at the clock on the wall of the library. It was eight minutes to nine and the trustee librarian was starting to blow out the lanterns on the tables. *It's Diego's first night to make a try for me.* He patted his shirt pocket to feel the folded Arizona Territory map page he had torn from the atlas earlier and closed the big leather-covered law book. He couldn't remember anything he'd read, but he'd made up his mind that if it came down to it, he would kill Diego. Now he pondered his possible alternatives when he left the library. Was Diego waiting outside tonight?

50

Would he really be alone? What would he have for a weapon? He was sure he could beat Diego if he knew he was coming at him. He took a deep breath and slowly let it out. *Time to go.* He stood, put the book back on a shelf and glanced at the clock again.

"C'mon, Deegan," the trustee said, and blew out another lantern. "Be glad when they get the electricity back on. These lanterns are a real pain in the ass."

"That clock right, Marty?" Deegan asked.

"Yeah, I checked it at six. You find that loophole in the law yet?"

Deegan chuckled. "No, but I got ten years to look for it. Best step on out because I only got about six or seven minutes to get to my cell." He stepped outside, knelt off to the side of the meager fan of light from the open door and worked with adjusting something with one of his boots. As he stood up, he brushed his hands on his pants and dropped handfuls of sandy dirt into his pockets. As his eyes adjusted to the light, he slowly looked around the yard trying to see anything in the maze of shadows. There were several lanterns giving out small circles of weak light hanging in the yard and a lantern in each archway to the cell blocks. He looked up at the guard towers, tonight

51

only lit by kerosene lanterns. "The guards won't be walking on the top of those dark walls tonight," he mumbled, as his eyes continued to search. *Stay in the middle of the yard.*

The fan of light beside him disappeared. The trustee librarian walked out, pulled the door shut and snapped a lock into the hasp. He said, "Good night, Charlie, I'm sure I'll see you tomorrow night. We got about four minutes before the whistle."

Deegan rolled his shoulders and flexed his hands. He had that feeling he was being watched. *Go. He's out there waiting.* It was silent, with no movement in the yard. *Move.* His eyes darted from side to side as he took his first tentative steps toward the dimly lit archway that led to the corridor of his cell. He stopped when he heard a gruff voice, "I am here, little mouse."

Deegan stopped and slowly turned in the direction of the voice from the shadows.

"I am going to step on you one last time, *raton chicito,* little mouse."

"Did you bring your sock, asshole?" Deegan asked. He could now see the bulky outline of Diego back in the darkness and he glanced quickly around to see if there was anyone else with him. "Did you bring all your friends?"

52

Diego chuckled. "No, I will do it myself. I thought about this time when I was in the snake den and when I was in solitary confinement. It gave me good thoughts."

"Well, step out here and let's get this over," Deegan said. "Come and do your worst."

Diego moved more into the dim light and Deegan could see something in his hand.

"You got a knife, Diego?"

Diego chuckled and stepped closer, tossing the long knife from hand to hand. "*Si,* I stole it from the kitchen a long time ago and have been saving it to cut out your guts, little mouse."

Deegan motioned with his hands for Diego to come at him and then lowered his hands to his sides and into his pockets.

Diego lunged and Deegan hit his face with handfuls of dirt, sending it into his eyes, nose, and mouth.

Diego threw his hands up to his face and the knife in his hand cut a gash up his forehead into his hairline.

Deegan grabbed the man's knife hand, twisted it and drove the blade up under Diego's ribs. He gave a choked groan and sagged heavily against Deegan, who pushed him aside, stepped back and watched him crumple to the ground. He reached down, straightened the man's legs, rolled him against the wall and looked around to see if there was anybody near them. *Alone.* He turned, dashed to the lighted archway of his cell block. As he passed under the lantern, he looked down at his hands and saw his right hand covered with blood. *Damn, I should have wiped it on his shirt.* Shaking his head, he ran to his dark cell.

"That you, Charlie?" Skinny Jimmy asked, as Deegan flopped onto his bunk.

"Yeah." Deegan fought to calm his breathing as the nine o'clock whistle blew a long mournful blast. "Just made it." His heart was pounding and his hands began to tremble. *What am I gonna do about the blood on my hand?*

"Find anything in the law books tonight?" Skinny Jim asked, as he sat up and swung his legs off the bunk above.

"No." *Calm down, calm down.* He took the map from his shirt pocket and slid it into the end of his straw mattress.

"I guess you didn't see Diego on the way in."

"Nope, didn't see anybody."

A guard carrying a lantern held it high in the door and looked inside. "Five in here now. That right?"

The three Mexicans laying on the bunks

54

across the cell raised their hands without turning from the wall.

"That's right," Deegan answered.

"Five," Skinny Jim repeated.

They heard the bar drop across the door, the lock snap and the light disappeared down the corridor.

Deegan put his trembling bloody hand out in front of him. *Now what?* "Is there a water jug in here tonight?"

"I didn't see one. Damn, this was Bob's week to fill and bring one in. I'll take his place tomorrow. Guess we'll just be thirsty tonight."

"Okay. Damn, I gotta take a piss." Deegan stood up, found the slop bucket, moved it into a corner, unbuttoned his pants and urinated on his bloody hand. He buttoned his pants, pulled a red bandanna from his pocket, thoroughly wiped his hand, dropped the bandanna into the bucket and used his foot to push it closer to the door. He stuck his hands into his pockets, filled his palms with the remaining dirt, sat on his bunk, vigorously rubbed his hands together and let the dirt fall to the floor. He lay back on his bunk and waited for his heartbeat to slow down.

The yard whistle gave three short blasts,

followed by a short pause and three more blasts.

"What's that for?" Deegan asked, as the horn repeated the signal.

"Damn," Skinny Jim said as he sat up and swung his legs over the edge of the bunk. "That's the escape signal. Somebody must've made a run for it."

Charlie Deegan lay back on his bunk, put his arm over his eyes and listened to the three continuing blasts. *How long before they find the body?*

CHAPTER SIX

A lantern lit the spaces in the cell door and Captain Knotts and two guards peered into the dimly lit room.

"Deegan," Knotts called. "Git up, the superintendent wants to see you."

Deegan rolled over, stretched and feigned waking up. "Huh?" he mumbled and stretched again. "What the hell time is it?"

"It's a little before ten. C'mon git up."

Deegan sat on the edge of his bunk and reached for his boots. He heard the bar being raised, the door open and the two guards grabbed him under his arms and rushed him out the door. "Damn," he said, "take it easy, I don't have my boots on yet."

Frank Ingalls sat at his desk looking at the long knife on a sheet of paper in front of him. The thin blade was black with dried blood. He looked up at the knock on his door. "Enter," he called.

Captain Knotts stepped into the room. "I have inmate Deegan here, sir."

"Bring him in."

Deegan shuffled into the room in leg chains and handcuffs, with a guard on each arm.

"Up here," Ingalls said, and pointed to the front of his desk.

Deegan stood looking down at Ingalls, who wasn't his usual dapper self.

Ingalls steepled his fingers and glared over the tops of them at Deegan. It was almost a minute before he lowered his hands and spoke. "Well, inmate Deegan, it's been a while since I've seen you, officially I mean. I'm told you've been almost a model prisoner."

Deegan looked at him with no expression on his face.

Ingalls picked up the knife from his desk. "This was taken out of a man tonight who you had a run-in with your first day in here, Diego Lopez."

Deegan looked at the knife, but showed no reaction.

"Did you kill him?" Ingalls asked, waving the knife at Deegan.

Deegan shook his head. "No, sir."

"Where were you tonight?"

"At the library, sir."

"Yes, that's been verified. You left a little before nine."

"I had to get back for lockdown."

"Did you go directly back to your cell?"

"Yes, sir."

"Did you happen to meet anyone on the way?"

"No, sir."

Ingalls leaned back in his chair. "This knife was reported missing from the mess hall several weeks ago. From the butcher section, to be exact."

"I don't work in the mess hall."

"I'm well aware of where you work, inmate Deegan."

"Another thing, sir, if I wanted to kill Diego, I could've made a usable weapon in the blacksmith shop."

Ingalls sat forward in his chair and nodded. "That's a good point."

"I think if a list was made of people who'd kill Diego, I'd probably be a ways down on it. He'd been bullying men a long time before I got here. What about those hard cases he hangs out and lives with? Maybe he crossed someone in his cell? It probably wouldn't take much to get one of them to stick him."

Knotts walked back into the room. "Excuse me, sir, but I talked to Deegan's cell

59

mates and they all verify he was in a little before lockdown."

The superintendent nodded. "Diego's face was covered with dirt. It was in his nose and mouth, so I would say that someone threw it in his face during the fight. Also, whoever killed him would have a lot of blood on his hands and clothing. Diego has a deep cut on his forehead, so his killer might have attacked him first. Do you have any blood or cuts on you, Deegan? Show us your hands and take off your shirt. I want Captain Knotts to take a good look at you."

Deegan held out his hands and turned them slowly for Knotts.

Knotts grasped Deegan's wrists, studied his hands and shook his head. "No blood."

Deegan held up his handcuffs. "It's a little tough to take my shirt off with these on."

Knotts signaled one of the guards to remove Deegan's cuffs.

Deegan quickly unbuttoned his shirt, pulled it off and spread his arms. "No cuts."

Knotts walked around Deegan, looking him over closely. "He's clean, sir. Not a cut or bruise on him."

Ingalls rose to his feet. "Take him back to his cell, but I may want to talk to him more in the morning."

■ ■ ■ ■

Charlie Deegan was never called back to Superintendent Ingalls's office.

CHAPTER SEVEN

Charlie Deegan, his shapeless hat pulled down low over his eyes, slouched in the shadow of the walls of the quadrangle, called the Bull Pen, at the front of the prison and watched the men loading the garbage wagon behind the mess hall. From time to time, he glanced up at the guard tower on the corner of the wall beside the main gate, known as the sally port. The sally port was a large concrete archway with two large sets of strap-iron gates with one-foot openings between the steel straps. There was a room between the sets of gates large enough to enclose a wagon and a team of mules when both sets of gates were closed. During routine jobs such as the garbage run, the inside door was rarely closed. A fact Deegan was counting on.

Unless someone was foolish enough to try to go over the wall, the sally port was the only way in or out of Yuma Territorial

Prison. The garbage wagon rolled through that barred space in the wall every morning at exactly seven o'clock. If Deegan had a watch, he could have set it by the movement of the garbage wagon and the gate.

Deegan nonchalantly stepped from the shadows and walked across the yard whistling tunelessly, kicking at small stones and secretly studying everything from under the brim of his hat. He stopped to scratch the nose of one of the mules hitched to the high-sided garbage wagon. He patted the animal's neck as he walked along beside it and drummed his knuckles on the side of the wagon as he continued on his way. One of the guards glared at him and he quickly dropped his hand and shoved it into his pocket. He stopped a short distance from the rear of the wagon and knelt to check the leather thongs around the ankles of his boots, hidden by his pant legs. He had stolen a rein from the stables earlier, cut it in half and tied the pieces tightly around his boot ankles. His boots were going to be an intricate part of his escape attempt. He stood, rubbed his thumb across the folded map in his shirt pocket and, with seeming indifference, watched the two men loading the barrels of garbage onto the wagon.

■ ■ ■ ■

For more than a month, Deegan had repeated this process with minor variations each day so as not to make himself conspicuous. Outside of the rotation of the men loading the barrels in the wagon, there was little change in the daily routine. The waste hauled to the river on a daily basis was from the buckets that served as toilet facilities in the cells at night. One galvanized slop bucket per six-man cell was emptied into the larger wooden barrels on the wagon each morning.

Wooden barrels were used because if they fell into the river they would float and be recoverable.

Although the prison had a water system, there was a constant problem with the muddy water of the Colorado River plugging it. A favorite comment was that the water was too thick to drink and too thin to plow. It had been decided that rather than having to work on a clogged pipe of cell sewage, it was easier to continue the old system of hauling it down the hill and dumping it in the river. There was always an average of six wooden garbage barrels on the daily trip and those barrels were usually only about half full. A half-full barrel was easier to lift and less likely to slop or dump the smelly contents into the bottom of the wagon or onto the men lifting it. The wagon could hold up to ten barrels if they were pushed tightly together, but most days there was a large space in the front of the wagon bed because the men didn't push the barrels any further into the wagon than necessary to get the tailgate hooked in place.

The waste from the mess hall, prison shops and trash cans was hauled down to the prison dump on Fridays.

Two convicts, in leg chains, would ride the half mile down the hill to the dumping spot on the river, sitting facing to the rear, under the driver's seat. A guard, armed with a shotgun, rode above them with the driver. At the river, the barrels were emptied, reloaded into the wagon and all returned to the prison to repeat the process the next day. On Saturday, the wagon would stop at the river and the convicts would haul the barrels into the water and scrub them. Garbage duty on Saturday could be considered a reward to some convicts. The water of the Colorado River, coming down from the mountains, was cool and refreshing and a man could wash himself while he scrubbed the barrels. It was much better than the silt-filled, smelly water that ended up in the bathhouse in the prison. Water for cooking came from a large settling tank on the prison grounds and was considered drinkable.

Deegan walked back past the wagon, stepped into the shadows beside the cell block nearest the gate and watched the convicts milling around waiting to go to their assigned duties at the sound of the seven o'clock whistle. He knelt, checked his leather thongs again, and picked up several silver-dollar-sized stones. He watched as the garbage-duty cons slid the tailgate down into its slot on the back of the loaded wagon, dropped the hooks in place, crawled over the side, tied restraining ropes around the barrels and settled in the front of the wagon bed.

The gray uniformed driver and a fat guard climbed up onto the seat. The driver gathered the reins and the guard swung the shotgun so it almost casually pointed into the back of the wagon.

Deegan stepped back deeper into the shadows, looked up for the placement of the guards above, and threw the first stone high into the air. It soared upward and fell rapidly toward a group of convicts gathered in the shade of the wall near the gate. The stone hit a man on the top of his shoulder. He cried out, grabbed his shoulder and spun to see who had hit him. His shout caused the others in the group to turn and look at him.

Deegan threw a second stone high into the air and watched it drop among the men.

Another man yelled, swore and pushed a man standing beside him.

Deegan threw two rocks at once and watched them fall into the cluster of men who were now shoving and shouting at each other.

A punch was thrown and a con went down. Another man, kicked in the shin, began to dance around and took an awkward swing at a man who was laughing at him. Within a matter of seconds, most of the convicts in the yard were fighting. Dust rose in the still air and shrill cursing echoed off the walls. The guards rushed out of the tower by the gate, trotted down the walkway on the top of the wall, pointed their rifles into the melee and shouted for the men to stop fighting. Guards from the other towers quickly joined them.

"Shoot a couple of 'em!" one guard shouted.

"Naw, let the bastards fight. It's good

exercise fer them and they's a hell of a lot more peaceful when they's tired," a guard shouted back.

Several of the other guards nodded and laughed.

"Yeah, let them git it outta their systems, let them fight."

The mules pulling the garbage wagon began to dance and strain in their traces and the driver sawed on the reins calling softly to try to control them.

The guards at the gate glanced nervously from the garbage wagon to the clock in the gatehouse and then back at the fighting convicts. One of them, armed with a shot-gun, started to run to the fight, but a guard in the tower waved him away.

Deegan stood in the shadows watching the men in the dusty yard yelling, slugging and kicking at each other.

The mules lunged and fought the reins at the outside door of the sallyport as the driver struggled to control them.

The driver shouted to the guard standing inside the sally port, "If you don't open those damned gates and let us out, we're gonna have a hell of a mess here with these damned dancing mules and all the shit in these barrels. They don't like that fighting! It's close enough to seven to let us outta here. Open the damned gates!"

The guard on the wagon was no longer casual about his shotgun. One tap with the barrels on the shoulder of the nearest convict as he started to stand was enough to convince both men it was smart to sit down to watch the fighting.

The guard at the gate glanced over his shoulder at the clock, looked at the men fighting, the driver struggling to control the mules, shrugged and unlocked the gates. He swung them open and motioned for the driver to go through.

Deegan bolted from the shadows into the cloud of dust. All eyes were on the fighting men and no one saw him run and slide under the wagon as it started to move. He rolled onto his back, reached up and grabbed the front axle of the wagon. He was strong from his work in the blacksmith shop and held himself stiff so only the heels of his boot were dragging on the ground as the wagon began to roll out through the gates. He knew the only dangerous time for him to be spotted was when the wagon cleared the sally port and turned onto the road down from prison hill. If the guards in the main tower were watching the wagon there was a possibility they would spot him when the wagon was rolling parallel to it. If the mules were trotting or running fast enough there should be plenty of dust from their hooves and the wheels to conceal him.

The driver shouted, "Yeehaw, mules," slapped the reins on the animals' backs and they bolted through the gate to get away from the noise of the fighting and the wheels skidded sideways in the dirt as the driver turned the team onto the main road. There was plenty of dust and Charlie Deegan knew if he could hang on long enough, he would soon be free.

CHAPTER EIGHT

The guards in the guard tower barely glanced at the garbage wagon as it passed below. It was something that happened every day at this time. The exercise yard where the men were still fighting was much more entertaining.

The driver swore and fought to bring the mules under his control as they raced down the road. The fat guard, his shotgun waving over his head, tried to find something to hold on to as he bounced up and down on the seat. The convicts braced their hands up against the bottom of the seat to hold themselves in the wagon as putrid liquid began to slop up out of the bouncing barrels and rain down on them.

The speed and bouncing of the wagon made it harder and harder for Deegan to maintain his grip on the square wooden axle and he could no longer keep his body stiff enough to keep from slamming on the rocks and ruts of the road. He began to cough from the dust, but the drumming of the mule's hooves covered the sound. His shirt was torn and shredded down the back, the buttons of his suspenders had ripped off and his pants pulled down to his ankles by contact with the rutted surface.

The driver managed to bring the mules to a trot but Deegan's blacksmith-strong hands lost their grip; he thudded down onto his shoulders and flipped over backwards as the wagon passed over him. The dust settled around him as he lay in the middle of the road, spitting dirt from his mouth and blowing dust from his nose as he tried to regain his breath and get to his feet. He finally stood and glanced over his shoulder at the cloud of dust behind the wagon as it rolled away. He took a step and fell to his knees, tripped by his pants gathered around his ankles. He stood again, yanked his pants up, bunched them at his waist with one hand and started to run into a patch of brush.

The driver brought the mules to a panting walk when the fat guard glanced back over his shoulder to see a man rise up from the settling dust, fall, stand again, pull up his pants and run into the brush. For a fraction of a second, he wasn't sure what he was seeing and then with a reflex action, swung the shotgun back and fired both barrels at Deegan as he disappeared into the brush. "Escape!" the guard shouted as he fumbled in his pocket for more shells.

The roar of the shotgun spooked the tired mules; they bolted hard against their collars and the driver fought to control them again.

As he ran toward the river, Deegan heard the buckshot cutting through the brush around him before he heard the shot and the shout of the guard. He turned, crouched and dodged back toward the road. *They expect me to go to the river!* His heart was pounding in his ears as he dropped to his knees and listened to the fading sound of the driver cursing as he fought to control the mules.

"Whoa, you sons-a-bitches!" the driver shouted as he jerked the reins of the running animals. "Whoa, damnit! Whoa!"

The wagon tipped up on two wheels as it skidded around a curve and the fat guard, arms flailing, flipped through the air and landed hard on his back, knocking the wind from his lungs.

The two prisoners gave each other a knowing look, grabbed their leg chains and leaped over the side of the skidding wagon.

The barrels tipped and slammed up and

over the side of the tilting wagon, spewing a smelly trail of garbage and slop as they rolled and bounced out across the desert.

A front wheel snapped from the axle and the corner of the wagon fell, digging into the dirt, twisting the wagon in a tight circle and breaking the tongue free from the front of the wagon.

The driver threw the reins into the air and dived away from the spinning wagon.

The mules, hooves kicking high, ran faster and disappeared down the road in a cloud of dust.

The two convicts managed to pick themselves up from the rocks alongside the road and began hobbling off toward the river as fast as they could move in their leg chains.

Jack, the fat guard, struggled up onto his elbows, gasping for breath, spitting dirt, shaking his head and trying to clear his thoughts. He saw the two men in the gray-and-white-striped suits shuffling off and looked around for his shotgun. He spotted it lying in the sand, scrambled over, broke it open, thumbed out the empty shells, dropped new ones into the chambers, snapped the gun shut, cocked the hammers, swung it up toward the two running men and pulled the triggers. The ends of the barrels split open and peeled back in a cloud of flame, smoke and dust when the loads of buckshot hit the sand plugging them. Jack flopped backwards to lie in the road blinking his eyes and shaking his head as he looked up at the rolled-back ends of the barrels.

The muttering driver came limping back up the road, slapping the dirt from his gray kepi against his leg as he walked. He stopped, adjusted the cap on his head and peered down at the guard. "You dumb bastard, Jack, why'n the hell'd you shoot that damned shotgun for?" he shouted, shook his head and continued to walk back up the road toward the prison. "Damn it, I'll tell you something, Jack, this stink here ain't nothing like the smell's gonna be when the warden gets done chewing on yer ass."

Jack struggled to his feet, looked with disgust at the peeled barrels of the shotgun and started to throw it away. He shrugged as he remembered he had signed for it, swung it up onto his shoulder and trotted to catch the driver.

"Sid, there's three of 'em got away. I shot at the one who's standing in the road back there," he whined as he tried to match the driver's stride. "I mighta hit him 'fore he got to the river. He's runnin' in the brush when I shot at him." He held the damaged shotgun out in front of him. "My shotgun blew up when I shot at the other two."

The driver stopped and turned, eyes squinted in anger. "You dumb ass!" he shouted. "There was only two cons in the wagon, not three." To emphasize his anger, he punched Jack on the side of his jaw.

The fat guard dropped to land on the seat of his pants. He wiped tears from his eyes and rubbed his jaw as he blinked up at the driver. "Damnit, Sid, why'd you hit me like that?" he asked as he struggled to get to his feet. "There's three cons. That's why I shot the first time. I looked back up the road behind us and there's a con standing there in the dust cloud pulling his pants up. Them other two was still sittin' in the wagon."

"You been drinking that damned rotgut mescal again, Jack. Damnit, you promised me you wasn't gonna drink while you was working! Yer damned shotgun spooked the mules and I wasn't ready for it. Now you're telling me you were shooting at a con standing in the middle of the road pulling up his pants and the other two cons were still sitting in the wagon. Why'n the hell didn't I see him when we ran over him, Jack?" Sid's face was bright red as he gasped for breath. "What was that con pulling his pants up for? Was he taking a shit in the road and we ran over him?"

"There *was* a con standing in the middle a the road pullin' up his pants, Sid, I swear!"

Sid shook his head. "Now we got us a damned busted-up wagon, a damned runaway team a mules and two, or three, damned escaped prisoners to explain to the superintendent when we get back. I know about two of them, but you'll have to explain to the warden about the third one pulling up his pants in the middle a the road. You been drinking, Jack, and I ain't gonna cover for you this time. I outta just kick your ass up around your ears! There ain't any way we're gonna find them now so let's go back to the prison and they can get a search party out looking for them." He spit at the other man's feet, turned and strode off. After a few steps, he stopped and turned. "Yer gonna have to explain that damned blowed-up shotgun, too!"

"I'm sorry, Sid, I was just tryin' to stop them prisoners."

"Where's yer damned cap?"

Jack patted his sweaty, bald head. "It musta blowed away when I fell off the wagon," he answered sheepishly as he dug out a dirty hanky and wiped at his face. "I best go look for it."

"That damned cap's the least of yer worries right now. You best be coming back to the prison and helping me try to explain this whole mess you created out here." The driver shook his head and started up the road. He stopped and turned back. "An' for sure I wanna be there when you explain to the warden about that con pulling up his pants in the middle of the damned road. You been drinking, Jack!"

Jack nodded, then shook his head vigorously and gave his face a wipe. He trotted back, picked up his kepi, brushed the dust off the bill with his thumb, pulled it down tight on his head and trotted, huffing loudly, to catch up with Sid.

Charlie Deegan watched the backs of the gray uniformed men trudging up the road and quickly ran to the other side. *Those other two headed for the river. There's a standing reward of fifty dollars for any escaped prisoner and once the word's spread they'll have both sides of the river covered for miles. There's no way those two'll get very far in those leg chains.* He squinted as he gazed out into the endless desert. *Lucky for me they decided to take off. They'll be easy enough to find and it'll take the searchers off my trail for a while.* He looked down at his ragged clothes and shook his head. *Besides a man'd be a fool to try to get away out across the desert this time of year.*

Superintendent Captain M. M. McInerney stood with his hands clasped behind his back looking out his office window. He had replaced Ingalls less than nine weeks earlier and this was his first crisis.

The driver, Sid Woods, and the fat guard, Jack Gomez, stood across the room nervously staring at his back. Another man in a shirt and tie sat on the edge of the desk. The superintendent turned and crossed his arms on his chest. "Our headcount confirms there are three convicts missing, so Gomez, your story about the third man has credence."

Jack Gomez nodded and grinned at Woods. "I told you, *amigo.*"

Woods glared at him, but said nothing.

"They've already recaptured Estrada and Monroe. A man can't get very far in leg chains. The other man is Charles Deegan, doing ten years for involuntary manslaughter. Near as we figure he must've gotten out by hanging under the wagon while the fighting was going on in the yard. He probably had just fallen free when you spotted him, Gomez. Do you think you hit him?"

"I don't know, Superintendent. He was already in the brush when I shot at him."

"Oh, one more thing, Gomez, the cost of that shotgun will be coming out of your pay."

Gomez nodded, dejectedly. "*Si,* Superintendent."

Woods grinned.

"I've put out the word of the fifty-dollar reward, so I'm sure the locals and the Indians will be looking for him. I figure he'll head down into Mexico or over into California. No man is foolish enough to try to get across the desert this time of year. Now you two get out of here and write up your reports."

Both men came to attention, turned and pushed out through the door.

The superintendent nodded to the man sitting on his desk. "Bill, get me Deegan's booking photos so we can get started on the reward posters. I'll put a hundred dollars on his head on those posters. A little more incentive."

"I'll get them and take them into the print shop in Yuma," the man stated, standing up and crossing to the door.

CHAPTER NINE

Charlie Deegan rolled the smooth pebble around under his tongue as he sat and paused to rest in the shade of a large rock. *That old Indian trick with the rock works good. I'm not really too thirsty yet.* He studied the sun nearing the western horizon. *Sun should be set in a couple hours and it'll make it a lot cooler for walking. Gotta keep moving,* he told himself and pushed to his feet. *They'll have the dogs out by now. I hope the trail smell of those other two is stronger and they follow it. Maybe I should head back to the river and get in the water for a while. No, they'd expect that. Just keep moving.*

Deegan had been using the large rock formation known as Castle Dome as a point of reference for a northerly direction, but he could no longer see it because of a small chain of high rock hills in his path. *That little moon tonight won't give me much light to see Castle Dome. I'm gonna have to try to find my way by dead reckoning until I can see it again.*

The sun set, putting a dark curtain over the desert and the air became almost cool as Deegan trotted on across the desert. To save his strength he had set himself a pace of running a hundred paces and then walking a hundred paces. *I ain't sweating anymore.* He rubbed his hand across his face, slowed to a walk and began to count aloud again. "One, two, three . . ." He made dry spitting sounds and rolled the pebble under his tongue. *I guess I can only fool my body for so long . . .*

A full moon showed through the clouds, lighting his way as he walked along a ridge that faded into the darkness ahead of him. He paused to rest and listen for the sound of dogs. It was so quiet the only thing he could hear was his own breathing. He held his breath and the beating of his heart drummed in his ears. *I know I heard those damned dogs. How could they've gotten on my trail so fast? God, maybe I'm going in circles.* He looked for something to use as a point of reference. *Use the moon; you fool, use the moon.* He smiled as he looked up at the moon and then dropped his eyes to study the area around him.

He heard the distinct baying of dogs and

he trotted on until a deep wash cut across his path. He stepped to the edge and, in the dim moonlight, tried to gauge the distance to the far side. *It's not that far. You can make it.* Pacing back and forth, working up his nerve, he stepped back a short distance, turned and ran. He leaped high into the air and crashed forward to sprawl on the rocky ground on the far side. He quickly struggled to his feet. "That should slow them down for a while," he muttered and began to trot again.

The sky in the east was getting lighter and Deegan knew the sun would soon burst over the horizon and bring with it the heat of another day. He continued to make spitting noises as he trotted and wished for something to drink. The sounds of the dogs were getting louder.

". . . ninety-nine . . . one hundred," he mumbled and slowed to a walk. His trotting pace was now a forward stagger with steps not much longer than his walking pace. He stumbled and fell on palms and knees now raw from falling in the darkness. He knelt, his head hanging between his arms, breathing deeply and trying to will himself to get back up and keep moving.

Deegan eventually pushed himself up and began to stagger forward. "One . . . two . . .

three . . ."

He thought he could smell water. *Mind's playing tricks . . .*

The baying of the dogs was louder, but not as frequent. He stopped in the shadow of a rock to look back and saw a lone dog top a distant hill. Another dog topped the hill, followed by another and another until there was a line of them walking slowly down the slope. The dogs raised their heads from time to time and howled, but it was obvious they were very tired and dispirited.

A lone horseman appeared atop the ridge and sat watching the dogs strung out in a ragged line below. More horsemen joined him until there were six riders on the hill. One of them drank from a canteen and passed it to the next man. He drank and passed it on. A man on foot walked up but stood off alone and watched the others drink.

Deegan knew the man was an Indian by his dark skin, hair and sparse clothing. *He looks like one a the Apache scouts from Fort Yuma.* He watched as the Indian moved down the hill, passed through the slow-walking line of dogs and started toward him at an easy trot. *God, some of those red bastards are better than the damned dogs.*

Deegan licked his tongue over his dry,

cracked lips and wished for some of the contents of the canteen the men were passing. He sniffed the air and smelled moisture. *Damned mind's getting to me. I can smell wet sand again.* He turned to look at the riders and dogs. *I make them out to be about a half mile behind me.*

The Indian was nowhere in sight.

One of the men raised a pair of binoculars and Deegan dropped behind a rock. *Keep moving.* In a crouch, he scrambled along behind the outcropping and when he was sure he couldn't be seen, slowly stood until he could study the terrain ahead. The rocks were steep and he knew he couldn't go up the face of the hill without being seen. He noticed a dark cut in the rocks ahead that could be the narrow entrance to a canyon. He rubbed his hand across his face, licked his dry lips and started forward in an almost drunken shuffle. "One . . . two . . . three . . ."

When he staggered into the mouth of the canyon, the air felt cool and he sniffed. *Must be raining ahead.* He moved into the shadowed hall, looked at the steep walls and knew there was no way he could go up them to escape the dogs, riders or the Indian. ". . . ninety-eight . . . ninety-nine . . . one hundred." The smell of wet sand was stronger.

"Gotta be rainin' someplace nearby," he mumbled as he forced himself to drag his feet through the soft sand.

He stopped and heard wind moaning softly in the canyon. *They gotta be back there.* Lights were beginning to dance before his eyes. *What number was I on?* "Twenty . . . twenty . . . twenty . . . something," he whispered as he stared blankly at the sandy floor of the canyon.

Deegan frowned and rubbed his eyes because he thought he saw a trickle of water seeping slowly across the sand at a bend in the wall ahead. He blinked his eyes rapidly as it flowed toward him. The water was almost hypnotic as it moved like a snake across the sand and then over and around the toes of his torn boots. He felt the water seep in through the holes and caress his burning feet. He gazed upward, took a deep breath and looked back at his feet as if trying to believe the feeling. He knew he had to be dreaming. This was like no mirage he had ever seen. He wiggled his toes and smiled. He dropped to his knees, pushing his fingers through the trickle of water and scooped up wet sand. He rubbed it against his face and began to chuckle. He dropped to his chest and lowered his face into the water. He took small tentative sips as if he didn't believe it was really there and he was lying in it. It was gritty and he spit particles of sand from his tongue. He sat up, spewed a stream of water into the air, lifted handfuls of water to his face and began to laugh hysterically. The water was now almost a foot deep and moving faster.

He heard a roar and looked up to see a wall of water smash against the far rock wall, climb upward, then drop and turn to roll toward him. He stood and scrambled through the wet sand to dive into a pile of large rocks just as the water smashed over them. He was pummeled and bounced among the rocks until he managed to thrust his arm into a space and hold on. His lungs felt as if they would burst when he pulled his arm free and let the water push him to the surface. He coughed, sputtered and spit as he wildly looked for a place to get himself out of the rushing torrent.

I gotta stop myself before this water carries me to the men and the dogs. He floundered and tried to get control of his movements. He kicked hard to his left and managed to climb higher onto the rocks and pull himself from the water.

"I guess they'll be having the same problems downstream," he muttered as he studied his surroundings. *There's no way in hell those dogs'll be tracking me now.* He sat wiping water from his face as he watched the stream of muddy water move down the canyon. *This is the monsoon season and it's sure been raining in the mountains someplace near here.*

When the water level had gone down, Deegan pushed off the rocks and paddled against the ebbing current into the middle of the canyon. He tentatively touched his feet to the bottom several times until he was sure that he could safely stand and walk in the water. As he pushed upstream, the water slowly receded until it was only slowly running around his ankles. *It goes away as fast when it goes . . .*

He found a trail that led upward through a cut in the wall and began to climb. When he reached the top, he turned and surveyed the canyon below. *There ain't a dog alive that'll be able to follow me now.* He smiled as he looked into the freshly washed canyon far below.

A bullet ricocheted off a rock beside his shoulder, breaking his sense of self-assurance and he dropped flat. "Where the hell did that come from?" he asked as he crawled backward to the protection of the rocks. "How'n the hell'd they get up here so fast?"

He slowly moved his head forward until he could look for the origin of the bullet. There was no sign of movement. *They must've gotten to the high ground before the water got to them. Damned dogs'll be able to smell me again and they ain't that far away now.* He cautiously peeked around the rock again and a bullet smashed into it, showering his head with particles of stone. "Damn!"

Deegan scrambled backward until he was under the shadow of a rock big enough to give him cover when he stood up to run. He heard the dogs baying as he began to lope across the sand. "Those dogs sound about as tired as I feel right now," he panted as he glanced back to see if they were in sight.

The rocks were closer together and he dodged between them to keep out of sight of the man with the rifle. The ground was getting steeper and he painfully went down on all fours in places to keep moving uphill. He stopped and tried to catch his breath. *It's rough for me and it's gotta be hard as hell for the horses.* He made dry spitting sounds and listened to the blood pounding in his head as he looked back in the direction of the sound of the dogs. *It'd be a helluva lot easier if you just give up.* Bright lights danced behind his closed eyelids. "Then you'd get to spend time in the dark cell, that is if you make it *back* to the prison," he argued. "Get moving."

He crawled over a large pile of rocks, stopped for breath and felt one of the rocks move under his feet. *These'd make one helluva rockslide if I could get them started. It'd slow them down some if they were dodging rocks and stuff rolling down the mountain.* He heard the dogs baying as he studied the rocks and tentatively moved the loose one again with his foot. He leaned his back against a boulder and pushed his feet up against a larger rock. He closed his eyes, took a deep breath and concentrated all of his energy into his legs. He felt the rock move slightly. He took another deep breath and pushed again. It moved farther. Once more," he told himself and put all his remaining strength into the muscles of his legs.

The rock moved, tipped over the edge of the pile, bounced and slowly began to roll downhill.

Deegan slid down the rock he was leaning against and landed in a heap when the pressure on his legs vanished. He breathed deeply as he listened to the growing sound of the rocks bouncing and crashing down the side of the mountain.

He laughed weakly as he struggled to his feet and looked down at the thick cloud of dust and an occasional rock bouncing in it. *That'll hold them for a while.* He turned and began to struggle up the steep rocks. *I ain't going back to the dark cell.*

The screaming of an injured horse came up from behind him and Deegan nodded as he continued to pick his way through the rocks. *They ain't gonna be moving very fast now, they're gonna be watching for more falling rocks.* He heard the sound of a shot, the screaming of the horse ceased and the sound of the shot echoed through the rocks.

CHAPTER TEN

Charlie Deegan paused and smiled to himself as he moved over to another large rock, leaned his back against it and raised his feet onto a rock on the downhill side. *One more good rock slide'll make them cautious and hopefully slow them down good.* He grunted with exertion as he pushed with his legs and felt it begin to move. A little more pressure and it broke free and began to bounce down the mountainside. As before, it started other rocks rolling and soon the side of the mountain was a noisy, dusty jumble of tumbling rocks.

He sat quietly catching his breath for a minute as he watched the cascade of stone bouncing below, then pushed to his feet and continued his journey.

If they're smart, they're gonna go around this mountain and cut me off on the far side. He looked up the mountain, turned and started down, being cautious and keeping a watch for the trackers and their dogs, just in case they didn't think the way he thought they would think.

Passing through the area of the second avalanche, Deegan moved from rock to rock scanning the area for signs of movement. Nothing moved and he noticed buzzards making large, easy circles in the sky. "The horse," he told himself as he pushed out of the shade. "It doesn't take them long to find death."

The first buzzard touched down, hopped quickly over to the dead horse and tore a small chunk of flesh from the animal's nose. Another landed and joined him in the feast.

Deegan carefully scanned the area and saw no other sign of movement. *Time to see if they left anything I can use.* He walked down the slope to the dead horse and stood looking at it as shadows of the circling buzzards crossed the ground around him. The rider had pulled the saddle from the carcass of the horse and stood it on end in the shadow of a nearby rock before leaving to join the others. The bridle and a canteen hung from the saddle horn and, although he knew it was empty, Deegan walked over and lifted the canteen by the straps. *Nobody's fool enough to leave a full canteen behind.* He shook it before pulling the cork and tipping the neck to his mouth. Several drops of water ran onto his tongue and he savored the feeling and taste. *I'll keep this with me because there's gotta be water in the rocks after that flood through here.*

He looked for tracks or signs of the direction of the search party's movement as he pushed the cork into the canteen. *If they're gonna cut me off going down the other side, they'll have to go left or right or maybe they split up to go both directions,* he reasoned as he looked around at the ground. *So I guess the best way to go is straight ahead.*

Deegan reached the floor of the canyon and studied the damp sand for signs that the trackers had come down into it. It was smooth as far as he could see in any direction. *Looks like I was right and they circled on the high ground to cut me off. The best thing is to go back down the canyon below them. Those high walls'll make good cover.* He stepped out into the sand and began walking close to the canyon walls.

He traveled a short distance before he found water in a rock indentation. The dirt and sand had settled to the bottom leaving a clear and inviting pool. He slowly lowered his face into it and took a long, unhurried drink. He lifted his face, pushed the water from his mustache and quickly looked around. *Keep moving.* He pulled the cork from the canteen and pushed it down into the pool.

As the water gurgled into the canteen, his eyes moved up and down the canyon and then up the walls to the high rim across from him. A shadow appeared on the opposite wall and became the outline of a man on horseback. Deegan dropped the canteen and pressed his back to the stone. *My God, he's on the rim of the canyon right above me.* He looked straight up and saw only rocks above him. *There's enough of an overhang to give me cover from up there. I hope nobody's coming from the other side.* Another shadow moved up and then one more joined the lineup on the far canyon wall. The shadow of a man on foot joined them and then the smaller shadows of dogs moved tentatively forward to sniff the air and look down into the canyon.

There were six of them on horseback a while ago, Deegan remembered. *I can't tell if the man on foot is the damned Indian or the man who shot his horse. It means there's two of them wandering around on foot. They might've gone around the other way to be the cutoff men for the search.* He raised his eyes up the rocks above him again to reassure himself that there was enough overhang to block their view of him. He could hear the muffled voices of the men talking, but couldn't make out what they were saying. As he listened and watched the shadows, he saw one dog lift his head and begin to howl.

How'n the hell does he smell me down here? He can't smell me down here, he's gotta be howling at something else.

A man on foot appeared on the far side of the canyon and shouted across to the mounted riders. Deegan crouched in the shadows of the rocks. The man walked to the edge and looked down into the canyon floor.

Deegan drew farther back and watched intently.

One of the men above him shouted something indiscernible to the man Deegan was watching.

"I left him about a mile back," the man answered. "He lost a shoe in the rocks and was starting to limp so I got off to walk. He's a good horse and I don't wanna ruin him. I'll go back and git him. You seen any sign of Deegan?"

Well, at least they know who they're looking for.

One of the men above him shouted an answer, but Deegan couldn't make it out.

"Mangas with you?" the one across the canyon shouted.

Deegan couldn't understand the answer. *That means there's three of them afoot now and they're split up. I gotta be very careful.*

Again, Deegan couldn't understand what the man above him shouted.

"Well, I ain't seen him for hours," the man on the far side answered. "Hard to tell where he's at by now. He's either hot on Deegan's trail or maybe he's got him a squaw hid out up here somewhere."

The men above Deegan laughed.

"I'm gonna go back and get my horse and head down the canyon to see if I can find a spot to cross," the man shouted. "We ain't gonna never find that sumbitch with these tired dogs and two of us afoot. Hopefully Mangas'll keep on the trail and leave sign for us to follow when we git back. I told him where to meet us at sunup in case we got separated. Maybe we'll be lucky and the damned buzzards'll get Deegan. Probably be easier on him than Mangas. C'mon, let's head back to Yuma for supplies, fresh water, horses and dogs. I'll meet you when I can."

The men above Deegan shouted something and the man across the canyon waved and disappeared from sight.

I was right. There's an Apache scout back

at Fort Yuma named Mangas. They must've gotten him to come along as the main tracker. I hear tell he's a mean bastard.

The shadows on the far wall disappeared and Deegan sank with relief. *If they're gonna go back to Yuma, they make it easy for me to decide which way to go in the canyon.* He stood up, lifted the canteen from the water, bumped the cork in and started to walk up the canyon. *The only one I really got to worry about is Mangas.*

CHAPTER ELEVEN

The shadows in the canyon were getting long and the sun was lighting only the very top of the wall to his left when Deegan got a feeling in the back of his neck that sent a chill down his spine. *I'm being watched.* He spun to look behind him. The darkening canyon was empty. He'd found years before he could sense when he was being watched and he had that feeling now. *It must be Mangas!*

The canyon curved and disappeared so he stopped and stepped back into the shadows to watch for movement ahead and behind him. The bright rim of sunlight disappeared from the top of the far wall and the canyon became dark.

Deegan strained his ears, but heard nothing. *I know you're out there, Mangas,* he mentally told his stalker. *Now we wait to see who makes the first move or the first mistake.*

A full moon began to move across the sky

and a band of dim, blue light slid down the canyon walls as it advanced. When the moon was directly overhead, the canyon was bathed in soft blue light and Deegan decided it was time to make a move. He got to his feet, stepped out several paces and began to trot toward a bend in the canyon. He ran in the center of the stone corridor so no one could miss seeing his tracks in the sand. As he trotted, he studied the rocks and shadows and rounding a bend, dived back sideways toward the stone wall. He landed, rolled, scrambled to his feet, and looked out into the canyon. The moonlight seemed to fill the indentations his boots had made coming around the curve to where they stopped abruptly, a short distance out in front of him. Staying low and close to the wall, he backtracked to the bend and knelt in the shadows beside a boulder.

The moon continued to move across the sky and the light and shadows in the canyon shifted and changed with its movement. The only sound Deegan heard was the thudding of his heart as he waited. He heard a soft shifting of something in the sand around the bend. He tensed, tightened his grip on the canteen straps and slowly rose to his feet.

A shadow moved cautiously in front of

him and Deegan knew it was the Apache tracker.

Mangas was naked except for his gray loincloth, high leather moccasins, a wide, folded band of faded red cloth around his head and a heavy leather belt with cartridges, a pouch and a knife sheath around his waist. The only things clearly visible were the whites of his eyes as they moved rapidly from side to side. He carried a rifle in one hand and a heavy knife in the other. The Indian took a slow step and stopped as he studied the distinct line of tracks Deegan had made up the middle of the canyon. He took several tentative steps and looked to his side into the shadows just as Deegan swung the canteen. Mangas started to duck and raise the rifle for protection, but the canteen glanced off it to impact sharply with the center of the startled Apache's face. He staggered and toppled to his back in the sand.

Deegan grabbed the knife from the man's limp fingers and pressed the blade to his throat. Trickles of blood from the Indian's mouth and nostrils ran down the sides of his face. *The hit from the canteen could've killed him.* Deegan eased the pressure on the knife and slowly rose to his feet. *I ain't the killer people say I am. I know he'd've killed*

101

me if he'd had the chance, but I can't cut his throat like this. I can't kill a man in cold blood.

Deegan stuck the knife in the sand, untied the man's moccasins, pulled them free and rolled him over onto his stomach. He lifted his arms onto his back, wrapped a wide moccasin lace around his wrists, tied it in tight knots and sat back onto his heels. He yanked the band of cloth from Mangas's head and knotted it around the Indian's ankles. *If I take his moccasins, it might confuse the dogs.* He looked down at his worn boots. *Besides these won't last much longer.* He lifted the knife from the sand, cut the thongs from the ankles around his boots and pulled them from his feet. He glanced at the ledge above him and threw them up out of sight. *Now with the Indian's moccasins on, the only scent leaving here will be his. That should confuse and slow the dogs and give me more time.* He slid his feet into the moccasins, wiggled his toes, smiled, cut the remaining lace in half and tied them on.

Satisfied, he pulled the Indian's belt around, yanked it free and dropped the knife into the sheath. He stood, quickly buckled and adjusted the belt, hung the canteen over a shoulder, picked up the rifle, worked the action to see it was loaded, and walked up the darkened canyon.

Deegan stopped and looked back to where he'd left the Apache. *You should've killed the bastard. That was a mistake you're gonna regret someday. He'd a killed you and been proud of it. He'd a done it slow and enjoyed it. Go back and do it. Go back and cut his damned throat.* "No," he muttered and continued to walk.

By the time the sun was putting a glow on the eastern horizon; Deegan had made his way through the canyon and was now on the far side of the mountains. The desert ahead was low rolling hills of rocky soil with formations of larger rocks with sandy washes and gullies running through them. Small sparse stands of ironwood, mesquite and paloverde trees and an occasional saguaro cactus broke the monotony of the horizon. Round barrel cactus, cholla and a variety of smaller cactus and bushes dotted the area.

Deegan climbed a high rock formation to survey around him for signs of his pursuers. He sat with his back to a rock and looked out over the desert. He saw a column of dust rise from between two hills but, as he watched, it began to spin and become a dust devil.

I don't know how much of a head start I got now because I don't know how long it took them to get back to Yuma and back out here.

103

Hopefully the smell from Mangas's moccasins'll throw a little confusion into the tracking dogs.

He took a small sip from his canteen and pulled open the leather pouch hanging from Mangas's belt. It contained a hooked piece of steel, several chunks of flint and a flattened brass button from a cavalry uniform. *Now I have fire.* He studied the button. *I don't know, maybe this is a good-luck piece. God, I wish I had something to eat. My belly button and backbone gotta be touching each other about now. A little sleep wouldn't be bad either.* He leaned his head back and closed his eyes.

Deegan awoke, on his second day of freedom, with a start. "God! How'd I let myself do that?" he asked as he looked around. He rubbed his face and tried to figure out how long he had been asleep. He took a sip from his canteen and looked up at the sun to try to gauge the time. *I must've slept at least three hours. Get moving!*

A flash of light in the distance caught his eye and as he watched, he saw another flash off to the left of the first one. *Probably sunlight on the lenses of binoculars,* he thought as he noticed another flash of light farther to the left. *They must be spread out and looking for me with glasses. Guess Mangas's moccasins worked and the dogs are confused.* He picked up his rifle and started down the rocks.

CHAPTER TWELVE

Hours later as the sun was beginning to sink behind the horizon to the west, Deegan climbed onto a high point of rocks to see if he could make out any sign of trackers.

With the sun behind them, they won't be giving me any reflections off their glasses anymore so I won't be able to see where they are. He scanned the land below and beyond him. *I sure as hell wish I had a pair of field glasses. I've gotta sleep for a while and move when the moon comes out again.*

He sat down beside a rock and settled his back into the heat it retained from the sun. He took a sip from his canteen and immediately fell asleep.

Deegan awakened with a start, looked around, listened and relaxed. He looked up at the large moon rising and nodded. "Guess I must've slept a couple hours. Not very damned smart, Charlie," he told himself, stretched and yawned. *I can be sure they've got Mangas with them again. If they didn't find him, he probably got loose and found them. I knew I should've done him in when I had the chance. He's been insulted now and the only way he's gonna save face is to kill me slow and painful. I should've killed that red heathen devil.*

Deegan crawled onto a higher boulder and lay on his stomach to study the area. He rested his chin on the back of his hands and only moved his eyes to search. A coyote yipped and howled in the distance. Another joined in and then another and another. He shifted his head and searched in a new direction. There was light from a fire dancing in a group of large rocks at a distance out across the desert. He stared at it in disbelief. *They're either dumber'n hell or it's something to get my attention.* He crawled back down the boulder, retrieved his rifle and gear and moved to see if he could still see the light of the fire. He found it and it appeared to grow brighter as he watched.

They must a brought wood with them for this. There ain't enough wood to be found around here to build a fire that big, so it's gotta be some kinda bait. Do they think I'm stupid enough to go over there to see what's going on? Kind of like a moth to flame, so to speak. Maybe they want me to keep an eye on the fire so Mangas can come out and find me. They gotta know I ain't so stupid as to go to that fire. I'll sit up here a while and see what comes about.

A dark shape moved around the fire.

At least one of them is down there taking care of the fire. I haven't heard any dogs, but they gotta have the dogs with them. Outside of the Indian, that's the only way they can find me. He sat back to mull over the situation and study the area he could see in the moonlight. *Maybe Mangas is gonna walk ahead of them across the desert to watch for me when they start out with the dogs in the morning. With all this moonlight, it won't be very hard to spot someone moving, but if I sit here all night I'm losing my advantage of time and distance.*

Deegan slipped through the rocks down to the level rocky surface of the desert. He hunkered in the shadow of a large rock to look and listen. Cactus and bushes were clearly visible on the moonlit desert and shadows began to play tricks with his eyes. "Don't let your imagination take over," he warned himself. The coyotes continued to call to each other and he thought he heard the deeper sound of a baying hound. "They can't keep those dogs quiet with all that damned coyote talk going on around them," he told himself and smiled.

Deegan heard the deep, distinct baying of hounds. The sound grew as more hounds joined in. He grimaced and shook his head. *I knew it.* He studied the surrounding area for his next move.

There was the sound of a distant shot and the hounds were silent.

They either shot a dog or fired a shot to get the dogs' attention. That shot would really get my attention if I hadn't seen the fire. He moved at an easy trot on the soft sand and then dropped into the shadow of a cut bank in a curve of the wash. He forced himself to breathe slowly as he watched and listened. He heard nothing but his stifled breathing and the pounding of his heart. As he waited, he could again hear the calling of the coyotes. He raised his head over the edge of the bank and watched for movement. Nothing. He lowered his head into the shadows and studied the wash ahead of him.

Satisfied, he started down the wash, dropped into the shadow of several large rocks, looked up at the moon and down at the shadows growing longer as the moon neared the far horizon. *It'll be dark as the devil's heart in another hour.* He settled back into the shadows. *I'm so hungry my stomach's forgotten how to growl at me.* He laid the

109

rifle across his knees and took a sip of water from the canteen.

After a few minutes, Deegan was again satisfied, stood and began to trot down the wash.

He repeated the process of trotting, waiting, listening and trotting again until the moon had disappeared beyond the horizon and it was dark. *Should I risk running in the dark?* He tried to see the shape of anything around him. *I gained a lot of ground on them tonight, but I'd better keep moving.* Deegan started trotting slowly down the wash, but after stubbing his toes and falling several times, decided it would be better to walk. He stepped carefully, almost feeling his way with his feet. He stopped frequently and strained his ears for sounds around him. When he felt it was safe, he cautiously moved forward again to a new position.

Deegan's head exploded in a great burst of white lights and he sagged to the ground.

CHAPTER THIRTEEN

As Charlie Deegan slowly regained consciousness, he became aware that the side of his face was pressing into dry sand. He slowly opened one eye and saw it was daylight. There was no feeling in his hands and he realized they were tightly bound behind his back. He could feel his ankles were also tied. He struggled slightly to move his arms and heard a laugh.

"Aha, you are alive again," a guttural voice stated.

Deegan rolled his face up from the sand to see who was talking to him, but he *knew* it was Mangas. A hard kick to his ribs drove air from his lungs and brought tears to his eyes. As he gasped for breath, a foot roughly rolled him over onto his back and he looked up at the battered face of Mangas. His eyes were almost swollen shut, but Deegan could read their burning hatred.

"I did not want to kill you until I knew

you would feel it," Mangas stated as he walked in a wide circle around Deegan, his knife hanging loosely in his hand. He wore a dirty, blue "trading post" shirt, a long gray loincloth and the faded red band of cloth was again wrapped around his greasy, shoulder length hair. He wore his high moccasins and cartridge belt and a rifle and canteen leaned against a nearby rock. "You think you were very . . . very . . . What is your word for it? Ah, yes, smart. Very smart to take my moccasins to fool dogs. I have trouble with dogs now. I have no trouble with the first dogs because they are after your smell, but the new ones do not know I am not the one being hunted. They are big half-wild dogs and I had to shoot one last night. The white trackers are not happy. One of them said they should have left me where they found me. You know where it was. The place you smashed my face. You should have killed me, Deegan."

I know that, Deegan thought as he studied Mangas's face.

"Your screams will bring the white trackers, but I will kill you before they are here," Mangas stated and kicked Deegan's shoulder. "I will hear you scream like a child, so I know you feel the pain." Mangas dropped to his knees, pinched a wad of flesh on Deegan's forearm between his finger and thumb, pulled it up and slowly cut off a piece the size of a silver dollar.

Tears filled Deegan's eyes, but he gritted his teeth and fought to keep from crying out.

An evil smile curved the corners of Mangas's mouth as he held the bloody piece of flesh for Deegan to see before throwing it over his shoulder.

Blood ran off Deegan's arm and turned the sand red.

"You are being strong, but foolish," Mangas said as he sat back on his heels and watched the blood drip. "I will see how many more cuts I can make before you scream."

Deegan forced a soft laugh and spat at Mangas.

Mangas rose to his feet, climbed to the top of the cut bank and looked around. He nodded, dropped back into the wash and began to circle Deegan. "I see their dust. No wind. It goes up like smoke. They are not good trackers. They are too easy to see. They go to the west and the river again. It will take them longer to get here when they hear you scream. Maybe they think you go to the river because you are thirsty." Mangas laughed as he lifted the canteen, took a

113

short drink, then tipped it to let the water pour into the sand beside Deegan's head. He laughed again and threw the canteen down the wash.

Deegan turned his head, looked at the wet sand and then up at Mangas.

"I won't scream for you, Mangas. I'll die quiet. You won't hear me scream."

Mangas moved closer and dropped to his knees. "You will scream. I have made stronger men than you cry and beg to die. The white trackers will hear you scream from far away. If I had time I would find an anthill to stake you on and cut off your eyelids so the sun could bake out your eyes." Mangas paused to study Deegan's face for signs of fear and then slapped him. "I cut out your tongue and let you drown in your own blood. Maybe I scalp your face," Mangas growled and yanked on Deegan's mustache. "You would welcome death." He reached out to get another pinch of skin from Deegan's arm.

Deegan swung his bound legs up and kicked the Indian under his outstretched arm.

Mangas grunted and rolled to the side from the impact. Instantly he was back up with the knifepoint pressed into Deegan's throat. A drop of blood formed at the tip of the blade and rolled down his neck.

Mangas nodded, released the pressure on the knife and sat back. "You almost made me kill you now," he said, with a wry smile. "You will die slow. I will kill you when it is my time, not yours."

A soft growl came from the cut bank behind Mangas and he turned to see a large dog launch itself at him. He shoved one arm into the gaping jaws of the dog and with the other, thrust the knife upward into the animal's chest. The dog died instantly, but the momentum of the animal pushed Mangas onto his back in the sand. He yanked the knife free, dropped it and used both hands to push the lifeless dog away.

Deegan rolled onto his shoulders and swung his legs hard at Mangas's head. The side of his ankles impacted solidly with Mangas's throat, crushing his windpipe and knocking him onto his back.

The Indian choked and gagged as his hands fumbled at his throat.

Deegan glanced at the knife and rolled toward it.

With great effort, Mangas rose to his knees and scrambled for the knife.

Deegan swung his legs at Mangas again, but missed.

Mangas grabbed Deegan's ankles and

twisted, turning him over onto his belly.

Deegan kicked back, but Mangas avoided his feet and dived toward the knife, a painful, gurgling sound coming from his throat. He grabbed the knife and turned to where Deegan had rolled onto his back. Mangas's eyes were glazed from pain in his throat and the air he wasn't getting into his lungs.

Deegan turned so his feet and legs were ready to defend him against the Indian's assault.

Another large dog was standing on the cut bank behind Mangas. The dog howled and leaped onto Mangas's back, knocking him facedown into the sand. In his reaction to grab at the animal, the Indian dropped the knife and struggled to free himself from the weight of the animal. The dog bit hard and growled as his fangs dug deeper into the man's upper arm. The Apache managed to get his hands up over his head, grabbing the dog's ears and trying to pull him free. The dog released his bloody jaws from Mangas's arm, snapped onto the back of his neck and began to shake his head, rocking Mangas's face back and forth across the sand. His hands dropped to the dog's muzzle and he struggled weakly to pull the dog's teeth from his neck. Blood ran from the corners of Mangas's mouth as he turned his head up out of the sand enough for Deegan to see fear in the slits of his swollen eyes as they began to lose their point of focus.

The dog gave a mighty shake of its head and Deegan heard the Apache's neck snap. His body shuddered and went limp.

Deegan never took his eyes off the dog as he pushed across the sand toward the knife.

The dog ignored him as he continued to growl and shake Mangas's lifeless head.

Deegan reached the knife and turned it enough to put the blade against the leather ties on his wrists and saw at them. They separated and he pulled his wrists free. He quickly reached down and cut the ties from his ankles as his hands began to tingle and burn as the blood returned to them.

The dog lifted the dead Indian's bloody head, gave it a final shake, and dropped it to the sand.

Mangas's lifeless eyes stared across the sand at Deegan.

Deegan looked at the dead Indian and shuddered.

The dog sat back, licking his bloody chops and glancing curiously from Mangas's body to Deegan, as he sat shaking and rubbing his hands to return the circulation to them. The dog stood, walked to the body of the other dog, smelled of it, circled several times and walked back to the body of the dead Indian. He nosed Mangas's corpse, lifted his leg, circled the body, sniffed, lifted his leg again, ambled back and nosed the dead dog. He slowly approached Deegan, a line of hair stood up the length of the dog's back and he growled deep in his throat.

Deegan flexed his fingers around the handle of the knife and prepared to defend himself from the inevitable attack, but the dog stopped, took a whiff of the air, raised his head, howled mournfully, turned and loped off up the draw.

He took a deep breath as he watched the dog leap up a cut bank and disappear. He looked at Mangas's lifeless eyes again and shuddered. "It's time to move on, fast," he told himself as he crawled over to sit beside the Indian's body. He tugged the moccasins free and tied them onto his feet. He tore several strips from Mangas's shirt and tightly bound the wound on his arm, pulling the knot tight with his teeth. He loosened the band of cloth from Mangas's head, shook it out and draped it loosely over his own. *Have to cover my head with something.* He freed the cartridge belt, buckled it around his waist, felt the leather pouch for the flint and steel, sheathed the knife, grabbed the rifle, checked the action and picked up the canteen. He shook it and tipped it up to his mouth, but nothing dripped from it. "Never can tell when I might find water left from yesterday," he muttered, tapped the cork in and slung it over his shoulder. "One . . . two . . . three . . . ," he chanted as he started to trudge up the draw.

". . . nineteen . . . twenty . . . twenty-one . . . oh, hell," Deegan mumbled, stopped and looked back. *It's good enough for the Indians and I've gotta eat, so I might as well try it.* He turned and returned to the site of the battle. He glanced at Mangas's body, drew the knife, knelt beside the dead dog, cut a large flap of skin from the animal's flank and sliced into the muscled meat under it. He lifted a thin strip of the meat to his nose and sniffed. *I smelled worse. I'll take some with me until I find enough wood to make a fire.* He cut several slabs of meat, tore another chunk strip from Mangas's shirt and tied it around the meat. He wiped the knife on the dog's skin, sheathed it, stood and started back up the wash, swinging the bundle of meat between his fingers.

CHAPTER FOURTEEN

Several hours later Deegan found a small pool of water in a tangle of rocks, knelt, sipped, savored and took a swallow. It was warm, but refreshing. He took several more swallows before he straightened and filled the canteen. He hefted the dripping metal container and made a wry smile. *It'll keep me going for a while.* He spotted a tangle of dried weeds wedged against a saguaro skeleton on a ledge and knew the saguaro remains would supply him with the wood he needed for a fire to cook the dog meat. He dug the flint and steel from the leather pouch and started a fire.

He gnawed the last of the scorched, stringy dog flank, wiped the knife on his pants and stood up. "The Indians may like it, but I doubt I'll ever develop a taste for this stuff," he told himself as he walked back to the water, lowered his face and sipped again before pushing his head cloth down into it. *Time to get moving.* He draped the wet cloth over his head and trudged off across the warm sand.

Later, Deegan looked back at the setting sun and decided it was time to find a high point to look for signs of his trackers. *They been awful quiet,* he thought as he struggled up the rocks. *Maybe they found Mangas's body and decided I'm more'n they could handle.*

Deegan sat on a high rocky hill and scanned the area. *I should head west and try to cross the river, but the Indians'll be working the river figuring that's what I'd try so I'll keep heading north.* He lifted his arm and looked at the strips of dirty cloth covering the wound on his arm. *Damn, this arm's starting to throb.* He slid the cloth off and found a softly scabbed wound with puffy, red colored skin around it. He tentatively pressed the edges and a large drop of milky liquid oozed from the center of the scab.

"Sure as hell looks like some sort of infection in there," he told himself as he examined it closer. "I should've known better than to put those damned dirty rags on it." He shook his head. *Not very smart, Charlie. I guess sun and fresh air'll probably be about the best thing for it for now.*

Deegan rolled the scab off, squeezed the wound and watched blood and pus run down his arm. He poured some of his precious water over the wound. *I need something to make a poultice and draw the poison out.* He gingerly wiped at the wound with a fingertip. "Damn, that stings!" he hissed through gritted teeth. *Seems to me I heard about the Pima making a poultice from cactus pulp.* He looked around at the variety of cactus growing in the rocks and sand. *Now what kinda cactus did they use?* He studied several different plants. *Guess this little one'll do as good as any of the others. It can't do worse'n kill me.* He gingerly shaved the needles from a cactus pad, cut it in half, laid the fresh-cut pulp on the wound and held it in place with his hand. It felt cool and soothing on the infected area. *Just a short rest and I'll be on my way again.* He leaned back against a warm rock and closed his eyes.

Deegan's eyes flashed open and he realized it was dark. "Damn, I went and fell asleep," he muttered as he scanned the sky for something to give him an indication of how long he'd been asleep. *The moon's not up yet so it must still be early.* He flexed his wounded arm and stretched. The chunk of pulp fell to the ground and Deegan brought his arm up close to try to look at the wound. It wasn't throbbing and didn't feel as hot. *Looks like that cactus poultice worked. I'll make another one.*

After tying a new poultice in place with a shirt strip, he took a sip of water from the canteen. He heard a coyote howl followed by the distinct baying of a hound, then a hound howled from a different direction. *Damn, they got more dogs after me.* He stood and gathered his possessions.

A hound bayed and was answered by another and then another. *All three are in different places. They must've added to the search party and those damned dogs'll move faster'n me in the dark.*

Deegan slowly made his way down the rocks to the floor of the desert and listened. He could hear the baying, howling and barking of the dogs more clearly. *They ain't that far off. How'n the hell'd they keep those dogs quiet for so long? I musta been sleeping sound and didn't hear them. It's hard to tell how far away they are because sound carries so good at night.*

There were no stars and the moon had not risen to guide him in the dark.

He was aware of barking ahead of him. He stopped and slowly turned to listen.

Dogs! He turned in a complete circle and heard dogs in all directions. *They can't all be following a scent. They must've spread out in a big circle and now they're moving into the center. How'n the hell do they know I'm in the middle?* He walked in a small circle, stopping from time to time to look into the darkness and listen to dogs. He wet a finger and held it up into the air. *I'll walk into the wind.* He stepped off, keeping the light breeze on his face. *Dogs downwind can smell me, but the dogs upwind won't know where I am unless they see me and I'll know where they are by the sound.*

The moon rose over the top of the mountain giving a soft glow to the night air, creating strange shadows and making it easier for Deegan to move faster. He would stop from time to time and listen as he studied the moonlit area. *I still can't tell how far away they are. I wonder if they'd move past me if I sat still and waited?*

He peered at the moon and saw a large bank of clouds moving toward it. From time to time the clouds would light up inside from bursts of heat lightning. *I wonder if it's gonna rain? It's that time of year. Hell, if it rains and washes out my trail again, I'll have to believe there's some sort a higher power looking over me for sure.* He chuckled at the humor of the thought. *Maybe I'll be a monk or a priest if I get outta here with all my parts.* He laughed out loud. *I can see me walking around in a long robe with my head bowed down, blessing people and doing saintly deeds.* He walked to a high point of rocks and began to climb to see if he could make out movement in the moonlight. The clouds had almost reached the edge of the moon and he knew that once it was covered it would be very dark. The lightning burst in the clouds more frequently and from time to time a jagged bolt of lightning would pierce through the bottom of the clouds and briefly bathe the area in a burst of brilliant light.

It was the desert monsoon season and Deegan knew there was a possibility of days of intermittent rain. Anything from a light mist to what the old-timers called *a frog drowner* when the water seemed to fall in solid walls. These rains higher up in the mountains made the washes run with flash floods downstream where it did not rain. Like the wall of water in the canyon that had saved him earlier.

CHAPTER FIFTEEN

A low rumble of thunder followed one of the flashes of lightning and Deegan knew it was going to rain soon. He reached the top of the rocks and hunkered down to study the area. The booming of the thunder was getting louder and the brilliance of the lightning breaking from the clouds made him squint as he searched for movement. *The dogs ain't gonna like being out in this storm.* He sniffed the air and caught a trace of the smell of wet sand. *Of course, the men working those dogs ain't gonna be all that happy either.*

The front of the storm was a cool wind that blew stinging particles of sand against his exposed skin. He wrapped the cloth from his head down around his face so there was only a narrow opening for his squinted eyes. He turned his back to the gale, slid down among the rocks and found a deep overhang for shelter. The smell of rain grew

126

stronger and a fine mist blew in ahead of the real rain, pushing most of the stinging sand from the air. Larger drops of rain began to slap down and he slowly unwound the cloth from his head and face. He wiped his hands over his wet face and tipped it back so the rain beat on it. He opened his mouth and felt the water run in. At first, it was dirty and salty from the dirt and dried sweat in his hair and on his face, but soon it was pure and fresh. Then a strange urge hit him. He scrambled back to the desert floor, untied, and kicked out of his moccasins. He untied the cord holding his pants, let them drop and flipped them away. He pulled off his ragged shirt and swung it in water-spitting circles above his head as he danced naked, laughing insanely. "You damned dogs can't smell me now!" he chanted and shouted repeatedly until he fell to the wet sand, exhausted. He lay spread-eagled on his back, letting the large raindrops pummel him as he fought to catch his breath.

He eventually sat up and looked out into the falling rain. "That must've been a sight to behold. God, I hope you ain't gonna hold me to my word when I said I was gonna be a priest or a monk if it rained and I escaped again," he said softly. "I really ain't cut out for that kinda life, but if I make it outta here, I will clean up my way of living. I give you my word on that."

A bolt of lightning cracked down from the clouds and smashed into the top of a large saguaro cactus. The cactus exploded and chunks of steaming pulp flew in all directions. Rows of needles on chunks of cactus burned briefly like small candles and hissed out in the rain.

Deegan rubbed his eyes, shook his head and looked up into the falling rain. *I take that as a sign, but I ain't outta here alive yet, so I ain't making any promises.*

As he sat in the downpour, he gently removed the cactus poultice to let the rainwater run over the wound. *The fresh, clean water should help.* He looked closely at the rain running across the wound during intermittent lightning flashes. *I don't think infection is gonna be a problem anymore. I must've gotten to it in time. Things are really starting to go right for me. I'm gonna head up north and get a job working cattle. I'll be a new man, a man nobody knows. All these things are gonna be long gone and far behind me. Get me outta this damned heat, yessir, get me outta this damned heat!*

Deegan found his clothes and hung them, with the moccasins and canteen over his shoulders. He remembered the map in his

128

shirt pocket, dug it out, looked at the sodden mass and threw it away with disgust. *This'll be a memory test now.* He buckled the belt around his waist, wiped water from the rifle and walked slowly through the pouring water. He found a small rivulet of water running from the rocks, put the open neck of the canteen under it until it filled and tapped in the cork. He could hear water running in the gully below him. *Think I'll go down and see if I can walk in that for a while.* He picked his way down the rocks to find the water was fast and he couldn't tell how deep it was. *I'll walk alongside it. It'd be stupid as hell to drown now after I've come through all this. Besides this rain'll wash away tracks for a while anyway.*

The body of the storm with the thunder and lightning moved off to the west and the sky in the east began to glow with the first signs of morning. Shivering in the damp cold Deegan plodded along on the wet sand.

Several hours later, another bank of dark thunderheads, lit by bolts of lightning, loomed over the horizon ahead of him. *Damn, one day I'm gonna die of thirst and the next I'm in danger of drowning. There just don't seem to be any justice around here.*

The sun began to brighten the morning sky

as Charlie Deegan awoke for the beginning of his sixth day of freedom. His teeth were chattering and he shivered from the cold and dampness of his clothes. The rain had fallen intermittently all the day and night before, but this morning there was not a sign of a cloud anywhere in the sky. He stood, rubbed his eyes, stretched, slapped his hands on his shoulders and stamped his feet to warm them. He examined his rifle and carefully wiped at it with his hand. *No sign of rust.* He peeled the damp, ragged clothes from his body and spread them on a rock to dry in the rising sun. He rolled his shivering shoulders and danced in a tight circle to get the circulation moving in his miserably cold body.

He stepped out into a clearing in the rocks and looked around to get his bearings. The sun was coming up to his right so he knew he was facing north, the direction he wanted to travel. He picked a path among the rocks, climbed to the summit and felt the sun begin to warm his naked body. He looked out over the desert and saw nothing moving. *Looks like they gave up. There's no way in hell those dogs'll pick up a scent anymore, the water washed out tracks and the chances of them stumbling across me out here in all these rocks and sand is damned near impos-*

sible. Looks like all I gotta do now is beat the desert and I'll be a free man. When he was warm, he climbed down the rocks, pulled on his ragged clothes, picked up his meager possessions and started to walk north. *Damn, I'm hungry.*

Later that morning he spotted a desert jackrabbit hiding in the brush and managed to kill it with a large rock. He skinned the scrawny animal, found enough wood to start a fire with his flint and steel, ate the stringy meat and continued on his trek.

The sun was nearing the western horizon as Deegan lay on the top of a high hill and studied a town in the distance. *I'm sure that's Wickenburg and that's the Date Creek Mountains beyond that. I'm doing well.*

Two days later, he was up off the desert and walking in trees. He rounded a steep, rocky hill and noticed what appeared to be a lodgepole pine corral set in the trees. He walked over, leaned on one of the cross-pieces and looked up at two wooden pack-saddles and a pair of hobbles hanging from wires in the trees. The gate poles were on the ground and the corral was empty. A metal pipe came down the hill and put a slow trickle of water into a small, natural stone basin. "Seems somebody lived around here at one time," he told himself as he looked around the area. A short distance away, he saw two long stone mounds with wooden crosses and a short distance from them a small stone cairn. *Somebody lived and died here.* He looked down in a small draw and saw rusted cans, broken bottles and other trash. He noticed what appeared to be a dark opening in the side of the hill back in the trees. He warily walked through the grove and found a large, man-made rock wall from the ground to the stone overhang above. In the middle of the wall was a shoulder-high opening filled with heavy wood and a cross-shaped gun port cut in the center. *Looks like somebody's been forted up in there.* A short, weathered split-log bench sat near a dark opening at the end of the wall. He raised his rifle and cautiously moved closer. "Hello," he called. "Anybody here?" There was no answer. He stepped to the opening and found a heavy, wooden door hanging back at an angle into a dark room. He rapped on the rough wood. "Hello, anybody in here?" Silence. He cautiously stepped into the room and stood as his eyes adjusted to the interior dimness. The air was very musty, but cool compared to the outside air. Dim light came in around him and through the gun port.

His eyes became accustomed to the dim light and he jumped back. "I'm . . . I'm . . . I'm sorry," he managed to stutter. "I didn't hear anybody answer my call."

There was someone leaning back in a chair at a table in the far corner of the room.

"Hello, do you hear me?" Deegan called.

The figure didn't move.

Deegan stepped forward and realized he was looking at a dead man. A man, dead long enough to have been mummified by the heat and the mountain air. He laid his rifle on the table, walked to the window and managed to raise and brace the wooden shutter open, filling the room with light. He turned to find the back wall was a jumble of various sized rocks that looked like the aftermath of an avalanche and the rest of the room was in shambles. A set of over-turned shelves, assorted canned goods, tin plates and cups, knives, forks and spoons, broken lanterns and chairs, dried boots and shoes, ragged pieces of bedding and clothing and assorted animal droppings littered the floor. Broken bottles glinted at the base of one wall. A good supply of cut firewood had been scattered about and a large oak barrel lay on its side, a trail of animal-chewed bedding fanned out across the floor. *Somebody was sure looking for something in here, but it coulda been Indians or someone just wrecking the place. They must've been afraid to touch the dead man. He looks like the only thing in here that wasn't moved.* He folded his arms across his chest and slowly studied the room. It was a small natural cave with a rock fireplace built into the fabricated stone wall in the front. A grate and a bed of ashes filled the center and a rod with several hooks was wedged across the top. A fire-blackened coffeepot hung from one of the hooks. A stack of three narrow bunk beds reached almost to the ceiling against the natural wall of the cave. "Bunks stacked just like in the damned prison," Deegan muttered and shuddered. "There must've been three of them living in here at one time. That explains the graves outside."

He stepped closer and studied the man slouched with his head resting on the back of the chair and his hands folded in his lap. Rats, mice and insects had chewed away at the dead man's clothes, but for some reason had not eaten from his body. His tight, hard skin was dark. Heavy white eyebrows topped his closed eyes; sparse white hair covered his head and joined into his white mustache and beard surrounding his tightly stretched lips. Lips pulled back from his teeth, giving him a permanent evil smile. The skin on his face had dried tight to his skull and he had the look of a man knowing and enjoying a great secret.

The mummified dead man was wearing the remnants of a patched and faded red cotton shirt, worn brown canvas pants and a matching canvas vest. Deegan saw a glint of gold in a hole chewed at the bottom of a vest pocket. He slipped his fingers into the pocket, brought out a gold watch and chain and turned so he could see them in light from the window. *This is a fancy one,* he thought as he pushed the stem and the gold cover of the watch popped open to reveal a fancy porcelain face. Inside the cover was a photograph of a smiling woman. *I wonder if she was his wife or his sweetheart?* He tried to wind the stem, but it wouldn't move. He looked at the face of the watch, smiled and gently laid it on the table. *The watch says two thirty, so I guess it'll be two thirty from now on.* He checked the other vest pocket and found a black-tarnished, silver match safe with the initials *A. M.* engraved on it. *He must be A. M. I'm sure I'll find out what those letters stand for,* he told himself as he slipped the match safe back into the man's vest pocket.

Deegan crossed his arms on his chest,

studied the man and then slowly looked around the cave. *That door must have been broken in recently. He had to be dead a long time to dry out like that and if the door had been open all that time, more of his body would've been eaten. Someone broke in here, but didn't touch him. Were they looking for something?*

He looked at the variety of cans scattered on the floor and knew that the square ones were probably corned beef and the flat square cans were sardines. He picked up one of the round cans, brushed his thumb across the remains of the label and made out the picture of a peach. "Peaches!" he exclaimed, setting it on the table, punching the point of his knife through the top and twisting it. With shaking hands, he lifted the can to his mouth and tasted the sweet juice of the peaches as it ran across his tongue and down his throat. He swallowed and began to cough. "Slow down," he warned himself. "There's more in here. Take your time and enjoy it! Go outside and let the place air out a little." He picked up his rifle, walked out, sat on the bench, leaned the rifle against the wall, turned the can up and slowly drank it empty. He cut the top, pulled it open and looked at the yellow color of the fruit. With the tip of the blade, he pulled a peach half from the can, slid it into his mouth and sighed as he savored the taste. *I don't ever recall anything this good.* He lifted another peach half out and slipped it into his mouth. He slowly turned his eyes up and stared into the greenery of the trees above him. "This is another one I owe You," he said softly. The temptation to rush in and look for another can of peaches was great, but Deegan fought it as he stood and walked into the trees to look around.

That water comes out of a pipe that goes into the ground. I'll have to try to find the source. He looked up at the packsaddles. *Those help explain how they got the table and all that other stuff up here. I wonder where the critters are that go under those?* He found a small pile of wood next to a hole in the rocks in another fabricated stone wall. He crouched, looked into the hole, straightened and moved aside a large slab of shale at eye level to reveal a smoke-blackened space with a steel rod and hooks. "I'll be damned," he said. "Now this is pretty damned clever, a smokehouse. Now all I have to do is shoot a deer."

Deegan walked back into the cave, grabbed a pick and a shovel from the pile behind the door and tossed them into the yard. "I'll eat something and then take you out and bury you with your friends," he told the dead man. He picked up one of the square cans, a frying pan, went out into the yard, started a fire and cooked the corned beef. When he finished eating, he wiped his knife on his pants, went back into the cave, knelt and lifted the fan of bedding to his nose. *Maybe when the smell blows out I'll be able to use this. Not sure what the bug count'll be.* He gathered it up, carried it outside, hung it on a low tree branch, lifted the pick and shovel and walked off into the grove.

He returned, stood across from the old man and looked down at his toothy, smiling face. "I don't know who you are, or anything about you, but you sure were a planner and I owe you a lot. I'm gonna take you out into the grove and give you as decent a Christian burial as I can there with your friends. I dug you a hole on the end by the other two."

Deegan put his hands under the man's arms and gently lifted. He was surprised at the lightness of the mummified body. The old man remained in a sitting position and Deegan swung his legs up to hold his body across his arms as he walked. He lowered the body on its side into the hole, filled it with dirt and built a mound of rocks on the fresh earth. "That oughta take care of you, old friend," he said, and lowered his head in a silent prayer. "Amen." He raised his head. "I'll make you a marker before I leave," he vowed and walked back to the cave.

CHAPTER SIXTEEN

Deegan sat on the bench beside the door and thought about all the things that had happened that day. He'd checked the bedding and decided it needed at least another day to air out. The distant rumble of thunder in the mountains brought him out of his reverie. *Damn, I'd best get the cave cleaned up in case I have to spend some time in there. No sense in sitting out in the rain.* He managed to fix the top hinge on the door so that it hung straight, righted the shelves, stacked the canned goods, dishes and utensils on them, hung the broken lanterns on the bunk frame, restacked the firewood and set the makings for a fire in place. The broken chairs, dried boots, shoes and bedding went into a pile outside for burning later. He found a broom in the pile of tools behind the door and raised a large dust cloud sweeping the gravel floor. Coughing, he walked back outside to wait for the dust to settle and saw a small doe drinking at the water hole. He slowly reached over for his rifle, raised and cocked it and dropped the deer with a single shot. "Now I've got fresh meat for supper and something to hang in the smokehouse for later."

The thunder was growing louder as Deegan finished a meal of cooked deer flank steak and a can of tomatoes. He washed his plate, knife and fork in the watering hole and as he walked back, looked at the smoke curling up from the rocks of the stone smokehouse and nodded. *That one should be okay, but I guess I'd best put a fire inside the cave to make sure I've got one later. This one could be a frog drowner. Best bring in my bedding too.*

Drops of rain began to patter on the tree leaves and make little dust puffs as they buried in the dirt. Deegan put more wood in the smokehouse fire, brought out a small log with a flaming end, trotted back to the cave and started a fire in the fireplace. *That'll hold, now time to do my laundry.* He pulled off his moccasins, stepped back outside, stripped off his ragged clothes and hung them in the trees. As the rain got harder, he scrubbed himself with his hands and laughed. "Life is good," he shouted.

"Life is good!"

An hour later, Deegan sat naked in the cave with his chair tipped back and feet up on the table. The sound of the rain was almost a roar, accented from time to time with thunder and flashes of lightning throwing bursts of bright light through the door and window. The air was getting cooler and the fire was down to a pile of glowing embers. He got up, put a chunk of fresh wood on the fire and walked around the cave to warm up. "Why not look around in here for a while," he asked himself and chuckled. "Maybe you can find what those other people might have been looking for."

There was a long trail of wax running down from a candle in a niche in the rock wall. "This'll help." He lit the candle from the fire and held it above his head to light the room. He glanced up at it and noticed the flame was bending away from the far wall of the cave. "That's odd, it's like there's air flowing out of that mess of rocks." He lowered the candle, put his hand between the flame and the wall and the flame went straight up. He did this several times with the same reaction. "There's air coming from over there someplace." He walked toward the wall, glancing down to look at the flame.

As he got closer, the flame bent back faster and farther. "There's got to be some kind of an opening back here someplace." When he reached the wall of loose stones, he could feel a soft breeze on his naked legs and knew it was coming around a wagon-wheel–sized slab of flagstone leaning in the rocks. He tilted the candle to drip wax on a stone above it, set the candle in the puddle and looked at the slab. *It's odd that a piece that big slid down in here. There's not another stone like it.* He grabbed the outer edges of the slab, gave it a tentative pull and it moved easily. He looked down, saw that one of the bottom corners was rounded and rolled the slab easily to that side revealing an opening that a man could crawl through easily. "Why you sly old bastard," he said softly, chuckled and dropped to his knees in front of it. "If they were looking for something, I know now what they were looking for, don't I?"

He brought the candle down with his hand cupped closely around the flame and crawled into the opening. He couldn't see much in front of him and the gravel scraped his knees as he crawled on into the tunnel. The roof of the tunnel disappeared and he could see a stone ceiling high above him. He stood up, lowered his hand from the front of the candle and his eyes widened.

There were four large metal trunks lined up neatly against the wall. On top of the end trunk was a lantern and three one-gallon kerosene cans. He grabbed the first can and could feel that it was almost full. He dripped wax, stood the candle in it, picked up the lantern and quickly filled it. He raised the globe, ran the wick up and down several times to fill it, lifted the candle and lit the wick. The room filled with light, he blew out the candle, set it aside and stood back to look at his treasure trove. *This must be what they were looking for.*

With shaking hands, he opened the hasp on the first trunk, lifted the lid and knelt to look inside. He lifted out a thick layer of wool blankets and set them on the next trunk. Now it was about half full and his hands shifted things: a tin of blasting caps, a coil of fuse, boxes of matches, a bundle of candles and boxes of rifle, pistol and shotgun ammunition, bandoleers, gun belts, holsters and two canvas bags with shoulder straps, rifle slings and several small leather, drawstring pouches. *For all this ammo and gear, there must be guns in here someplace.* He laid the blankets back in and closed the lid.

The next lid opened to reveal a row of books, a tin of hardtack and almost-empty bags of rice, flour and beans. There was an assortment of canned goods: peaches, tomatoes, corn, and baked beans. *More peaches.* A small wooden box contained cans of salt, black pepper and sugar. *When these bags were full, the trunk would've been full. Looks like he was about due to make a supply run.* He hefted another bag, sniffed it and grinned. As little was in the bag, there was no mistaking the smell of coffee. He knew things were getting better by the minute. He pulled out each of the books: a Bible, an atlas, a home-remedy book, four books on campaigns of the Civil War, and three leather-covered logbooks. He quickly opened and skimmed through the atlas, looking for a map of Arizona Territory. The page for Arizona and half of New Mexico Territory was gone. *Damn!*

Angus McKenna was printed in bold letters on the cover of the logbooks. "I think I now know the name of my grinning friend." He opened each of them, found dates on the first page and put them in order by date. The first book started in 1865 and the last entry in thc third book, barely discernible, was 20 July 1888. *Angus McKenna may have been sitting in that chair for three years. These will be interesting reading.* He put the books back in place and lifted out a small stack of threadbare towels. *I guess I can use these.* He opened a metal box to find a variety of shaving and barber supplies. He found a shaving mug, brush and soap. The box also contained a razor strop, an assortment of razors, a pair of mechanical hair clippers, a partial bottle of bay rum aftershave lotion and a box with three bars of "Fine Milled Bay Rum and Glycerine" soap. He pulled the stopper from the bottle, waved it slowly under his nose and took a deep breath. *Damn, between the soap and the aftershave I'll smell mighty damn good when I get done cleaning up.*

He shifted the lantern, opened the latches on the third trunk and inside pressure popped the trunk partially open. He lifted the lid and found three sheepskin-lined canvas coats; one blue, one black and one brown. Inside the coats were fur-lined gloves and tightly rolled wool storm king caps. He unrolled one of the blue caps, put it on his head and pulled down the bill in the front. *Looks like they were ready for winter.* He set the coats on the next trunk and looked down at an array of folded shirts. "Whoa, look at these," he said as he held a blue one to his chest. "No way will this fit me." One by one, he held them up and disgustedly laid them on top of the coats. "Were all three of these men small?" The fourth shirt, brown cotton, matched up to his shoulders. "Aha, this one'll fit." He found two more shirts that would fit, both blue cotton, and he was pleased. Next were layers of folded blue canvas pants, tan canvas vests, underwear, a pair of leather suspenders and rolls of socks. He set the underwear aside and chuckled, "I haven't worn these things in so long, I probably wouldn't know how to operate them." Shoes and boots finished the trove, but he knew by looking at them that none would fit him. Minutes later, he had three shirts, two pairs of pants, a vest, suspenders and four rolls of socks sorted onto piles of clothes. These were his clothes. *This old man was really well supplied with everything.* He shook a bar of soap out of the box and tossed it from hand to hand. *Now I'm going outside and take a real shower while it's still raining. I'll leave the last box for morning.*

Charlie Deegan, his wet hair pulled straight back on his head, sat on the chair in the main cave and rolled up the legs of his new canvas pants. He stood, looked down, and satisfied with their length, pulled the brown cotton shirt over his head. He adjusted the neck, rolled his shoulders, grinned and looked up at the ceiling. "You've done it again, haven't You?" he said softly. "I think You're pushing me to be a man of the cloth, but it ain't gonna happen." He buttoned on the suspenders and shrugged into the vest. "I think I'm a human being again."

CHAPTER SEVENTEEN

The next morning Charlie Deegan, dressed in his new clothes, stone-ground enough coffee beans to brew a small pot and enjoyed it with a deer steak. He folded his new blankets on the bottom bunk and looked at the opening in the far wall. *Time to go in there and see what's in the last box.*

He set the lantern on a trunk and opened the last one. It contained a variety of well-oiled guns and more ammunition. He hefted and examined each of the weapons. *Damn, he could have held off a small army for a while with all of this.* He worked the action of one of the rifles and smiled. *I guess I can put up Mangas's rifle.* He chose and laid aside a Hopkins and Allen hammerless .32-caliber. *This'll make a good pocket gun.* He looked over the rest of the guns and chose a .44-caliber Colt and a lever-action Winchester of the same caliber. Lastly, he laid aside a ten-gauge, short-barreled Greener shotgun.

Now I'm well armed. He brought out cartridge belts and other gun gear from the
other box, filled belts with cartridges and
distributed ammo in the leather pouches.
He chose a holster for the Colt and a sling
that fit over the barrel of the rifle. He broke
the Greener down, wrapped the barrel, action and stock in a piece of oily cloth and
pushed it down into one of the canvas
packs. He used another oily cloth to give all
the remaining weapons a good wipe down,
put them in the trunk and snapped the lid
shut.

He lifted the lantern and held it high
above his head. "Now let's see what else is
in here," he said and heard his words echo
back at him as he stepped deeper into the
cave. He found a small ledge with rows of
half-lemon-sized mounds of sand and small
rocks scattered on the remains of small
leather bags. He moved closer, set the
lantern on the ledge and took a deep breath.
"I'll be damned," he muttered, pushing a
finger into one of the piles and seeing the
light reflect off it. "Gold! It's gold the mice
have eaten the bags away from!" He pushed
on another pile and saw the glint of the gold
as the grains and small nuggets shimmered
in the light. *Angus must've put his gold in
leather bags for safekeeping back here in this*

cave. That explains his hidden door. A show of gold in town and he'd had claim jumpers following him for sure. He must've walked these washes and canyons for miles looking for nuggets and panning for the finer grains after the rains. God, I'm rich! I thought things couldn't get any better than those damned canned peaches and now I'm gold-fever rich.

"I'm rich!" he shouted and his words echoed back to him. "I'm rich! I'm rich!" He set the lantern on the shelf and scooped one of the piles of small nuggets into his hand. He began to dribble the small nuggets and dust from one hand to the other, marveling at the weight and color as it glittered in the lantern light. *I can't believe my change of luck. There looks to be enough gold in here to make me a man of leisure! Now all I gotta do is bag it up and get it to a town.*

Deegan studied the pile of gold in his hand. "Steady up a minute, Charlie," he told himself. "You can't just dance into a town with all that gold and not cause a ruckus of sorts. People are gonna wanna know where you got all that gold. What if they got reward posters with your picture plastered all over the place? You ain't a man can just go walking the streets. You ain't that long out of Yuma Prison, and it's not like the warden shook your hand, gave you a

151

new suit and five dollars and told you to make something good of yourself now that you've learned your lesson. Settle down. Just settle down. You got nothing but time right now. Do it smart."

Deegan lifted the lantern and began a slow circuit of the cave, looking carefully at the walls and ceiling. As he neared the back corner of the cave, he felt a faint breeze from a dark space in the rocks. *There's a breeze blowing from back there someplace.*

He saw a candle stuck on the wall near his head and could tell from the cascade of wax down the rocks that many candles had been burned in this spot. He heard dripping and turned to see a pool across the cave. Water dropped, a large drop at a time, splashing and making circles of ripples move slowly out to the edge of the pool. When the water was almost still, another drop would hit the surface and the circular waves of water would move out again. *This must be the source for the water at the corrals.* A wooden bucket and two metal pails sat on a rock ledge beside the pool. *If he had to fort up, he could get water without going outside. Smart.*

He again felt a soft breeze on his face. *There's fresh air coming in up there some-place,* he thought as he gazed at the ceiling.

152

There's got to be another way out of here up there. He walked back to the short tunnel for the main cave and wondered at the pile of large rocks placed on the overhead ledge. *He could've sealed himself up in here and held out for months and there's obviously another way out if he wanted to go. He was a crafty old fox who thought of all the answers.* He hefted a large metal bar standing beside the pile of rocks. *This is probably a lever to move the rocks to close off the passage and then again, to open it when it was safe. He's really thought everything out carefully.*

CHAPTER EIGHTEEN

Charlie Deegan spent the next four days exploring the cave, the area around the cave and slowly reading the three logbooks. From the first book he learned that Angus McKenna had come over from Scotland in 1860, at the age of fifteen and eventually worked as a bartender in New York City until he joined the Seventy-Ninth Highlanders, a New York Scottish unit known as the Highland Guard. There he had met his two now-dead partners, Matt McArthur and Karl Gilmore. After the war, in 1866, they headed west to seek their fortunes. They had heard the rumors of the sands covered with gold and set out with youthful enthusiasm to become rich. They quickly learned they were very weak rumors so they traveled to Texas and hired on with Charles Goodnight, working as cowboys driving cattle up to the railheads in Kansas. After three years of pushing cows and eating dust, they decided to give mining another chance.

They went back to the desert, found this canyon and built the stone wall on the cave that became their home. They named their camp Cibola, after the Seven Cities of Cibola, the legendary cities of splendor and riches sought by the sixteenth-century Spanish conquistadores. There were Indian problems at first, but the migration of white people into the area soon forced the Indians to move on. The first few years they eked out a fair living by panning nearby streams and searching dry streambeds and rock formations in the canyons. Then one day they came across a small cave in a deep canyon that contained a mother lode of gold ore. The quartz walls had heavy veins of gold and the old, dried-up stream that had run through the cave had layers of gold in nuggets and dust.

They quickly amassed a fortune and knew they had to be very careful with it. When they went to Date Creek, Wickenburg, Gillette, Bumble Bee, Prescott or other small towns in the area, they worked the same plan. They always alternated towns, one of them walking in an hour or so earlier to have gold assayed and turned into cash. He would then meet the others, with the pack animals, outside of town, pass them the cash and hide along the trail while they shopped for supplies. He would then watch to make sure they had not been followed on their return trip to Cibola. This system worked fine because none of them was ever seen with large amounts of gold or money. Like so many others, they were just crusty old miners, eking out a living somewhere in the desert.

In book two Deegan learned that by the end of the third year at Cibola, Angus, Matt and Karl decided they had more than enough money to last each of them for a while and it was time to see other parts of the country. With plans made, they went into Gillette for needed travel supplies and a few drinks.

Unfortunately, they were not as cautious and didn't use their usual system of watching the trail returning home.

Early the next morning Cibola came under a state of siege. Bullets splintered the wooden door and shutters and slugs ricocheted off the walls and ceiling. Voices outside called for them to come out, but they knew they were safe inside their stone fort. When it was dark, Matt went out through the hole in the ceiling of the inner cave and returned to tell his friends there were five men sitting around a fire just beyond the corrals. They discussed it and agreed the only way they could win was to sneak out and shoot them down in cold blood. They had tried to kill the three friends so turnabout was only fair. It was bad luck that Matt hadn't stayed out long enough to see two other men who were waiting and watching closer to their cave. There was a half-moon when they crept out and moved up to a place for their ambush. Their first volley killed three of the men at the fire and the other two escaped into the darkness. The two men watching the cave moved up and opened fire, killing Matt. Angus and Karl hid in the shadows in the rock and returned fire, killing one of the cave watchers. They did not know how many men were in the second group so they split up to move through the rocks and trees to try to kill the remaining gunmen. The battles lasted for several hours. Karl killed both of the men who escaped from the fire, but not before he was badly wounded.

Angus was wounded in the lower arm and upper leg before he shot down the man he was after. He managed to get Karl back to the cave and dressed their wounds. Karl died the next morning. Angus managed to dig two graves for his friends and used one of the pack animals to drag the bodies of the other dead men a ways from the camp and drop them down a steep canyon.

For the next month Angus did little but rest and heal from his gunshot wounds. He also decided it was time for him to move on away from this place that had so many memories for him. He wrote about sealing up the back cave and all his supplies. He'd decided to leave the front cave as it had been during the time they'd lived in it. He took the pack animals into Gillette and traded them for a saddle horse to ride as he searched for a new life.

The rest of the second book and most of the third book told tales of Angus's life and adventures as a bounty hunter throughout the southwest.

In the third book, he told of deciding to live a quiet life for a time and do some mining so he returned to Cibola after a seven-year absence. He found the main cave to be in good condition with signs that it had been occupied at times, but no one had found the large back cave. He refreshed the graves of Karl and Matt and, out of curiosity, went to the canyon where he dumped the bodies of the seven gunmen who had laid siege to Cibola. Angus saw the canyon littered with the bleached bones of the men and, after careful consideration, and a bout with his conscience, rode down into the canyon and looked closer at them. He dismounted, spread a blanket and put all seven skulls and lower jaws on it. He returned to a place not far from where Matt and Karl were buried, dumped the skulls in a pile and built a cairn of rocks over them. "I really don't know why I did that," he wrote in the book. "But for some reason I felt better."

He kept in contact with several law agencies and from time to time, and when the reward was large enough, would leave the security of Cibola to search for fugitives. He wrote in the book of some of the reward money he had garnered in his pursuit and capture of criminals.

Deegan fanned the next few pages and found that the tales of Angus McKenna were about over and he continued to read. In the spring of 1888 Angus was having terrible bouts of coughing and began to cough up blood. A doctor in Prescott informed him he had lung cancer and probably a few months to live. He loaded his packhorse with a large supply of food and two cases of good Scotch whiskey. He'd decided if he was going to die, he would do it in his own way.

■ ■ ■ ■

Charlie Deegan ate supper, sat on the bench beside the cave door, opened the book to the last of the written pages and began to read:

July 20, 1888

Getting weaker. Have accepted what is coming. Made my peace with the Lord. Wish I could hear the pipes one more time before I go. Finished the last bottle of good Scotch whiskey. The pain in my chest is bad at times from this terrible coughing. Other times I don't even feel it. Time doesn't seem to matter anymore. I lived a good life and regret very little except that we never moved to San Francisco as we'd planned. I did some things I now know were wrong, but were necessary and seemed right at the time. Matt and Karl have been dead for more years than I can remember. Turned the horses loose. Had to chase them off. Hope they survive. Wish I had more whiskey for the pain. Wish I had one of them pretty little Mexican women who work the saloons in Yuma. Too late now for wishes. Read someplace if wishes were horses, then beggars would ride. Will read from my Bible and put this book away with it. Hope someone finds this so they know my story. Tried to seal off the big cave but have no strength left. I think I can hear the pipes calling. Whiskey would be good! Have to put this away so the mice don't make a meal of it. Pesky little bastards. I hear the pipes . . .

The handwriting was now so shaky it was almost indiscernible. Deegan gently closed the book, laid it on the bench and went back into the cave.

CHAPTER NINETEEN

Days turned into weeks as Deegan enjoyed his freedom and furthered his plans to travel north to the big ranches and find a job as a cowboy. With the anonymity of a working cowboy, he could move north with a cattle drive until he got to Kansas or Nebraska and leave the herd for a good life with his hoard of gold. No one would be looking for an escapee from Yuma Territorial Prison that far north. *Hell, the coyotes are probably gnawing on Deegan's bones out there in the desert right now.*

One day, while walking up a narrow canyon, he began to whistle and realized the sound was echoing back at him. He stopped, whistled a series of notes, listened to the sounds coming back at him and smiled. "Hello!" he shouted and his greeting returned. He laughed and the sound of mirth bounced from the rocks. He began to whistle again as he continued his journey.

"I guess I don't have to be alone anymore," he told himself. "You're gonna make it, Charlie, you're gonna make it." Later when he was shaving, he looked at his long hair and ran his fingers through it. "About time to find a real barber," he told himself. "Time to hit the trail."

He carefully gathered the gold piles from the ledge, put them in the toes of four socks and tied the tops of the socks in pairs. *Now they'll be easy to carry under my shirt when I leave.* He held them up and saw each sock had about four inches of gold in it. *I am now a rich man.* He explored the inner cave looking for possible hiding places for the cache of reward money that Angus may have hidden. He dug into the rock cairn out by the graves, found the first of the skulls and decided not to dig any farther. "I don't think that if he hid the money, he'd put it anyplace so obvious. I could go crazy searching for money that I really don't know exists. The monsoon season is about over and it's time for me to move on."

He carefully organized the supplies he was taking and packed them into a canvas bag with shoulder straps. Shirts, pants, socks, four cans of corned beef, five cans of sardines, a can of tomatoes and his last can of peaches. He picked the best rifle, a Model

163

1873 .44-40 Winchester Carbine and loaded it with eleven rounds. He chose a .44-caliber Colt pistol, loaded five cylinders and let the hammer lay on the empty one. The same ammo for both guns made it easier. He put a dozen cartridges in the belt for the holster he was going to wear. He broke down the short-barreled shotgun and put it in the canvas bag along with a box of ammunition for all the guns. He still carried the small canvas sling for the rifle and carried the small .32-caliber pistol in his pants pocket. The four socks of gold dust and nuggets would hang around his neck under his shirt.

He broke up one of the chairs from the cave and on the seat laboriously carved:

ANGUS McKENNA
A FINE HONEST MAN
1845–1888

He stuck the carved monument in the pile of rocks on Angus's grave. After one last look at the lady's picture inside the gold watch, he hung the watch and chain on a small nail on the side of the seat. "This is about all I can do for you now, Angus. I'll leave you and your lady to rest here in peace. It's too bad I never did figure out who she was. Godspeed."

164

The day before he was going to leave, he had a long discussion with himself. "Should I seal up the back cave like Angus started to do? I don't really know why he wanted to seal it, but it seemed to be his last wish, so I'll do it. I'll close the window cover and the door and leave this cave the way I found it."

Deegan held the lantern high and gazed around the great stone room. He watched the reflection of the lantern as the ripples in the pool rolled through it. It was now time to see if he could seal off the big cave.

There were places on the walls marked by trails of wax dripped from candles that had burned there in the past. He hung the lantern on a hook, dug a handful of candles out of a box and began putting them in the spaces above the long, dry wax waterfalls. *I'll light it up in here like Angus and his partners did from time to time. Kind of a final tribute for the man I never knew, but owe so much to.* He lit the last of the candles, lifted the lantern from the hook and stepped into the middle of the cave. He slowly turned and scanned the room. "I don't see a thing more with all of this extra light," he muttered.

Then he noticed something glinting from

one of the ledges high up on the far side of the cave. He walked to where he had seen the glitter, reached up and slowly felt back until he found what had glinted in the lantern light. It was a coin leaning against a rock. He brought it down, with a cascade of dust, to where he could look at it closely. He brushed the dust off and smiled. It was a twenty-dollar gold piece! He put his hand up and searched for more coins. The ledge was empty.

He held the gold coin close to the lantern to examine it. "What the hell's the reasoning behind this gold coin?" he asked as he rolled it between his fingers. "Is this some sort of a sign or a clue there's more gold hidden in here, or is this the last of their gold coins?

"Why was it standing up?" Deegan asked. "Is this Angus's way of keeping me in here to look for treasure or was it the old man's idea of a joke? Why in the hell did I have to find this thing the day before I was gonna leave?" He held the lantern over his head and made a slow circuit of the stone room, carefully looking for anything he might have missed in the past. "I said I was leaving tomorrow. I'm packed, I'm leaving, and that's all there is to it, Angus!" he shouted and listened to his voice repeat back to him off the walls. "Angus, I think you left this gold coin for someone to find as a joke to make them stay and look for more gold. So my dead friend, I'm not gonna fall for it. I owe you my life for all the things you left, but I'm gonna seal up this cave and go away from here first thing in the morning. I have enough gold dust and small nuggets to live comfortably for a long time. If there're more gold coins hidden in here, I didn't find them. Nice try, Angus."

Deegan set the lantern in the small tunnel into the cave, lifted the steel pole, studied the piles of rocks beside and above the tunnel, pushed the bar into a space, put his shoulder under it, and braced it upward. Several of the rocks high on the pile shifted slightly. *This is what he planned.* He moved back and took a last look before he started the avalanche that would seal off the cave. The candles still burned brightly, giving an eerie, flickering light to the great stone room.

"Let's do it." Deegan slid the bar back into the space and put all of his strength into a hard, upward push. The rocks on the top of the pile moved and began to rattle and crash down in a cloud of noise and dust. He ducked back into the tunnel to watch the stones tumble and bounce down to close off the entrance and block his view of the cave. Coughing from the dust, he backed out in search of clean air.

Inside the cave, one of the tumbling rocks released a cascade of fist-sized, soft deerskin bags, each containing fifty twenty-dollar gold coins. The bags rolled and bounced down through the dust and falling stones to land heavily on the floor. Many of the bags were mouse-chewed and split on impact, releasing gold coins that rolled, skidded and spun across the floor to circle and settle in the dust-dimming light of the candles. One of the bags burst on the stones at the edge of the pool and a cascade of gold slid into the water, making a rainbow of shimmering gold across the bottom of the pool. The cave became silent, the dust settled, one by one the candles burned out and the circles of bounty gold were gone.

CHAPTER TWENTY

Charlie Deegan proceeded north for two days and then turned northeast. By the end of the third day, he was walking through scrub oak and other small trees at the edge of the mountains. All things appeared right to him and he was happy and content. His clothes were clean and he had guns, water and food. The bill of the blue storm king cap kept the sun from his eyes. The soles on his moccasins were still intact and he patted the lumps on the front of his shirt. *My start for my new life, my four socks of gold.* He dug the gold coin out of his pocket and rolled it between his fingers.

He stopped at the edge of some trees and looked down at a small adobe village resting beside a narrow river in a valley not far below him. *Time for a rest.* He dropped his pack, laid his rifle on it, and took a drink from his canteen as he studied the settlement. People worked in gardens and several women washed clothes in the water moving slowly past the adobe buildings.

As with most towns and villages in the southwest, the largest building was a church built on a square and surrounded by about a dozen or so houses and outbuildings. The village was mainly adobe or stick-and-mud houses roofed with clay tiles or wood covered with brush and dirt. Several had stick and pole corrals and pens for goats, sheep and other livestock. Chickens of assorted sizes and breeds picked at the dirt around the houses. Each house had a small area screened by an adobe wall or a thick wall of branches and brush a short distance behind it. No sense in wasting good adobe or wood for an outhouse and what was the need for a roof in this part of the country? Besides, it gave the little boys a reason to hide, peek and giggle whenever a girl or woman went into it. There was no bell in the tower of the church, but the roof was made of clay tiles showing a sign of what could be considered exorbitant spending. A lone dog sniffed his way from house to house, occasionally lifting a leg to mark his passing. He paused at a small pole corral to sniff noses with a burro that appeared to be asleep, chased a lone chicken and then disappeared behind a house.

The door of the church flew open and a group of children burst out onto the bare dirt of the churchyard. A rotund, old nun, hobbling on a cane, followed the children, shouting and motioning at them with the cane as if trying to herd a flock of wild ducks. The children were all dressed in white clothing that appeared to be threadbare but clean, and they quickly scattered across the open area pushing, shoving and shouting at each other in the ways of all children.

Deegan noted there didn't appear to be any men in the village. *Strange, I wonder where they are? I don't see any large fields so maybe they work away from the village. Probably in a mine or a big ranch nearby.* He found a tree and sat to lean against it as he watched the children cavorting in the churchyard. A tall, thin, white-haired, black-robed priest appeared at the door of the church and shouted to the nun who looked over at him and waved her cane as if dismissing his message.

That's a lot of children. They must bring them in from other villages or maybe it's an orphanage. With the old priest and nun, I'd have to guess it's an orphanage.

Satisfied with his conclusion, he wiggled his shoulders to find a comfortable position, pulled the bill of his cap down over his eyes and immediately fell asleep.

As Deegan awakened, he had that inner feeling he was being watched. He opened one eye and fingered up the cap bill. Startled, he snapped his head back to the side of the tree away from the eye staring into his. He realized he had been eye to eye with a goat. High, almost musical laughter came from behind him and he turned to look around for the source of the sound. A beautiful Mexican girl stood with a hand over her mouth trying to muffle her laughter.

Deegan smiled sheepishly as he stood up, pulled the cap from his head and nodded to the girl. "I guess that must've been pretty funny," he said, with a soft chuckle.

The girl nodded and smiled.

"Ah, do you speak English?" he asked. "You *hables* English?" He had learned limited Spanish in prison, but he still had a hard time with rapid speech.

"Is that a mission school down in the village?" he asked, pointing below.

The churchyard was empty and quiet.

"Ah, no, that is a school for *huerfanos* . . . ah . . . ah . . . what is the word for a child with no mother or father?" the girl asked.

"An orphan?" Deegan offered.

The girl nodded. "*Si* . . . ah, yes, an orphan. Most of them are orphans. Some of them are children from the village."

Deegan studied the girl for a minute and then looked down at the empty churchyard. "Is it just the old priest and nun that care for them?"

"*Si,* Father Alfredo and Sister Manuela. The people in the village do what they can, but we are a poor people. Most of the men have gone off to work in the mines at Prescott. My mother and I have a small garden and I tend these goats."

"You have no father or brothers?"

"No," the girl answered. "I must go down to the village now. It is time to milk the goats."

Deegan nodded and smiled. "Is there a store in the village? A place where I can buy supplies?"

"We have no store and there is no market until . . . ah . . . Saturday. Two days. Everyone comes to the village for market in two days. That is when I sell goat milk and cheese."

"Is there a town or village close by where I can get supplies?"

"There is a town called Date Creek about a two-day walk to the east. There is another village called New Virginia about a day and

173

a half north across the river. Prescott is four or five days away. It depends on how fast you walk. That is where I lived with my aunt and went to a mission school for several years."

"What is the name of the river?" Deegan asked, in the hope the name would help him figure out his location.

"It is called the Bill Williams Fork. Do you need food, s*eñor*? I will give you some *tortillas.*"

The name of the river meant nothing to Deegan. "What is the name of your village?"

"It does not have a real name," she answered. "We call it *San Raphael* because of the church. The church is named for Saint Raphael, one of the seven archangels. His name means 'God heals.' He is the patron saint of travelers."

Deegan rolled his eyes skyward and shook his head. *You're still trying.*

"*Señor,* I asked if you would like some *tortillas?*" the girl stated, almost indignantly.

"Yes, I'd like some *tortillas,*" he answered and smiled.

"We will go to the village," she said and began to shoo the goats with her hands.

He thought about the twenty-dollar gold piece in his pocket. *If I paid her with this, she wouldn't have any change and if I gave it to*

174

her for a pile of tortillas it wouldn't take long for the story to get around about the rich gringo passing through and showing off his money, he warned himself. *What do I have to trade for her tortillas? A small gold nugget would be a good trade and really nothing to make me out to be a rich white man. Just a hungry gringo passing through.* He nonchalantly patted his shirt as if to reassure himself that the socks were still there. *Now how do I get a nugget out?*

Deegan looked around and saw the girl moving through the trees, gathering the goats back into a herd and starting them down the hill toward the village.

"I'll come down for some *tortillas,* but I'll leave my things up here," he shouted to the girl. "I've gotta keep moving on so I'll hide them and come back later," he said lamely.

The girl shrugged and motioned for him to follow as she shooed the goats ahead of her.

Deegan grabbed up his pack and other gear, ran back into the trees and hoisted it to hang hidden in the leaves. He stretched to lay his rifle across branches, hung his cap from it and started to unbuckle his gun belt. "This is hardly the time to start going into a strange town unarmed," he told himself. He saw the girl was almost to the end of the wide dirt trail that was the main street of the village. She motioned for him to join her. He turned his back, quickly unbuttoned his shirt and pulled a pair of the socks free, untied them and fingered one of them open. He dribbled a small nugget and a few grains of gold into his hand. He stuck the nugget into his mouth, brushed the grains off on his shirt, knotted the sock and swung them back around his neck. He waved to the girl as he ran out of the trees buttoning his shirt and looping Mangas's faded, red headband around his neck. He spit the nugget into his hand. "Go ahead," he called, "I'll catch up!" He looked down at the small, bird-egg–sized nugget. *This'll pay for a few tortillas and give her some extra money when she cashes it in.* He closed his hand and trotted down the hill to join her.

As they walked down the dirt street Deegan looked at the houses with their low crumbling street walls. Many of the roofs sagged and had tiles missing. Several had roofs of thatched scrub oak, mesquite, ocotillo and straw. The plaster had fallen off much of the walls, leaving the brown adobe bricks exposed. The winds had rounded off the corners of the bricks and blasted the gray wood around the windows and doors. *This place could really use some work,* Deegan told himself as his eyes scanned the buildings.

The dog he had seen earlier rushed from behind one of the houses and made a barking charge at the goats. In one swift motion, the girl scooped up a rock and threw it, hitting the dog in the ribs. It yelped in pain and scurried off in the opposite direction.

"Like some men, that old fool never learns," the girl stated, smiling at Deegan.

Deegan was a little taken aback by the girl's statement, but nodded in agreement. *She must've learned a lot in that mission school.* He studied her out of the corner of his eye. "You throw very well."

The girl appeared to be concentrating on the movement of the goats, but her slight smile showed she was proud of what she had said and guessed it had surprised him. She also liked his compliment. She herded the goats into a pen behind a small crumbling house, pulled the gate shut and slipped a loop of wire over it. "I will milk them after I get you something cool to drink," she stated, motioning toward the house.

A frail, dark-skinned, white-haired little woman with a deeply lined face stepped out onto the sagging steps of the house and rattled off several sentences in rapid Spanish.

The girl answered, speaking even faster. "This is my mother," she said, motioning to the woman. "She says welcome to our home."

That's not exactly what she said, Deegan told himself, smiled at the wrinkled woman and bowed slightly. *"Buenos tardes, señora. Gracias."*

The aged woman rattled off more quick Spanish and the girl threw a long string of words back at her. The old woman made a face, turned and disappeared into the house.

"Please, sit down," the girl said, motioning toward a bench in the shaded area beside the door. "I will bring you something cool from the well."

Deegan sat on the bench and watched as she pulled a rope until a clay jug with a cloth cover appeared. She unhooked it and pointed to a tin cup hanging in the eaves above him.

He stood, lifted the cup, glanced in it and held it out to the girl. She removed the cloth from the jug and poured white liquid into the cup.

Deegan looked down at it questioningly. "Goat milk?"

"*Si,* you were expecting water, *señor*?" she said, with a laugh. "Or maybe *tequila*?"

Deegan shook his head, raised the mug

and took a sip. It was cool, almost sweet. "Not bad," he said and took a deep swallow. "Not *tequila,* but not bad." He laughed, drank the rest of the liquid and turned the cup over. "It's good, but that's all I want."

She took the cup, refilled it from the jug, drank it empty, smacked her lips, smiled up at him and offered him the cup again.

He shook his head and smiled. "Thanks, but I ain't that thirsty."

"My mother has fresh *tortillas* in the house," the girl said. "What is your name, s*eñor*?"

"Jefferson," Deegan lied. "Ah . . . Thomas Jefferson."

"Just like the American president," she stated, keeping a straight face.

"Like the American president," Deegan replied, knowing she knew he was lying.

"Please sit down while I go in and bring you some *tortillas.* Would you like beans?" she asked.

"That would be good," he answered and nodding, held out his closed hand.

She looked at his hand questioningly.

"This is for all of your troubles and the food," he said and motioned her to put out her hand.

She held out an open hand and felt the gold nugget drop into it. Her eyes grew large when she saw what he had given her. "Oh, no, *Señor* Jefferson," she said holding it between her fingers and offering it back to him. "This is too much!"

"It's for you and I'll be greatly offended if you don't take it," Deegan told her. "I found it and I can find more. Take it, please."

She looked closely at the nugget, smiled, turned and ran into the house.

Deegan could hear the fast Spanish conversation inside and the mother's voice appeared to be softening.

The girl reappeared and motioned to him to come inside. "My mother has fresh *tortillas* and beans. She would be honored if you would sit and eat with us."

Deegan smiled and followed the girl. The house was clean and filled with the smell of well-seasoned beans and fresh *tortillas*. The mother's toothless grin was immense as she took his arm and led him to a chair. A plate of *tortillas* was set in the middle of the table and the old woman brought a pot of beans from the small cooking fireplace in the corner. *I guess the size of that nugget must've softened the old girl's heart a bit.*

The girl crossed herself, folded her hands and bowed her head.

Deegan quickly followed her example.

When they finished eating, the mother

handed Deegan a neatly tied cloth bundle, smiled her toothless smile and rattled off several quick sentences to the girl.

"My mother has made you food to take with you. It is *tortillas* filled with beans. She says you are very . . . ah . . . ah . . . generous and she thanks you very much."

Deegan smiled. *"Gracias, señora."*

The two women walked outside with him and the old woman gave him another toothless smile. *"Via con Dios,"* she uttered softly.

"She says . . . ," the girl started.

"I know that one," Deegan interrupted, smiled and bowed to the old woman. *"Gracias."* He turned to the girl. "It's time for me to go. You know my name, but I don't know yours."

"Helena, my name is Helena Gallegos," the girl answered, with a coy smile.

"Well, Helena Gallegos, I hope that I see you again one day," Deegan said and held up his little bundle of food. "I thank you again. *Gracias.*"

CHAPTER TWENTY-ONE

Charlie Deegan left the house and walked toward the main dirt street when two gunshots cracked the air. He ducked behind a corner of the house, motioned the two women to go inside and drew his pistol. *I sure as hell hope I don't have to use this thing. Now's when I should have the damned shotgun up in my pack.* He checked the shells, lowered the gun down and peeked out into the street.

A tall man, dressed entirely in black with a large black *sombrero* set on the back of his head, rode a prancing black horse in the street, a smoking, silver pistol raised high above his head. A second silver pistol was holstered on his gun belt. As the horse danced in circles, he shouted in Spanish and old men and women stepped out to stand in the street with their hands raised.

"It is the evil man who calls himself *El Loco Lobo,* the Crazy Wolf."

Helena's voice startled Deegan and he spun, his gun pointing at her face. "I'm sorry," he whispered and lowered the gun. "Don't sneak up on me like that."

"He comes through here every two or three months and demands money from the people," the girl explained, quietly. "This time he is telling us he has heard of a silver crucifix in the church and he wants it. Last time he came, we had no money to give him so he burned one of the houses and shot one of my goats. Then his men shot a burro and when the man who owned the burro shouted at them, *El Loco Lobo* shot him in the stomach so he would suffer and die slowly. He and his men took two young women into the hills and did bad things to them. Later, one of the girls walked into the river and drowned. The other one never comes out of her house. Her mother says she is going to have a baby and she cries all the time. I am the only other young woman in the village, but I have always been able to hide when they have come here so they have not seen me."

"*You* better go hide."

"They do not know I am back here," Helena argued.

"How many other men does he have?"

"Sometimes there are three or four, sometimes six or seven," the girl whispered.

"Do you know where they are?"

Helena's eyes grew large and Deegan felt something poke against his back. A guttural voice spoke loudly in Spanish and Deegan slowly raised his hands. The man reached over his shoulder, yanked the gun from his hand and roughly prodded him into the street. He waved the pistol at Helena and she quickly stepped up to walk beside Deegan.

El Loco Lobo yanked the reins and spun his horse to face them.

Deegan could see the *bandito*'s sweeping black mustache and the hard set of his eyes. He wore large, silver *charro* spurs with heavy, silver-decorated straps, but his black clothes were threadbare and patched in several places. He was not so elegant up close. He pushed his *sombrero* back off his head with his pistol and his long, black hair was dirty and greasy, with a lock of it hanging down across one eye. He tried to flip it away with the back of his hand as he shouted something in Spanish to the man prodding Deegan.

The man yelled back and both of them laughed.

El Loco Lobo needed a shave and showed stained, broken teeth under his mustache when he laughed and spit a cud of tobacco in the general direction of Deegan and the girl. He spoke again, pointing at Helena and both men laughed.

Deegan understood enough to know what they had in mind for Helena.

El Loco Lobo began wheeling his horse and shouting at the people again.

Stars came to Deegan's eyes and his knees folded when the man behind him hit him sharply over the ear with the barrel of his own pistol. He shook his head and tried to stand, but the man kicked him in the back and he flopped forward into the dirt.

"Do not get up, Mister Jefferson," the girl whispered, dropping to her knees and putting a hand on his arm. "They will push you down again and next time it may be worse."

Deegan turned his head to look up at the girl and then at the man standing over him.

El Loco Lobo spoke; the man laughed and kicked Deegan in the ribs, bent down, ran his hand over Helena's breasts and shouted something to the bandit leader.

Helena recoiled and spit at him.

Deegan folded up as if to cover himself from more kicks, slid his hand into his pants pocket and grasped the small pistol. *I don't even know if this thing shoots.*

185

El Loco Lobo called out, the door of the church opened and the old nun hobbled out on her cane followed by a line of subdued children.

A roughly dressed man, with a pistol in his hand, walked out, followed by the white-haired priest who was being prodded with a pistol by another man in ragged clothes.

The old priest's head was bowed; blood ran from his nose and one of his eyes was swollen shut. The man behind pushed him sharply into the street and he staggered, but managed to regain his balance before he lifted his head to look up at the man on the horse.

The first man said something to *El Loco Lobo.*

"He says there is no crucifix in the church and the priest will not tell him where it is hidden," Helena whispered. "The priest tells him the crucifix is only a story. It does not exist."

Deegan nodded that he understood what had been said.

The priest spoke softly.

"The priest says to kill him, but leave the children alone."

El Loco Lobo shouted and the man standing over Deegan swung his pistol up and shot one of the old men standing at the edge of the street. The impact of the bullet lifted his bare feet from the dirt and dropped him to the ground a foot away. A woman wailed and fell to cover the dead body with her own.

The bandit leader spoke again in rapid Spanish and his men laughed. "He says he would shoot us all, but they do not have enough bullets," the girl said, quietly. "He told the priest he would not kill a man of the church, but he does not mind shooting others. It is up to the priest to decide how many people will die today."

Deegan slid the small pistol from his pocket, cocked it, tilted it up beside his arm and squeezed the trigger. The sound of the shot was almost like a handclap and the man standing over him screamed, grabbed his crotch and fell to his knees.

CHAPTER TWENTY-TWO

Charlie Deegan grabbed the gun the man had dropped in the dirt, rolled and shot at *El Loco Lobo.* The slug tore a hole through the ear of his horse and it reared, snorted and bucked.

A barking dog ran into the street and snapped at the hooves of the bucking horse.

El Loco Lobo dropped his fancy silver pistol to the dirt street, grabbed the saddle horn and fought to stay in the saddle.

Deegan fired again, under the rearing horse. The slug tore into the *bandito* standing beside the priest and he dropped into the dirt.

My God, I hit him! I've never hit anything at a distance with a damned pistol. Deegan's hands began to shake as he realized what he had just done.

The children screamed and scattered in all directions, as the people fell flat where they stood.

The old nun dropped her cane and hobbled with amazing speed back to grab the hand of the white-haired priest and pull him toward the church.

The crotch-wounded, kneeling man made a gurgling sound and Deegan looked over to see Helena standing behind him. She held his head back by the hair with one hand and a bloody, long-bladed knife was gripped in the other. The man's throat was cut from ear to ear.

The other *bandito* fired wildly from across the street, the slug punching into the man with the slashed throat, shoving him backward into Helena and toppling both of them to the ground.

Helena pushed free of the man's body, knelt and spit in his face. "You pig! You will never do to me what you did to Margarita and Yolie. I will never drown myself or cry in my house for a pig like you," she screamed in Spanish, spit, dropped behind the body for cover and continued to shout at the dead man as she pounded her fists on his chest.

Deegan fired and missed the *bandito* running for cover behind a house.

The *bandito* shot back at Deegan as he dived and disappeared behind the building.

Deegan fired and chunked adobe from the

189

wall as the man vanished. He scrambled to his feet, ran to the opposite corner, raised his gun with his shaking hands and waited for the man to circle the house.

El Loco Lobo cursed as he held on and fought the horse, bucking up and down the street, the dog still barking and snapping at its hooves.

A boy appeared around the corner of a house, threw a rock at the kicking horse and rider and disappeared again.

El Loco Lobo cursed at the boy, the dog, the horse and everything in general as they disappeared behind the church.

"Mister Jefferson!" Helena cried, and Deegan turned to see the *bandito* run around the corner and fire a shot at him.

Deegan rolled to the ground, lifted his pistol with both hands and fired, hitting the man in the chest and dropping him onto his back. His hands were shaking harder as he stood and looked at his smoking pistol. "I've never hit anything with a pistol and now I've killed two men in a minute with one," he said through nerve-chattering teeth.

"Mister Jefferson!" Helena shouted.

Deegan spun to see a dirt-covered *El Loco Lobo* standing in the street, his second silver pistol clutched in his hand. The *bandito* grinned, showing his stained teeth, yelled something in Spanish, raised the pistol, cocked it and aimed at Deegan.

Deegan crouched, swung his pistol up, thumbed the hammer and squeezed the trigger. The hammer snapped down, but nothing happened. "Damn, I'm empty." Deegan's fingers went to his gun belt.

El Loco Lobo laughed as he squeezed the trigger. His pistol snapped, but there was no gunshot. The *bandito* swore, cocked his pistol and squeezed the trigger. Snap! Continuing to swear, he repeated the process. His second gun was empty!

Deegan couldn't believe his good fortune. With wagging fingers, he managed to clear an empty casing from his pistol and fumbled at his belt for a bullet. One bullet was all he needed to kill the *bandito.*

He pulled a bullet and it fell into the dirt by his foot. "Damn." He glanced down to find the dropped bullet as his fingers searched for another bullet in his belt. He slid it free of the belt loop and it fell from his trembling fingers.

With a roar, *El Loco Lobo* threw his silver pistol, drew a long-bladed knife and charged Deegan.

Deegan looked up and his hand brushed against the small pistol he'd stuck in his gun belt. He pulled and cocked it as he prepared to meet the *bandito*'s charge.

El Loco Lobo bore down on him, swearing and swinging his knife in wide arcs.

Deegan leaped to one side, spun and fired at the running man's back as he passed. The bullet made a small puff of dust as it tore into his shoulder.

El Loco Lobo grunted with pain and his knife hand dropped. He took several steps and raised his other hand to feel the small wound in his shoulder. He glanced at his bloody fingers, turned and switched the knife to his good hand. He glared at the people standing in the street. He hefted the knife as if to assure his courage, gave Deegan a broken-toothed smile and muttered in Spanish.

Deegan knew the wound hadn't hurt the *bandito* enough to stop him. He glanced at the cartridges in the dirt, tossed the small pistol aside and dropped to his knees. He looked at the *bandito* as he felt for more cartridges.

The smile faded from *El Loco Lobo*'s face. The *gringo* had gone to his knees and thrown the small gun away. His big gun was empty. Was he giving up? He glanced around at the people. The girl who had called out to warn the *gringo* was nowhere to be seen. He shouted curses at the people to get back on their bellies, but they didn't move. They were no longer afraid.

Two boys appeared in the street, determined looks on their faces and rocks clutched in their dirty hands.

El Loco Lobo cursed louder and swung his knife, but the boys stood their ground. The braver boy even laughed and threw a rock. The *bandito* ducked under it. They were not afraid of a man who no longer held his fancy silver pistols. *These people will all be afraid of me again when I kill the gringo.*

A group of boys appeared from behind a low wall and one of them raised *El Loco Lobo*'s first silver pistol with both hands, pointed it at the bandit leader and pulled the trigger. Nothing happened. The pistol was not cocked. One of the older boys grabbed it from him, managed to cock it, lift it in both hands and pointed it at the *bandito* leader, who laughed and waved his knife at the boy. The boy pulled the trigger, the gun roared with a ball of flame and smoke and the bullet kicked up dirt beside *El Loco Lobo*'s foot. The recoil caused the boy to stagger backward and fall to the street.

El Loco Lobo, shouting curses, ran toward the boy holding the smoking pistol.

The boy scrambled to his feet, the pistol

still clutched in his hands, and pushed through his friends.

El Loco Lobo knocked children aside and a rock bounced off his head as he passed.

The boy glanced over his shoulder to see *El Loco Lobo* dive at him and he skidded in the dirt trying to change directions.

The *bandito* landed in a cloud of dirt, but grabbed one of the boy's ankles and yanked his legs from under him.

The boy tried to throw the pistol, but the *bandito* grabbed his hand and twisted the gun free.

The boy stood and ran off to join his cheering friends, who threw rocks and ran to hide.

El Loco Lobo, covered with dirt, struggled to his feet and checked his pistol. Still cursing, he turned to find Deegan standing with his pistol clutched in quavering hands. He knew he hadn't had time to reload.

"You stupid *gringo perro, you dog,*" *El Loco Lobo* shouted in Spanish. "I have one bullet in my gun. How many do you have in yours?"

Deegan, his jaws clenched against his chattering teeth, shook his head.

Laughing, almost hysterically, *El Loco Lobo* raised his silver pistol.

Deegan swung his pistol up with both

hands, crouched, aimed and pulled the trigger. Flame and smoke burst from the barrel of Deegan's gun and cut off the laughter.

There was a look of surprise on *El Loco Lobo*'s face as the slug tore through his chest, lifted, and dropped him unceremoniously to the dirt street.

"Uno bala," Deegan told him in Spanish. "One bullet."

CHAPTER TWENTY-THREE

The boys ran to circle the body of the dead *bandito* where it lay in the street. Several of them kicked dirt on him and soon they were all kicking dirt. One of the boys spit on him and soon they were all spitting.

Deegan pushed through the children to look down at the sightless eyes of *El Loco Lobo* staring up at the cloudless sky.

The children scattered, the boys making gunshot sounds and shooting at each other with finger pistols, the girls gathering to whisper about the adventure they had just been through and trying not to look at the dead men lying in the street.

Deegan heard a cry and twisted around in time to see Helena come running from behind a house, a pitchfork held in front of her at waist level.

Deegan raised his hands. "Whoa, slow down there, Helena!" he shouted. "Everything's over!"

Helena slowed to a walk and noticed all the staring people. She was embarrassed as she lowered her eyes and the pitchfork. She made a series of zigzagged lines in the dirt with the tines before looking up and smiling sheepishly. "I . . . I wanted to help you *Señor* Jefferson, but I could not find a gun. This was all I could find," she said, lifting the pitchfork. "I'm sorry I took so long."

"Don't worry about it, Helena. It makes no difference now anyway," Deegan said softly.

"I thought you were out of bullets for your big *pistola.*"

"I loaded it while he was chasing the boys."

The people dragged the bodies of *El Loco Lobo* and his three gunmen over to the church and lined them up beside a low wall. The priest gave them the last rites, and when the boys thought the priest wasn't looking, they threw rocks at the bodies. The old nun hobbled out, retrieved her cane and shooed the children away with it, only to have the boys circle the church and throw stones from the other side.

The boys were not afraid of the dead *bandito.*

El Loco Lobo was not so bad anymore.

One of the old men walked up, spoke

197

softly to Helena and handed her the *bandito*'s silver pistols.

She looked at them, nodded and brought them over to Deegan. "Juan brought *El Loco Lobo*'s *pistolas* and showed me something," she said and handed him one of the guns. "This is the second *pistola.* Look at the bullets."

"It wasn't loaded," Deegan said. He noticed his hands were no longer trembling as he held them out for the gun.

"Look at the bullets," she insisted.

Deegan took the pistol, opened the loading gate and looked at the indented primers as he turned the cylinder. "So?" he asked. "They've all been fired. He must've forgotten to reload it the last time he shot it. That's why he was using his knife."

"Take the bullets out of the gun and look at them," she instructed.

Deegan watched the loaded cartridges as they fell into his hand. He stuck the pistol in his belt and examined the primers. "These didn't fire. Are you sure this is the second pistol?" he asked.

"*Si.*" She held up the other gun. "This is the first *pistola.* It had been fired four times before he dropped it. The boy fired it once in the street." She lifted it above her head with both hands, cocked it and pulled the trigger. The gun roared. She cocked it again and pulled the trigger. Click! She lowered the pistol.

"You see, *Señor* Jefferson, there were two bullets left in the first *pistola* and they shoot. Why don't the bullets in the second *pistola* shoot?"

Deegan shrugged his shoulders and looked carefully at the second silver pistol. He cocked the hammer, squeezed the trigger and it snapped down. *Something ain't right here.* He carefully watched the action as he slowly cocked it. "Aha!" he said and grinned. There was a small stone in the mechanism at the base of the hammer. "This would keep the hammer from hitting the primers hard enough," he said, pointing out the stone. "It must've gotten in here when it was dropped." He worked the action several times and the stone dropped free.

He reloaded the cartridges, cocked it, pointed it in the air and pulled the trigger. Bang! In rapid succession, he cocked and fired the pistol five more times. The sixth time the hammer clicked down on a spent cartridge and he lowered the pistol.

Helena pointed upward. "Someone is watching over you, *Señor* Jefferson. You have a guardian angel. You are a man who is being watched over." She made the sign of the cross on her breast.

Deegan nodded. "I need some time by myself to think, Helena. Here." He handed her the pistol, turned and looked up at the empty bell tower of the church. "I'll be in the church for a while."

Charlie Deegan stood beside the hard bench at the front of the church and watched the old priest walk through a side door.

He carried a tall silver crucifix slowly to the altar, settled it carefully into place, wiped his finger marks from it, crossed himself, genuflected, spoke softly to the crucifix, crossed himself again and turned to Deegan. "You . . . are a man . . . who . . . God . . . watches over, s*eñor,*" he said in halting English. *"Via con Dios."* The old priest made the sign of the cross on Deegan, shook his hand, walked up the aisle and out of the church.

When he heard the door close, Deegan looked around the dim interior of the church, lit only by light through four small windows and a short row of flickering prayer candles. He sighed, sat on the bench and held his hands out in front of him. They were steady. He lowered his hands and bowed his head. He raised his eyes and looked at the crucifix. "I know I owe You even more now than I did before, but I told You I wasn't meant to be a man of the church. I've been on the wrong trail for too long to change my ways. I killed a man in a bar fight and then killed a man in prison before I escaped from there. I'm a man on the run," he said. "I just killed four more men in the street here, but those men needed killing. I know this ain't right, but I'm gonna try to buy my way outta this." He unbuttoned his shirt, pulled a pair of knotted socks free and swung them loosely from his fingers. He felt the weight and wondered what the gold was worth. He sighed, stood, walked to the altar and laid the socks at the base of the crucifix. "There, now I figure we're about even," he stated flatly, turned and started up the aisle.

Deegan paused with his hand on the door and turned to look back at the altar. A lone beam of sunlight came through a hole in the tiles of the roof and spread across the crucifix. "Oh, damn," he whispered and looked up quickly. "Sorry." He shook his head, dug his fingers back into his shirt and brought out the second pair of knotted socks. He walked back down the aisle, gently laid them on the others and looked up at the crucifix. "I hope this makes us a little more closer to even." He shrugged his shoulders, smiled, walked up the aisle and pushed the door wide enough to see outside. There was no one in sight as he slipped through the door and turned around the corner of the church.

Deegan stopped and looked at *El Loco Lobo*'s black *sombrero* lying in the dirt. *What the hell, it's more like a cowboy'd wear. Better than that cap.* He picked it up, slapped some dust off, reformed the top to his liking and slid it on his head. "It doesn't fit too bad. I'll get used to it."

When he reached the trees, he turned to make sure no one had seen him or was following. Satisfied, he walked to his gear hidden in the tree, brought it down, shouldered his pack and canteen, picked up his rifle and looked back down at the village. "Goodbye, Helena," he said softly. "Maybe I'll be seeing you again someday. Damn, I forgot my tortillas and beans. Oh, well." He glanced at his blue cap, still hanging from the branch and shrugged. "Not the kind of headgear a cowboy'd wear." He put his hand into his pocket, brought out the twenty-dollar gold piece, and as he strode off, flipped it into the air and deftly caught it. "This's a hell of a lot more than I left prison with," he told himself, smiled and began to walk. "One, two, three, four . . ."

CHAPTER TWENTY-FOUR

Charlie Deegan's feet hurt and he was tired from three days of hard walking. He'd worn holes in the soles of Mangas's moccasins and now had two pair of socks inside them. He'd given a wide berth to several small towns, but he could now see a town in the distance and knew from the map in his mind that it must be Pine Spring. He started a mental argument with himself. *It's time to go into a town and buy a decent pair of boots. A bath and a haircut would top it all off. That gold piece ain't getting any fatter by itself in your pocket. You're far enough away from Yuma. Besides, they probably think you're dead by now 'cause nobody can survive that long in the desert. You gotta do it sooner or later. You're gonna ruin your feet if you keep walking in these old moccasins. Damnit, Charlie, go into town and get what you need done.*

An hour later Deegan walked down the

main street of Pine Spring. He stopped and looked at items in the windows of stores and shops that he hadn't seen for a long time. He paused, stared carefully and nodded at his reflection in a window. He couldn't remember how long it had been since he'd seen this much of himself. *Clothes ain't the greatest, but you look okay.* He adjusted his collar and pulled his vest straight. *No need to buy new ones, these'll do for now.* He tipped *El Loco Lobo*'s hat back to have a better look at himself as he thumbed his mustache. *A bath, shave and a haircut are long overdue.* Walking down the board sidewalk, he would sneak sideways glances at his reflection in store windows.

Deegan touched his fingers to the brim of his hat to a woman sweeping the doorway of a store. "Morning, ma'am," he said, with a smile.

She nodded, glanced at his feet and returned a weak smile.

Deegan slowed his pace at a corner and stared across the street at the swinging doors of a saloon. He heard the sound of a tune being beat from an off-key piano. He looked up at the sign above the door:

THE MINE SHAFT SALOON

In his mind, Deegan knew all the sounds and smells inside those swinging doors. Shouting, the raucous laugh of a whore, loud piano music, singing, the click of billiard balls, shuffling of cards, the rattle of poker chips, the snap of coins on the bar, the clink of glasses and bottles. The stench of stale beer, cigars, whiskey, cigarettes, tequila, pipes, unwashed bodies, manure, cheap whore perfume, kerosene lamps, spittoons. . . . He remembered them all very well.

Well? he asked himself, with a shudder. *Can you do it? Can you go over there and have a drink? One drink? It's been over a year since you've tasted liquor. Remember what liquor's done to your life already.* "No," he muttered and shook his head. *I came into town to get new boots, not get drunk.* He turned and continued down the boardwalk until he found a window with a display of shoes and boots. He walked in, set his pack, canteen and rifle by the door and began to look at boots.

The man behind the counter gave him a long look, up and down. "You need any help, just holler," he said as he wrapped a bundle for a woman.

Deegan laid the twenty-dollar gold piece on the counter and slid it toward him. "I'll

206

need a pair of good boots. Had a fire at the cabin and lost my good ones."

The clerk smiled, put the coin in a vest pocket and nodded.

Deegan laid two pair of heavy socks on the counter.

The clerk leaned over and glanced at the new boots on Deegan's feet. "Those boots will be three bucks, the socks are forty-two cents." He scrawled some figures on a sheet of paper and turned it to Deegan. He pulled Deegan's coin from his pocket and laid it on the paper. "Anything else I can help you with?"

Deegan surveyed the shelves. "Let me see, three cans of corned beef, three cans of sardines, a bag of dried apples and a bag of Arbuckle's coffee. Oh, yes, peaches, canned peaches. How much?"

"Ah, sixteen cents a can. A dollar and seventy cents a dozen."

"Gimme a dozen cans . . . No, that's too heavy. Gimme six cans."

"Better deal on a dozen."

"No, just six cans. I don't have that much room left in my pack."

The clerk nodded, stepped to the shelf and set an armload of cans on the counter. "You must really like peaches. Anything else? Tobacco? Ammunition? How about a new hat? That one you've got's seen better days."

Deegan put his hand to the brim of the battered black hat and shook his head. "No, this one carries a few memories that I'm not ready to get rid of. That'll do me for now."

The clerk brought out Deegan's gold coin and looked at it. "Don't see many of these now days." He did some writing on a paper and turned it to Deegan. "You've got fourteen dollars and forty-two cents change coming." He slid the gold coin out of sight, brought up a handful of coins and thumb-counted them out on the counter. "There you go. Looks like you've got enough for a beer or two before you head out."

Deegan recounted the coins and dropped them into a vest pocket. "Where's the closest place I can get a bath, haircut and a shave?" he asked, as he stowed the goods in his pack.

"Down the street to your left is Bradley's Barbershop. Shave and a haircut and a hot bath'll cost you two bits."

Deegan brought his pack over to the counter and stuffed the socks and canned goods in it. "Thanks," he said, as he slung his pack on his shoulders and walked to the door.

"You going far?" the clerk asked.

"No, I'm just looking for somebody needs a body to work a cattle drive. Like to go up to Kansas, Nebraska, even the Dakotas. Someplace to get outta this damned heat. You know of anybody around here's looking for help?"

"Nobody around here that I know of, but I hear tell of a lot of cattle moving up from Texas into Kansas and Nebraska and places north. Good grazing up there. They put them on trains for the east. That's probably your best bet. Head northeast into Colorado."

"Thanks."

The merchant nodded and began to work his pencil again.

Deegan lifted his pack, walked out the door, stepped to the edge of the sidewalk and sat down. He dug Angus's moccasins in the dirt. He dug Angus's knife out of his pocket, opened it, pulled a can of peaches out of his pack, cut the top open and slowly drank most of the juice. *Damn! That's good.* He speared a peach half with the knife, slid it into his mouth and smiled as he savored the flavor. He finished the last of the peaches and drank the juice, stood, threw the empty

209

can on a pile in the alley and looked down the boardwalk for the barbershop.

An hour later Charlie Deegan stepped out onto the board sidewalk, adjusted his gun belt and looked up and down the street. He was shaved, mustache and hair trimmed, bathed and smelled of good bay rum after-shave lotion. He had his pack and canteen hanging from one shoulder and his rifle on the other. He realized from the talk of the barber that he had very little knowledge of what was going on in the country. He didn't know that Benjamin Harrison was the president. When was the last time he'd read a current newspaper? He now looked forward to all the things that he would learn. While he had soaked in the steaming tub, he'd thought about the taste of a beer. He now asked himself, "What could it hurt for me to have one beer? I'm stronger now. I've learned from my mistakes. One beer and out the door would prove how strong I am now."

The Mine Shaft Saloon was across the street. "Do it." He hooked his thumbs under the straps on his shoulders, stepped off the boardwalk, crossed the dusty street and stood with his hands on the tops of the bat-wing doors. It was quiet inside; not what he remembered in his mind when he had first looked at it across the street. A man sat on the piano stool, leaning back over the keyboard and drinking from a large beer. Another man stood at the bar staring at the life-size painting of the naked woman reclining provocatively above the mirror. The bartender was stacking glasses neatly on the end of the bar.

One beer, that's all, just one beer. He pushed in, strode to the bar, dropped his pack by his feet, leaned his rifle against it and laid several coins on the bar.

"What'll you have?" the bartender asked.

Deegan separated a dime from the pile and slid it across the bar. "Beer."

The bartender filled a foaming mug and sent it sliding down the bar. "You got one more coming. Beer's only a nickel."

Deegan nodded, lifted the beer to his mouth, took a sip and smacked his lips. The taste of the beer was strange, yet, oh so familiar. He took another sip through the foam and wiped the white residue from his mustache. "Damn, that's good," he said, and took a deeper swallow.

The big man down the bar dropped his gaze from the naked lady and slowly turned his head to look at Deegan. "Ya say somethin' t'me?" he asked with a slurred voice.

Deegan shook his head. "No, just saying this beer's damned tasty. Been a long time since I had one."

The big man grunted and returned his stare to the naked woman above the mirror.

Deegan turned the beer up and set the empty mug back on the bar. *What the hell. I got one more coming.*

The bartender was talking intently to a well-dressed man who had just come in and was standing at the far end of the bar.

Deegan rapped his empty mug on the bar.

The bartender glanced at him and raised his hand. "I'll be right there," he called and returned to his conversation.

Deegan studied himself in the mirror behind the bar, gazed up at the naked woman and turned his attention to the reflection of the big man standing down the bar. He had obviously been at the bar for some time. He lifted his beer, drained it and slammed the mug onto the bar. "I wanna 'nother beer!" he shouted.

The bartender hurried down the bar. "I think you've had enough. Go sleep it off and come back later when you've sobered up."

The drunk stared at the bartender. "Yer not gonna gimme 'nother beer. Wha' if I jis' took ya by the neck an' shook the shit outta ya? Would ya gimme a beer then?" he asked, belligerently.

The bartender nonchalantly brought a short-barreled shotgun up and laid it on the bar. "If you can reach across this scattergun and get me by the neck, you can shake me," he said, with a sly smile.

Deegan took a quick step away from the bar.

The drunk studied the bartender's face, nodded and pushed away from the bar. "I be back," he slurred. "Coun' on it."

The bartender rapped the barrels of the shotgun on the wood. "Don't do anything stupid. Go across the street to the Rusty Spur. They'll serve anybody."

The big man turned, lost his balance and staggered down the bar to where Deegan held up his hands to stop him. He grumbled, straightened and pushed off the bar. When he turned, one of his spurs caught on a strap of Deegan's pack and he fell forward onto his hands and knees. With a roar, he was on his feet again, glaring down at what had tripped him. Cursing, he kicked Deegan's rifle across the floor, grabbed the pack and swung it to crash out the front window. He spun to face Deegan. "Now I'm gonna throw ya inta the damned street right behin' it," he shouted and swung a hard punch.

Deegan ducked back and raised his hands. "Let it go, friend. I ain't gonna fight you."

The man put his head down and charged.

Deegan sidestepped and the man sprawled across a chair and onto the floor.

Deegan looked beseechingly at the bartender, who only shrugged and grinned.

The drunk managed to get onto his hands and knees and glare up at Deegan.

"I told you, I ain't gonna fight you," Deegan repeated, shaking his head. "I'd whip your ass sure. You ain't a fighter; you're just a damned mean drunk. Let it go."

The man staggered to his feet, his hand coming out from behind him holding a large knife. He moved the knife from hand to hand, as he stalked Deegan.

Deegan's hand brushed against the gun on his hip. *If you shoot him, it'll be self-defense. He pulled the knife first, but they might lock you up until they decide.* He retreated until his legs contacted the pool table. He reached back to get his balance and his hand rolled across a pool cue. He brought it up and swung it, making swooshing sounds as it cut through the air. "All right, you sumbitch, I'm telling you to back off!" he shouted, swinging the cue. "This thing'll peel your scalp back like a knife! This is your last warning. Drop the damned knife!"

The saloon doors slammed open and a short Mexican wearing a gold star on his vest and carrying a shotgun across his arm stepped into the room. "What seems to be the problem, James?" he asked the bartender.

"Well, Sheriff Baca, the drunk cowboy threw the other man's bag out through the window and now he wants to throw him out behind it, but he doesn't seem to want to cooperate so now they're having a standoff. I'd say the fella with the pool cue has the advantage right now."

Deegan stared at the little man with the shotgun. *Baca? Is this the sheriff that smashed Bob's face? I's warned he's a mean one.*

"I would advise you, *señor,* to drop that knife," Sheriff Baca said, motioning to the floor with his shotgun. "And you, *señor,* please put the pool cue on the table. It is hard to find a good cue in this town."

The bartender and the man at the end of the bar chuckled nervously.

The man with the knife looked at Sheriff Baca and then at Deegan.

"I will not ask you again, *señor,*" the

sheriff stated softly and cocked the hammers of the shotgun. "I give you two choices. Jail or a grave."

The knife clattered to the floor.

Deegan immediately laid the cue on the table behind him.

"Now the gun belt, *señor,*" the sheriff instructed, pointing the shotgun at Deegan, who quickly unbuckled his gun belt and let it drop to the floor.

"That's his rifle," the bartender said, pointing across the room. "The drunk kicked it over there."

"I will be back for the guns later. Now, *señores,* you will go with me to the jail where we will discuss some important points of the law here in Pine Spring." Sheriff Baca motioned toward the door with his shotgun. "You, *señor,*" he said to Deegan. "Pick up your bag from the sidewalk and bring it with you to the jail."

CHAPTER TWENTY-FIVE

Sheriff Baca closed the door of the jail, stood in front of the tall drunken cowboy and smiled up at him. "*Señor,* I do not like problems in my town. You are a problem." The stock of the shotgun was a blur as it came up to smash into the side of the man's face. Totally unprepared, the drunk slammed backward and slid down the cell-block door. Blood ran from his nose and a deep cut on the side of his face, as he lay unconscious on the floor.

Deegan braced himself.

Sheriff Baca pulled a hanky from his pocket, wiped the blood from the stock of his shotgun and stood it in a rack beside the door. "I have been watching him for two days now. He is a troublemaker. He started fights in other bars in my town. Today was his last day to cause fights. I do not like a man who gets mean when he gets drunk. What about you, *señor?*"

"Uh, no, I don't like a mean drunk," Deegan answered.

"You have the face of a fighter, *señor*. Are you a mean drunk? A bar fighter?"

"No, Sheriff, I was just having a beer before I headed north. Matter of fact that was the first drink I've had in over a year. I stopped to buy some new boots and a few supplies I needed," Deegan explained, pointing at his new boots. "He started it and I's doing everything I could to avoid a fight. Ask the bartender."

"Do you like what I did to him?" Baca asked, motioning to the man lying with his face in a growing pool of blood.

Deegan shook his head.

"What is your name, *señor*?"

"De . . . Devries. Devries. Martin Devries."

The sheriff nodded. "Have you ever been in prison, *Señor* Devries?"

Deegan shook his head. "No, Sheriff, I never been in prison."

The sheriff studied him through narrowed eyes. "How did your face get so beaten, *Señor* Devries?"

"I was a boxer in the army."

The sheriff nodded. "I see. Did you win your fights, *señor*?"

"At first, Sheriff," Deegan answered, with

a slight smile.

"Why do you smile at that?"

"They just kept matching me up with faster and tougher fighters," Deegan answered truthfully. "They kept getting younger and faster and I just kept getting older."

"And slower?" Baca said. "Why haven't you had a drink in over a year?"

Deegan looked carefully at the sheriff. *He's trying to trap you. Be careful how you answer him.*

"I am waiting for an answer, *señor.*"

Deegan nodded. "I got out of the army and went into the mountains to look for gold. I was drinking too much in the army anyway."

"That was the answer to my next question. What do you do for a living? Now I know you are a prospector."

Deegan nodded.

"You do not mind if I look through your bag, do you *Señor* . . . I am sorry, I do not remember your name."

"Devries. Martin Devries. No, go ahead, I got nothing to hide."

Sheriff Baca dumped the contents of Deegan's bag on the floor, knelt and quickly sorted through it. He laid the two parts of the shotgun and three cans of peaches on his desk. "I like peaches and you seem to have enough to share."

Deegan nodded and smiled weakly. *They were cheap, so let him have what he wants. It might get me outta here. Don't do anything to rile the little bastard.*

"You may pack your bag again. Oh, *Señor* Devries, do you have another gun?" he asked tapping his fingers on the shotgun. "Besides those over in the saloon?"

"No, Sheriff . . ." Deegan remembered the small pistol in his pocket. "Wait, I just remembered, I've got a small pistol in my pants pocket."

"That is very stupid, *señor.*"

"I . . . I'm sorry, Sheriff," Deegan stuttered. "I honestly forgot I had it. That's the truth. It's so small . . . It's mainly for snakes and it's usually in my pack. I took it out earlier and forgot it was in my pocket."

The sheriff put his hand on his holstered pistol. "I would advise you to put it on the desk. Very slowly and very carefully."

Deegan nodded as he slid his hand into a pocket, brought out the little pistol between his finger and thumb, laid it on the desk and raised his hands.

Sheriff Baca motioned for him to step back and picked up the pistol. He examined it and laughed. "I think the only thing this

220

pistol is good for is to put rust stains in your pocket. You are lucky because I believe it when you tell me you forgot it was in your pocket. A gun like this is good to forget." He dropped it back onto the desk.

There's a dead Mexican back in San Rafael who might not agree with you, Deegan thought as he nodded in agreement with the sheriff.

"Now, *Señor* Devries, pack your bag."

Deegan quickly stuffed all the things back into his canvas bag.

"Why do you keep those old moccasins?"

"They remind me of part of my past life."

"How so?"

"My old shoes wore out and those were all I could find to fit me."

The man on the floor stirred and moaned.

"Help me move him back into a cell," Baca ordered.

They dragged the man through a door and into the first cell. "Leave him on the floor. I do not want a bloodstained mattress in my jail. It makes for bad rumors." The sheriff pointed to a pail in a corner of the cell. "Take that out back and fill it from the pump. Then put it in here for him to clean up if he wants to."

Deegan returned with the pail full of water and carried it into the cell. As he set it on

221

the floor, he heard the door of the cell slam and the sheriff turn the key.

Deegan spun to see Baca standing with his hands on his hips, smiling at him.

"Wha . . . what in the hell's the meaning of this?" Deegan stammered, sweat forming on his forehead. He stepped forward and gripped the bars. He heard a moan behind him and glanced over his shoulder to see the man had regained consciousness and was glaring at him.

The sheriff grabbed a handful of rags from a shelf and threw them at the bars.

"Clean yourself up, *señor,*" the sheriff ordered. "I will be back later to see if I need to get a doctor to sew up your face. That scar will always remind you about my laws in Pine Spring."

"What about me?" Deegan asked. "You've got no reason to lock me up."

"I still have some questions about you, *Señor* Devries. Help your friend get cleaned up." Baca chuckled as he opened the door to his office. "Maybe he will want to finish your fight."

The door to the cell room closed and Deegan shook the barred door. Sweat was running down his back. *God, I can't be locked up again. Not back to the prison at Yuma.*

He heard the man behind him move and

spun to face him.

The man with the bloody face was on his feet, eyes filled with anger. He rolled his shoulders and raised his hands.

"I'm telling you if you come after me I'm gonna beat you to death," Deegan hissed, pointing a fist at him. "So help me, I'll beat you to death."

The man saw the look in Deegan's eyes, his scarred face, his stance, balled fists and decided he was probably capable of doing what he said. He slumped back on the bunk and tentatively ran his fingers over the puffy cut on his cheek.

Deegan pulled the rags through the bars, wiped his face with one and threw the rest at the man on the bunk. "Here, clean yourself up. You look like hell!"

An hour later, drenched in sweat, Deegan sat on the floor lost in deep, nervous thought.

The other man slumped on the edge of the bed holding a bloodstained rag against his face. "Why'd the little Mexican bastard have to hit me with his shotgun? He had me here in his damned jail. All he had to do was lock me up and lemme sleep it off. He didn't have to hit me like that."

Deegan shook his head. "I don't understand him." His mind had become his worst enemy. All he could think about was going back to Yuma Prison. *The snake den. I can't do more time in the dark cell. I'll go crazy. I'll make a run for it on the way back and hope they shoot me.*

The door to the cell room opened and Deegan scrambled to his feet.

Sheriff Baca stood in the open door and another man stepped up to look over his shoulder. "I don't have to tell you which man to look at, Doctor," Baca said. "That was a terrible fall he took back in my office. Drunks, you know how they are sometimes when they try to walk."

The other man grunted as he stepped up and looked at Deegan. "Anything wrong with you?"

Deegan shook his head.

"Why are you sweating so bad? It's not that hot back here. Matter a fact, it's rather cool."

"I'm fine," Deegan replied weakly. "Take a look at him."

The sheriff unlocked the cell door. "Come with me, *Señor* Devries, while Doctor Murdock looks at the cut on your friend's face."

Damn, this man's cold, Deegan thought as he stepped past him.

The contents of Deegan's bag were again

224

strewn on the floor and he saw there were no cans of peaches, one can of corned beef and one can of sardines. *The little bastard took most of my food.* He saw a definite bend in the barrel of his shotgun.

The sheriff sat at his desk and motioned for him to sit on the other chair.

"*Señor* Devries, you have seen how I handle justice problems here in Pine Spring. I would say that you are not very comfortable being locked up. Am I not right?"

Deegan nodded.

"I didn't hear your answer, *Señor* Devries."

"I've seen how you handle justice, Sheriff."

"What about being locked up, *Señor* Devries?"

He's playing games with you, Deegan thought. "No, Sheriff, I don't like being locked up," he answered matter-of-factly. "I don't like it at all."

Sheriff Baca nodded. "I will give you some advice, *Señor* Devries. I would suggest that if I decide to let you go, you never come back to Pine Spring. Do you understand?"

"I understand."

Sheriff Baca pointed at the bag on the floor. "Pack your bag, *Señor* Devries. As soon as you clean up the blood on the floor,

225

I think I will let you go. There is a mop and bucket out by the pump. You know where it is. Go do it now."

Deegan finished mopping up the blood and Sheriff Baca nodded his approval. "Put the mop and the bucket back and we will talk more before I let you go."

When Deegan returned, Sheriff Baca asked him, "How much money do you have, *Señor* Devries?"

"Fourteen dollars and change."

"The window in the saloon will cost you three dollars to repair."

"Wait a minute," Deegan argued. "The man back in the cell broke that window."

"It was your bag, wasn't it?"

Deegan nodded. *Don't be stupid, pay the damn fine and get outta town.*

"Good, we have an understanding about the window." Baca exclaimed and slapped his hands down on the desk. "There is also a five-dollar fine for being drunk and disorderly and a five-dollar fine for a concealed weapon. A fine and confiscation of the weapon."

Deegan paled. "Wha . . . ?"

"The five-dollar fine for the concealed weapon or thirty days in jail," the sheriff stated. "Think how much you would sweat being in jail for thirty days. For all I know

226

you are a wanted man with a reward on your head." He pointed at a thick wad of reward posters hooked on a nail on the wall. "In thirty days, I can get many letters of inquiry sent to places like the Territorial Prison at Yuma. It is your choice. Thirteen dollars or jail."

He's playing with you. Just take this as a lesson and keep moving.

"You will still have money left, *Señor* Devries. Who knows, maybe you will find gold after you leave here." The sheriff put his hands behind his head and leaned back in his chair. "I know you are much smarter than the man back in the cell. Thirteen dollars, please."

Deegan pulled the coins from a vest pocket, counted out thirteen dollars and laid them on the desk.

Sheriff Baca looked at the money, smiled and waved at the door. "Good luck with your prospecting, *Señor* Devries."

As Deegan turned the doorknob, the sheriff raised his hand. "One more thing. You should get some better prospecting tools. You cannot pick too much gold from the rocks with the barrel of that shotgun in your pack. I don't think you can shoot much with it anymore either. Oh, and don't forget to go back to the saloon for your other guns.

Tell James I said it was all right for him to give them to you. Tell him I will stop in later with the money for his window your bag destroyed. You may need those guns because prospecting can be a very dangerous business." Baca waved his hand at the door. "Go now."

Deegan opened the door and slowly stepped out onto the boardwalk. *He's playing with you.* He pulled the door shut and stood thinking about what had happened. *Get out of town before the little Mexican bastard changes his mind.* He grimaced at the sound of Sheriff Baca's laughter behind the closed door.

CHAPTER TWENTY-SIX

Charlie Deegan's feet no longer hurt from his new boots and Sheriff Baca and the Pine Spring jail were three days behind him. He had not seen another person on the road today and whenever he had heard or seen anyone, he would slip off into the brush and hide. He walked into the trees, shrugged out of his pack, leaned his rifle against a tree and sat down. He looked up at the sun to figure the time, leaned back against his pack and promptly fell asleep.

The crack of a gunshot awakened Deegan. He sat up, instantly alert and listening. Several more shots and an Indian war cry. He worked the action of his rifle and trotted to where he could see out. Another volley of shots and more war cries. He stared in the direction of the din. Small puffs of smoke came from a wooded area across a small valley followed quickly by the rattle of gunfire.

Unexpectedly a mule, loaded with a large canvas-covered pack and dragging a lead rope, bolted from the trees, galloping headlong down the side of a steep hill. A running Indian whooped as he ran in pursuit of the runaway animal. He dropped to one knee, raised his rifle and fired.

As the sound of the shot reached Deegan, the mule plunged forward, flipped end-over-end and rolled sideways down through the rocks and thick brush. The pack broke open, leaving a trail of spilled boxes as the animal bounced and tumbled down the slope.

The Indian leaped to his feet and charged toward the mule. The beast thudded to rest against the trunk of a large tree.

The noise of more shots in the trees caused the Indian to stop and look back. He stood as if trying to decide which way to go before giving a cry of triumph and bounding down the hill toward the dead mule.

I'm sure those were army markings on that animal's pack, so that means soldiers are fighting over there. I'd best head across and see if I can lend a hand. Course there's no real reason to get involved in something that ain't any of my concern.

Deegan watched the Indian stop by the dead animal and pull at something on the pack. He leaned his rifle against the carcass, drew a knife and began to saw at the ropes.

Deegan raised his rifle, took careful aim and squeezed the trigger.

The slug punched into the tree above the Indian's head and he vaulted over the mule and disappeared.

Deegan dropped to his knees, jacked in a fresh round, rested against a tree and watched over the end of the barrel for the Indian to make a move. *Drop the next slug a little.*

A dark hand snapped up and grabbed for the rifle.

Deegan quickly aimed and squeezed the trigger, but the rifle was already out of sight. He shook his head as he jacked in a fresh round. "Damn, that was a waste of a shot," he muttered to himself. "Why don't you just hand the damned thing to him?" There was no sign of movement around the carcass and the gunfire continued higher in the trees. "You could just slide back there, get your stuff and skedaddle outta here and nobody'd be any the wiser," he argued with himself.

As he watched, the end of a rifle barrel slowly slid up over the shoulder of the dead animal. *Looks like the sumbitch wants to do battle.* He gritted his teeth, took a careful aim, adjusted his sight and slowly squeezed the trigger. He watched the mule through the smoke from the rifle barrel. The slug cut into the animal's shoulder, the wide-eyed Indian snapped upright from behind it and settled backward out of sight. There was a small dark hole in the dirty yellow cloth wrapped across his forehead.

"Yeah!" Deegan shouted. "That's where I wanted it to go!"

The gunfire across the valley was becoming more sporadic. "Oh, hell, I best get over and see if I can help," he muttered to himself as he stood and swung his bag onto his shoulder.

Deegan reloaded his rifle and as he got closer to the battle, the shooting was down to one or two well-spaced shots at a time and then it was silent. He could hear loud voices he couldn't understand. He dropped his bag and slipped from tree to tree until he could see movement in a clearing ahead. At the edge of the opening, he saw dead horses laying in a circle and five Indians animatedly arguing and gesturing. The Indians wore breechcloths, moccasins and a colored piece of cloth wrapped around their foreheads and long black hair. Each had a distinct pattern painted on his face. They all had rifles, four of them wore cartridge belts around their waists and the fifth, the tallest, had two cartridge belts crisscrossed on his chest.

Deegan could see boots and yellow-striped pant legs sticking out from behind one of the horses.

The tallest Indian kicked the boots as he shouted at the others. Two of them pulled knives and motioned downward. The tall Indian nodded. They shouted and dropped to their knees behind the dead horses. The third pulled his knife and knelt beside them. One of them lifted a soldier's head by the hair, sawed his knife through the skin on the man's forehead, snapped the bloody scalp free, held it high over his head and screamed in victory.

Deegan could see the blue collar of a uniform, a red bandanna and shoulder boards before the bloody head dropped from sight. *An officer! That's probably why they're arguing. Who got the honor of scalping the officer?*

Another Indian lifted a soldier's head by the hair and began to cut into the man's scalp.

Deegan raised his rifle, aimed and squeezed the trigger. The slug hit the tall Indian just above the crossed belts and threw him over backward outside the circle of dead horses. He jacked the action of his rifle and fired low at the other standing Indian, who glanced at the smoke and dropped for cover. The slug went through the side of the man's face and he flopped against the carcass of a horse. The other three Indians vanished.

Deegan worked in a fresh round and waited for movement. A bush wiggled slightly beyond the dead-horse fort. He fired a quick shot at the bush and darted to another tree. *That sure as hell sounded like I hit something.* He reloaded as he ran from tree to tree to circle the bush he had fired into. He took a quick peek around the tree and made out a dirty yellow piece of cloth and dark eyes glaring at him from under it. He spun to the other side of the tree, swung his rifle up and fired at the yellow blur.

The Indian's head jerked back and he fell forward.

Deegan jacked the action of his rifle. *Two more.* He could see inside the circle of dead horses where three dead soldiers were sprawled. *Sorry I got here late.*

An Indian burst from behind a tree to his left, screaming and firing his rifle as he ran.

Deegan swung his rifle up and fired, the slug catching the Indian in the side of his chest and spinning him to the ground.

"One more," he muttered, reloading and squatting with his back against a tree for protection. *He's gotta be coming after me. It's a matter of honor for him now.*

A squirrel jumped from one branch to another, scampered to a higher limb on a tree not far away and sat chattering at something below him.

"Thanks," Deegan whispered as he concentrated on the area the squirrel was scolding. He brought his knees up and laid the rifle on them pointing into the woods. He looked up into the tree to see if the squirrel was still there. The little gray animal lay on a branch intently watching something below. Deegan lowered his eyes to where the squirrel was looking and shot into the brush.

Before the smoke cleared, the Indian rose, returned fire and dropped from sight. The slug dug into the tree above Deegan's head and he rolled to the ground. *That red bastard knows where I am now.* He reloaded, scooted backwards to find cover and looked up at the squirrel.

The animal was looking to his right and chattering.

Deegan crawled to his left. *I'll just stay on the opposite side of the circle.* He glanced up at the squirrel and then back to where it was watching. *That Indian's got to know the squirrel's telling me where he is.* He detected movement and slowly slid the barrel of his rifle through the branches of the bush in front of him.

The Indian had seen the rifle barrel slide out of a bush pointing slightly away from him. He knew the white man was watching where the squirrel was looking. The Indian had seen the coyote gliding through the brush following his nose in the direction of the fresh blood of the horses at the same time the squirrel had seen the animal from above and he was now watching the coyote. The Indian slipped silently through the brush to the tree beside the rifle barrel. He leaned his rifle lightly against the tree, slid his knife from the sheath and poised himself to spin around the tree and sink it into the white man. He took a deep breath, swung around screaming a war cry and found himself looking down at a rifle resting in the branches of a bush. He spun back around the tree and looked into the eyes of Charlie Deegan standing with a pistol raised in both hands. The Indian saw the flash of the muzzle, the slug punched through his chest, bouncing him back against the tree and he toppled to the ground. He coughed blood from his nose and mouth, his eyes rolled back and he died.

"Things ain't always what they seem," Deegan muttered as he stepped over and looked down at the dead Indian. "Bad a shot as I am with a pistol, I couldn't have missed from that distance." He kicked the knife away from the Indian's hand, lifted the rifle, glanced at the brass tacks on the stock and swung it with both hands against the tree. The stock broke free and flew through the air. He turned and threw the barrel off into the woods. *This battle's over.*

CHAPTER TWENTY-SEVEN

Charlie Deegan returned to the horse fort and looked down at the three dead soldiers and the dead Indian. The body of the Indian with the crossed cartridge belts lay outside the circle. The soldier with no stripes lay on his side with his fly-covered scalp in the dirt beside him. His lower shirtfront was a mass of blood. *Looks like the poor bastard was gut shot. Helluva way to die.* The soldier with the three stripes lay on his back, a large circle of blood on his chest. His pistol lay beyond his hand and his pant pockets were pulled out. A folding knife and several coins lay in the dirt. "He was too busy going through your pockets to take your scalp before I shot and interrupted him," he told the dead sergeant as he knelt and pushed the items back into his pocket. The dead captain lay on his back, his head leaning against a dead horse. The flies covered the mass of blood where his hair had been. Deegan shoed the flies away, only to have them circle and return. A rivulet of blood ran from a small dark hole in front of the captain's right ear. "Well, Cap'n, it looks like you and your men really got your asses kicked today. You probably didn't know what hit you," Deegan said, pulling him away from the horse and laying him flat. "Must've been a pretty slick ambush you rode into because you never even drew your pistol." He studied the dead officer, knelt, took the pistol from his holster, fired it in the air until it was empty and put it into the captain's hand. "Now, Captain, at least it looks like you put a little bit into the battle."

Deegan stepped over a dead horse, grabbed the Indian with the crossed bandoleers by the ankles and dragged him a distance off into the brush. He returned and dragged off the second body. To finish the battle scene he gave each of the dead Indians a gun. "Now at least it looks like there was some distance in the battle." He returned and freed the men's bedrolls to cover their bodies. "That'll keep the flies off you."

Deegan paced around the covered bodies and considered his situation. Then decided it was time to go down the hill and look at the other dead Indian and the army pack mule. He lifted a canteen from one of the horses and could tell by the weight that it was probably full. He slung it over his shoulder and started down the path of scattered boxes to where the carcass of the mule wrapped around the tree. He gave a cursory glance at the dead Indian before picking up his rifle, breaking it against a tree and throwing the barrel off into the grass. He sighed as he looked over the scene.

Who in the hell's stupid enough to send a mule loaded with cases of ammunition through this territory with only a three-man escort? He hauled and hid the six marked ammunition boxes in the bushes. He returned to the last box, unhooked the latches and found it filled with rations. He smiled as he carried the box up the hill away from the smell of the dead mule. "Some civilized food for a change," he told himself as he sat on the ground and spread food items on the grass. He opened a cloth-wrapped, smoked ham. "Now this'll be some good eating." He cut off a chunk of meat and his grin widened as he chewed. He ate from a bag of dried apples and took several swallows from the canteen. More ham, apples and water. He looked into a box of hardtack, but decided it wasn't something he wanted to chew. He put the ham and apples back in the box, latched the lid and sat on it.

"Wait just a minute, what the hell was that on the dead Indian's neck?" He leaped to his feet and ran down to look at the dead man. A leather thong was tied around his neck and a glint of gold shown in the shadow of his hair. He bent down and pulled the thong up to see three twenty-dollar gold pieces strung on the leather lash. "Now if that don't beat all!" Deegan shouted. "I got money for a horse!" He snapped the leather, stared down at the coins and raised his eyes skyward. "I don't understand my luck, but thanks." He wadded the coins and the thong into a ball and pushed them into a vest pocket.

Deegan walked back, retrieved his bag and started to trudge up the hill to the soldiers' bodies. He stopped and turned when he was sure he heard the sound of horses across the valley.

A lone Indian carrying a rifle across his knees, dressed in a blue cavalry shirt and a feathered kepi rode into sight, carefully examining the road ahead of him. A few hundred yards behind him rode an officer and a sergeant. A short distance behind them was a double column of twelve cavalry troopers and four extra horses with empty packsaddles.

Looks like they came expecting the worse. Deegan waved and fired his pistol into the air.

The Indian scout wheeled his horse and swung up his rifle at the sound of the shot.

The officer raised his hand and the column came to an abrupt halt. They looked across the valley and saw a white man with a smoking pistol above his head, waving and motioning them to join him.

The officer shouted something to the Indian, who spun his horse, rode down the hill and across the valley at breakneck speed. The Indian reined his horse to a dusty, skidding stop and sat looking down at Deegan.

"What you want?"

"Tell your officer there's been a battle here and I've got three dead soldiers back up yonder," Deegan answered, pointing up the hill with his pistol. "Go tell him *now.*"

The Indian wheeled his horse, raced back across the valley, and spoke to the officer and the sergeant with much gesturing at the man standing on the hill.

The three men rode back across the valley and reined their horses in front of Deegan.

The captain leaned his hands on the front of his saddle and looked down at him. "Nantajae says you've had a battle here and there are three dead soldiers." He raised his eyes, looking out beyond Deegan for signs of the battle. "I'm Captain Amos Bailey. This is First Sergeant Odell. We're here from Fort Wingate to look for a contingent of three men transferring in and bringing some supplies. I have a bad feeling you may have found them."

Deegan pointed over his shoulder. "Those soldiers' bodies are a little ways back up in the woods. A captain, a sergeant and a private. They put up a hell of a good fight before they died. There're dead Indians up there and one down the hill by that dead pack animal. I hid six cases of ammunition in the bushes back in the woods. They won't be hard to find since you know what you're looking for."

"Take charge, First Sergeant," the captain ordered. "Then join me to look over the battle scene."

"Yes, sir." First Sergeant Odell signaled the troopers and called out with his strong Irish accent. "Blessing, take half the men down there, look over the dead pack animal and load up anything that's salvageable. The rest of you come with the cap'n and me to look after the bodies up there."

"You got it, Sarge," a corporal answered, wheeled his horse and began to assign tasks to the men.

"The ammo cases are in the bushes to the south," Deegan shouted.

"What's your name?" Captain Bailey asked.

"Devries. Martin Devries," Deegan answered.

"Well, Mister Devries. You wait here. I'll want to have a little talk with you when I get back from looking over the battle area."

Captain Bailey returned, swung down and offered his hand to Deegan. "Well, Mister Devries, you did a helluva job here, hiding that ammo and all. Were you here for the battle?"

Deegan nodded and shook his hand. "I killed the last Indian. At least I think he was the last Indian. He's the dead one down by the pack mule. He didn't hear me coming up and I shot him. I went up there where the bodies are, but didn't see any more Indians. I don't know how many there were."

"The captain up there was a friend of mine, Kirk Warner, transferring in from Fort Concho, Texas. It's going to be hard to write to his wife about this. At least it was a quick and probably painless death, and he died fighting."

Deegan nodded his understanding.

"Several things are strange to me, Mister Devries," Bailey stated, digging a pipe out of a pocket and tapping it against his hand. "My friend, Captain Warner, and the private had been scalped. I'd guess the sergeant was the last to die because he wasn't. Warner must have died instantly from that shot to his head, but at least he'd fired all the bullets in his pistol, so he died fighting. We found a total of five dead Indians scattered in the brush. I'd guess you killed the Indian that did the scalping. He must have left to go after that pack mule."

"Yeah, that could be. He probably knew that he could do the scalping after he got the mule. Maybe he thought the other Indians were still alive. I don't know, Captain . . . The only thing I did up there was cover the bodies to keep the flies off of them."

Captain Bailey nodded. "Where's your horse?"

"I'm afoot."

"How did you happen to be here in the first place, Mister Devries? You being afoot and all."

Deegan studied the captain's face. "Sheriff Baca ran me out of Pine Spring and I'm walking north until I find me a cattle drive and get a job."

"Why did Sheriff Baca run you out of Pine Spring?"

Deegan relayed the story of his run-in with Sheriff Baca starting with the incident at the bar and ending with his departure from Pine Spring. He chose to omit the part about Baca's threat to lock him up for thirty days and all the things the sheriff could search out during that time.

Captain Bailey was chewing on his unlit pipe and smiling as Deegan finished his story. "Yes, the army has also had some problems with Sheriff Baca. We've learned that it's best if the army doesn't spend any nights in Pine Spring. We always make it a point to camp far enough away so the men can't get into Baca's domain after dark. He's extracted some stiff fines from soldiers in the past. We had ten men listed as AWOL for four days when we got word from Baca that he had them jailed in Pine Spring for disturbing the peace. Colonel Patterson wasn't very happy about the amount of time it had taken the sheriff to notify the post. Baca charged the government one hundred dollars in fines to get them out and the men had the money docked from their pay until it was repaid. There was a rumor they were trying to put together a party to burn Pine Spring, but it was just whiskey talk. Now they make it a point to stay away from there. I'm surprised Sheriff Baca let you leave town with any money at all."

Deegan nodded. "Yeah, maybe he thought stealing all my canned peaches and other food was enough."

"I didn't know about Kirk and those two soldiers coming over until I was informed they were late. I don't know who in the hell was stupid enough to send them out when we knew there were small bands of marauding hostiles here in the area. I'm sure he would have asked for a bigger contingent if he had known about it. I should have gone out to meet him. Why didn't they check with us? Damnit!" The captain tucked the pipe in a pocket, clapped his hands and remounted his horse. "I'll find out who authorized this and there'll be hell to pay!"

First Sergeant Odell reined his horse and saluted. "Everything's ready to go, Cap'n. We've recovered and packed all of the gear and supplies, sir. It's a damn good thing we brought four extra horses, because we used them all. We laid the Indians out over there in the trees. Their people can take care of them, I guess, if they come looking for them at all. Buzzards're circling high, looking over the area. I'd say the Indians and animals will be picked clean by this time tomorrow."

"Very good, First Sergeant," Captain Bailey stated. "Mister Devries is afoot, so have a couple of the men double up and give him a horse. He'll accompany us back to Fort Wingate. I'm sure General Carr will want to have a few words with him. And see that he gets a room in the visiting officers' quarters. He'll want to be rested and clean when he meets the general."

"Won't take but a minute when we git back, Cap'n," First Sergeant Odell answered.

"All right," Captain Bailey said. "Let's get back to Fort Wingate. I want Mister Devries to meet General Carr."

"That's really not necessary," Deegan stated as he took the reins of a horse a soldier handed to him. *All I really want is to get the hell out of this area.*

"Don't be modest, Mister Devries," Captain Bailey asserted. "You arrived too late to help the men, but you did a great service in saving the ammunition and killing the last of the Indians. The general will like that. He'll definitely want to meet you."

CHAPTER TWENTY-EIGHT

Charlie Deegan and his cavalry escort arrived back at Fort Wingate just after dark. Captain Bailey made an excuse that he had to do the paperwork on the day's expedition, set up a meeting for the next day with General Carr and try to write a letter to Captain Warner's widow. "It's going to be damned tough, but at least he died fighting" were the last words over his shoulder as he started for his office.

First Sergeant Odell took Deegan to the mess hall and saw to it that he was fed a good meal.

"Mister Devries," he said, as they left the building, each working a toothpick in their mouths. "Would ya be likin' a wee shot a whiskey to finish off the day?"

Deegan looked at Odell out of the corner of his eye. *What the hell can one shot of whiskey hurt?* "I think a small drink of whiskey would top off my day," he answered, patting his stomach. "And be sure and tell the cook again what a great meal that was."

"We'll be going to the company stables, then," Odell stated and pointed at a nearby building. "I happen to keep a bottle hidden in there for just such an occasion."

Sergeant Odell pointed at the top rail of a feed bunk. "Have yerself a seat, Mister Devries, while I fetch me bottle," he instructed as he disappeared into a nearby room.

I seem to recall somebody else who used to keep a bottle or two hidden in the stables. Look how that all ended up. This isn't very smart, Charlie . . . Oh hell, one drink won't hurt anything. You have to prove to yourself that you're a strong man. One drink. That's all. Just one drink.

Odell reappeared, smiling and dusting straw from a bottle. "Here, it is, m'boy. I never take it with me when I go off the post, but it sure as hell gives me something to look forward to when I git back."

Take a hike, Charlie.

Odell handed the bottle up to Deegan and pulled himself up onto the rail beside him. He took the bottle, twisted the cork free, wiped the mouth of it with his sleeve, tipped it up and took one long, noisy swallow. "Ah, nectar a the gods," he said, smacking his lips. "Here, m'boy, have a swallow," he said, again wiping the mouth of the bottle with his sleeve and handing it to Deegan.

Deegan took the bottle and lifted it in a toast to Odell. *One drink.* He tipped the bottle and took a slow swallow. He handed the bottle back to Odell, smiled, took in a long breath and wiped at the tears in the corners of his eyes. "That's mighty fine, strong whiskey, First Sergeant, mighty fine."

First Sergeant Odell held the bottle out. "It says in the Bible, Mark, three seventeen: *No man can walk on one leg.* I've always taken that to mean no man should have just one drink." Odell grinned and tipped the bottle up for another noisy swallow. He again smacked his lips and proffered the bottle to Deegan. "A man will believe anything if ya quote it from the Bible."

Deegan hesitated as he looked at the bottle in Odell's hand. *One more won't hurt, if you stop then and go back to your room.* Deegan laughed and took the bottle. "This is only because of your Biblical interpretation." He took a short swallow, handed the bottle back to the sergeant and dropped off the rail to his feet. "Thank you, First Sergeant. It's time for me to turn in. I've had a long day and this is the first time in a long time I've had the pleasure of a real bed.

Good night."

Sergeant Odell started to argue, but decided there would be more for his own pleasure if he were alone. "G'night, Mister Devries. Sleep well. I'll be seeing ya in the mornin'."

Deegan sat on the cot in his room, pulled off his boots, blew out the lamp, lay back on the cot and put his arm back under his head. *Just go to sleep. Whiskey got you in trouble more times than you can count, but tonight you proved you could walk away from it. Go to sleep.* He tossed and turned until he sat up and hung his feet off the side of the bed. *I can't sleep. There's got to be someplace the soldiers go for a drink. A little conversation and maybe a beer would help me get to sleep. I proved tonight that I could control my drinking. A beer wouldn't hurt,* he argued with himself. *It'd sure help me sleep. I know when to quit now. I can handle it. One or two is all I'll have.*

The guard at the main gate told Deegan he could leave the post after informing him the gate was locked at ten o'clock and not opened again until six o'clock the next morning.

"What time is it now?" Deegan asked.

The corporal pulled out a watch. "About

ten after eight. You got a couple hours. Actually a little less. You, being a civilian, you got no problem staying out all night though. If a soldier misses bed check at ten o'clock, he's in deep shit. That's a law General Carr enforces to the letter. I seen more than one man busted for not being in his bunk when they do bed check."

"How far is the nearest watering hole?"

"About a quarter mile right down this road. Place called the Lost Cabin Saloon. You'll git a fair drink for your money."

Deegan ambled down the road and was soon following the sound of a melody being beaten from an out-of-tune piano. He stepped off the road and stood looking at a dimly lit log building. A kerosene lamp beside the door barely lit the sign above it:

LOST CABIN SALOON

This is the place. You know you had best go back to your room and go to sleep. He moved closer to the building, taking in the sounds and smells reaching him through the door. *But you couldn't sleep. That's the reason you came out here. To get something to help you sleep,* he argued with himself. *Hell, one or two drinks ain't gonna hurt. You'll know when you've had enough and it's time to go home.*

You've proved you can do it.

Deegan shrugged, stepped onto the porch, opened the door and stepped inside. All eyes in the smoke-filled room turned to look at the stranger who smiled weakly and walked to an open space at the bar. He pulled several coins from a vest pocket and laid them on the bar. "Beer cold?" he asked, sliding a quarter forward.

The bartender gave him a gap-toothed grin. "Yeah, I hafta wear a damned glove to pour it."

The men at the bar all laughed.

Deegan gave them a fleeting glance in the dirty, cracked mirror behind the bar. They all wore army blue. "Well, then put your damned glove on and pour me one," he retorted and smiled.

Again, the men at the bar laughed and the soldier standing next to him slapped his hand on his shoulder. "Ya tell 'im, buddy," he slurred.

The bartender filled a mug and leveled off the foam head with the edge of his hand. He set the beer in front of Deegan, picked up the quarter, flipped it in the air and dropped it into a cash drawer below the bar. "Ya got two more coming; ten cents each, three for a quarter," he stated and moved down the bar to talk to a soldier wearing sergeant's stripes.

Deegan looked down at the beer and started to say something to the bartender about how he'd leveled the foam on the mug. "Ah, hell," he muttered and drank half of the beer slowly, turned it up and drained it in two swallows. He held the empty mug out; the bartender nodded, stepped down, refilled it without leveling the foam and returned to his conversation.

Deegan lifted the mug and turned to rest his elbows on the bar behind him. He took a sip of beer and studied the people in the room over the top of the mug.

Several soldiers were in a heated card game at a table in a far corner. A man in a derby hat, a semi-white shirt and a flowered vest was dealing and arguing with one of the players.

The soldier leaped to his feet, pulled a knife from his boot, waved it at the dealer and shouted louder.

The man in the derby hat shook his head, said something, his hands disappearing under the table and quickly reappearing with a pair of short-barreled, silver pistols. He grimaced as he said something and rested the ends of the pistol barrels on the table.

Wonder where he keeps those? Deegan

took a sip of beer. *He sure got them up there in a hurry.* He glanced quickly at the door. *I'd better get out of here 'fore this goes much farther. My luck they'll have another lawman here like Baca.* He drained the beer and set the mug behind him on the bar.

The bar became silent, and as if by a signal, the piano player quit beating the keys and turned to watch the confrontation.

"I can't help it if you don't know how to play cards, soldier," the dealer declared. "Why don't you just take a couple of dollars out of the pot and go to the bar for a few drinks. I wasn't cheating. You just don't know how to play cards. Let it go at that!"

"Ya bastard!" the soldier shouted, waving the knife. "Ya's dealin' off'n the bottom a the deck. I seen ya!"

The dealer raised the pistols until the barrels were pointed at the soldier's chest. "I don't want to shoot you, soldier, but if you keep waving that knife at me, I'll be forced to do it in self-defense. I'm going to count to ten and then shoot you with both of these. One . . ."

The bartender quietly stepped around the bar, tiptoed up behind the soldier, cracked him in the back of the head with a heavy wooden club and stepped back as the soldier crumpled to the floor.

"Sorry, Bennie, but I can't let you be shooting any soldiers in my place. General Carr'd run me off and burn the place down," the bartender declared. "He's done it before to others."

"I wasn't really going to shoot him, Wayne, I's just trying to bluff him, scare him off. I sure as hell don't want the army after me for putting a bullet in one of their soldiers," the dealer responded. "Everybody belly up to the bar! A round on me!"

With a shout and a cheer, the men moved to the bar, the piano player drained the glass put in front of him and began pounding out a song. The bartender worked his way down the bar until he was standing in front of Deegan.

"Whiskey," Deegan ordered.

"You were drinking beer before. You'll be drinking beer now," the bartender countered.

"I'll pay for my own damned whiskey, then," Deegan said as he dug the wad of leather and gold pieces from a pocket. He leaned forward and held his arms up to help hide it as he slid one of the gold pieces from the thong and handed it to the bartender.

The bartender looked at the coin, bit it and nodded. "This hole in it makes it worth about, oh, I'd say about fifteen dollars."

"The damned hole ain't that big," Deegan argued. "It's worth at least eighteen."

"Sixteen."

"Sixteen dollars and two shots of whiskey."

"Done," the bartender answered and slammed his hand on the bar. He rummaged in the cash drawer and laid coins on the bar.

Deegan quickly pocketed the other gold coins. "And two shots of whiskey," he reminded the bartender.

"And two shots of whiskey." The bartender put two shot glasses in front of Deegan and poured an amber liquid from an unmarked bottle into each of them.

Deegan lifted one of the glasses and sniffed it. He smiled, nodded, tipped the glass to his lips and drained it. "Ahhh . . . ," he sighed as he set the glass back on the bar, lifted the second glass and drained it. He slid a silver dollar forward and waited until the bartender returned. "How many drinks?" he asked.

The bartender looked at him through hooded eyes. "Twelve beers or four shots of whiskey."

"Ain't that a bit costly for whiskey?" Deegan asked. "Two bits a shot? And out of a bottle without a label."

The bartender put his fingertip on the

silver dollar. "The nearest place where you can get it cheaper is in Gallup, a goodly number of miles west of here. You want beer or whiskey?"

Deegan raised his eyes as if in deep thought. "Whiskey."

CHAPTER TWENTY-NINE

Charlie Deegan watched as the bartender brought up two more glasses and lined the four up in a neat row and with a smooth run of the bottle over the glasses, perfectly filled them all and laughed. "Drink up, my friend. The price could be higher and the distance could be farther." He chuckled as he pushed the glasses toward Deegan and moved down the bar looking for more empty glasses.

Deegan looked at the neat row of glasses. *Now's when you've got to start watching your actions,* he thought as he reached for the first glass. He drank it down and felt the warmth spread slowly outward from his stomach as he let the din of the saloon begin to wrap him in its cocoon. He tipped the second glass and emptied it into his mouth.

"They got any whores in here?" the soldier next to him asked.

"I ain't seen any tonight," Deegan an-

260

swered, twirling his third shot of whiskey back and forth between his fingers. "Of course, this's my first time in here so I really don't know much about what goes on. Maybe they got cribs out back and they don't come in here."

"Well, a bunch of us just got in here from Fort Yuma a couple a days ago and we're lookin' for a little action without having to go all the way to Gallup," the soldier said, looking around the room. "We had us some real pretty little Mexican whores down there in Yuma. You ever been to Yuma?"

Yuma set off an alarm in Deegan's mind. *Time to get the hell out of here.* "No," he answered, shaking his head and quickly swallowing his third shot of whiskey. *Damn, I wish I didn't have that fourth one on the bar.* He realized he was beginning to have trouble focusing his mind. *Damn, Charlie, you should've known you couldn't hold your liquor now like you used to.* He stared at the last glass of whiskey. *It's been too long and you just can't handle it like before.* He was having a problem with the fact there were now two full glasses on the bar. He closed his eyes and when he opened them, one glass slowly became two. "I gotta git outta here," he slurred as he pushed away from the bar and turned toward the door. *There might be somebody from Yuma that'll recognize me.*

"Hey, Deegan!" someone shouted.

A chill ran up his back as he stood looking at the door. *Oh, shit, just walk out. As drunk as you are, maybe that was your imagination. Walk out that damned door!*

A tall, skinny, pimple-faced soldier stood in front of him surrounded with a wall of his friends. "Hey! Deegan, ya remember me, Landom?"

Deegan fought to focus on the man's face. He shook his head. "You . . . you . . . you . . . talking to me?" he stammered.

"Yeah," the soldier answered. "Hey, this here's Private Deegan, the straightest shooting sumbitch in the army. Least he used to be." The soldier paused and stared at Deegan. "Hey, wait a minute," he said cocking his head and smiling. "As I remember, Deegan here got in a fight over a little Mexican whore back in Yuma and ended up gutting some guy. He got put in the Yuma Prison fer a pretty good stretch . . . I remember something else. Deegan escaped a while back and they never found him. The last word was he died in the desert. You got a reward on yer head, Deegan?" the soldier asked, stepping closer and putting a hand on his chest.

The adrenaline rushing through Deegan's

body was quickly sobering him. He glanced down at the man's hand on his chest and hit him with a strong uppercut to the jaw.

The soldier sagged back against one of his friends.

Deegan hit another soldier, dropping him to the floor.

With a roar the rest of the soldiers moved in and the bartender stepped around from behind the bar, smacking the wooden club into the palm of his hand.

Deegan kicked a soldier in the shin and bounced a short jab off the jaw of another. He glanced at the mirror behind the bar and saw the bartender start to swing the club. He ducked, the club hit a soldier in the mouth and he flopped backward and crumpled to the floor. He threw a punch at a soldier in front of him, the soldier ducked and his fist glanced off his shoulder. Someone smashed a chair over Deegan's shoulders and he fell forward in a shower of stars. A boot scraped across his ear, he grabbed the foot and twisted hard. A soldier dropped across his chest, another across his legs and a third man joined the pile. He curled and tried to get an arm above him to protect his head. A boot heel collided with his shoulder.

An elbow crashed down on the side of his head and he turned his head and bit into the man's arm.

A man screamed and smashed his fist into Deegan's mouth.

A shotgun blast roared and silenced the room. The bartender stood on the bar in a cloud of gun smoke, a stream of blood running from a cut over his eye and a smoking shotgun held above his head. "I'm gonna blow a hole the size of China in the next son of a bitch throws a punch!" he shouted. "I've got one more shell in here and I wanna use it! Somebody try me!"

The standing soldiers shook their heads, raised their hands and began backing toward the door.

The soldiers piled on Deegan pushed clear of him and stood up.

"Take this bastard out and hang him or turn him over to somebody at the stockade," the bartender yelled, pointing the shotgun at Deegan. "He's the bastard started all this. Do it fast or I just might use this last shot on him."

Deegan struggled to his feet and glared up at the bartender. "Do it!" he shouted holding his hands on his chest. "I got nothing to lose. Shoot me!"

The bartender lowered the barrels of the shotgun until they pointed at Deegan's hands.

"Well?" Deegan challenged. *I'm not going back to that dark cell.*

Private Landom struggled to the front of the crowd. "Wait a minute! Take him over to the fort and lock the bastard up!" he screamed. "There's gotta be a reward on his head and I'm *claiming* it!"

Two soldiers grabbed Deegan's arms and rushed him toward the door.

CHAPTER THIRTY

Charlie Deegan sat in the corner of a dark stockade cell muttering to himself. *You dumb bastard! How many times you gonna let liquor put you in this kind of a mess? Haven't you learned anything?* He looked at the dark shadowed bars of his window through swollen eyelids and felt a chill run down his back. *You pushed your luck and now they know who you are. You're gonna go back to the dark cell at the prison.* He clenched his fists and rubbed his raw knuckles on his pant leg. *Why didn't you learn? Why didn't you learn?*

Deegan thought about the fight that had put him into a cell again and shook his head. He gingerly ran his fingers over his face feeling the cuts, scrapes and swelling. He ran his tongue over his teeth and found several were loose. *Guess I could be worse, but I've got to get out of here.* He ran his fingers over the remnants of his vest. *Damn!*

Somebody stole those gold coins I had in my pocket. Charlie, when your luck changes it sure as hell goes in a full circle.

The door to the cell block opened and a soldier carrying a kerosene lamp entered, followed closely by First Sergeant Odell.

"Well, Devries or whoever in the hell ya are, ya got yerself in some real hot water. They got me outta bed 'cause there's a man over at the orderly room who claims yer an escaped prisoner from Yuma Territorial Prison. He's demandin' any reward on yer head. Ya got any denials?" Odell asked, leaning against the bars and peering down at Deegan. "Here, gimme the light," Odell ordered the soldier. "Ya go back out to the front office and let me talk to this man alone."

The soldier nodded, handed the first sergeant the lamp and left the room.

"Ya did a pretty good job a bustin' up a couple a those soldiers. Did ya knock the teeth out of that one or did the bartender do it like the man claims?"

"It was the bartender and that club he's so handy with."

"I figured as much. How're ya feelin'?"

Deegan shrugged. "I'll be okay, but I'd be a hell of a lot better if I was down the trail a ways. Any chance of you letting me out on

267

account of all I did for those dead soldiers?"

Odell shook his head. "Well, much as I'd like to help ya git outta here, I'm afraid I can't do much for ya now. I didn't tell ya to sneak out and get drunk. When ya left the stables, ya told me ya were going to bed. They've sent a wire to the prison and Fort Yuma to git information to positively identify ya." The sergeant studied the man shrunken back into the corner. "The doc'll be by to take a look at ya in the morning." Odell pulled a watch from his pocket. "It'll be sunup in an hour or so. Try to get a little sleep. I'll stop back later."

Deegan stared at the door after it closed. "What're you gonna do now, Charlie?" he asked himself. "You're as good as back in prison." He crawled over to the bunk and drifted off to a troubled sleep.

Deegan awoke with the feeling someone was watching him. Through the slits of his swollen eyes, he peered up at the barred pattern the rising sun spread across the ceiling of the cell, closed them again and shuddered. It seemed his whole body ached. He rose up on his elbows, opened his eyes, swung his feet over the side of the bunk and slowly sat up. *God, I hurt in every part a my body.* He tried to organize his thoughts as he pushed up from the bunk, grabbed the

268

bars of the door and steadied himself as he looked around. He was startled to see a man, his arms folded across his chest, sitting cross-legged on a bunk in the next cell. He was an Indian with matted hair, a beaten face and torn clothes. Obsidian-like eyes studied Deegan.

"Hey," Deegan called, softly. "Can you hear me?"

The Indian didn't move.

"Do you understand English?"

The Indian remained stoic.

"Ah, the hell with you," Deegan muttered as he stepped over and looked down into the empty metal pail beside the door. "Hey!" he shouted. "Anybody out there?"

The handle of the door rattled several times and was silent.

"Hey!" Deegan shouted. "I know you're out there."

The door opened and a soldier, with an eye swollen and colored like a plum, stepped into the cell block. He smiled crookedly at Deegan. "Ya want sumpin'?"

"I need a drink and that bucket's empty," Deegan stated, pointing at the pail.

"I can give ya sumpin' to drink," the soldier declared, unbuttoned his pants and proceeded to urinate in the pail.

Deegan made a lunge and grabbed

through the bars, but the soldier stepped back, laughing and urinated on Deegan's pants and shoes. He leaped away and fell onto his bunk. "You . . . you . . . you . . . bastard," he managed to stutter. "I'll kill you, you little son of a bitch!"

"Like ya tried to do last night?" the soldier taunted as he buttoned his fly.

"If I ever get my hands on you, you're a dead man, you little bastard," Deegan seethed. "You're a dead man!" He kicked the pail and it bounced off the bars, tipping and spilling the liquid on the floor.

The soldier laughed as he left the room, slamming the door behind him.

Deegan glanced over at the Indian who lowered his eyes and appeared to be examining something on the back of his hand. "Were you in the fight I was in last night?"

The Indian raised his eyes and looked at him blankly.

Deegan sighed. "How'd you get beat up so bad? You got any water in that bucket of yours? That damned guard pissed in mine. I'll kill the little bastard if I ever get my hands on him." He began to pace. *You're wasting your time talking to him. He doesn't understand a word you're saying.* He stopped and leaned against the bars. "Firewater get you in the mess you're in?" he asked.

"Firewater got me in my mess. Bad thing about it is that it ain't the first time. Why'n the hell didn't I learn the first time? Why didn't I learn the third or fourth time?"

He began pacing again. "Why in the hell am I telling *you* this? I gotta get outta here. I can't take more prison time. I've just gotta get out of here."

Deegan was drenched in sweat as he tried to shake each bar in his cell, but they were all solid. He sat on the bunk and held his face in his hands. *The sons-a-bitches even stole the last of my money.*

CHAPTER THIRTY-ONE

The door rattled, opened and First Sergeant Odell entered the cell block. "The doc'll be a little later than I thought," he announced.

The soldier with the swollen, purple eye followed Odell into the room carrying two small metal pails and two large, steaming metal cups.

"Beef stew, bread and coffee," Odell announced.

The soldier slid a pail and a cup between the bars into the Indian's cell and stepped over to Deegan's. As he slid the metal containers into the cell, Deegan launched himself through the air, grabbed the man's wrists and yanked him forward. The top of his head collided solidly with the metal bars and he slumped to the floor.

First Sergeant Odell stood frozen, shocked at Deegan's sudden action. He fumbled at the flap of his holster and drew his pistol, but Deegan had already dropped the man's wrists and sat back on his haunches, his hands in the air.

"What the hell's wrong with ya?" Odell demanded, holstering his pistol and dragging the unconscious man away from the bars.

"The little bastard peed in my water bucket a while ago. I should've killed him."

Odell looked at the unconscious soldier, the Indian and Deegan.

"What?"

Deegan lifted the metal cup with shaking hands and took a sip of the hot coffee. "He came in here this morning and I told him I was thirsty and needed water. He said he'd gimme something to drink and started to pee in my bucket over there. When I grabbed for him, he peed on my pant leg and boots."

Odell shook his head. "I never've guessed Milligan was that ornery."

The man on the floor moaned and stirred.

First Sergeant Odell nudged him with a boot toe. "Milligan, do ya hear me?"

"Uh-huh."

"Sit up."

The soldier struggled up to his hands and knees.

"Sit up, so I can talk to ya," Odell commanded. "I wanna ask ya a question."

Milligan rose to his knees, sat back on his

heels, and glared through the bars at Deegan. "What do ya want, First Sergeant?"

"This prisoner tells me you peed in his water bucket earlier this morning."

Milligan gingerly put his hands to the top of his head. "He's lying, First Sergeant. I never saw him until I came in here with you to bring him his breakfast."

"You lying little bastard," Deegan sneered. "You told me I gave you that black eye last night and it was your way of getting even."

"Did this man give you that shiner?" Odell asked.

"How in the hell'd I know who hit me in a fight like that one last night?" Milligan asked as he struggled to get to his feet. "It was every man fer himself, if ya know what I mean, First Sergeant. I'm told ya been in a couple of those yerself in yer time."

"My old fighting record is not the question right now, Milligan, I just wanna know if ya peed in this man's water bucket."

"So help me, First Sergeant, I'd never do anything as bad as that," Milligan wheedled. "I'm just not that kinda person."

"Well . . . ," Odell said, studying the face of the soldier.

"C'mon, Odell," Deegan said. "You can't believe that little weasel. Do you think I tried to pull his head through the bars 'cause I don't like his looks? I'm a peaceful man until I get riled and that little bastard riled me good when he peed in my water bucket."

"Well, Devries, or whatever name ya go by now, he's a fairly good soldier and I'm told yer an escaped murderer. I'm gonna have to side with a soldier and go with his story." Odell turned and reached for the door handle.

"Little blue shirt bastard lies," the Indian stated.

All three men turned to stare at the Indian sitting on the cot, eating from his fingers.

"What'd ya say?" Odell asked.

"Hell, I didn't think you understood English," Deegan interrupted. "Why didn't you answer when I talked to you?"

The Indian shrugged, tipped up the small pail and took a long swallow of stew broth. He wiped his arm across his mouth. "You talk plenty. I say nothing."

"What'd ya say about Milligan?" Odell asked.

"Little blue shirt bastard is like dog with him," the Indian stated, pointing at Milligan and then Deegan.

Odell turned to Milligan. "I wanna see ya in my office in ten minutes. Go change into yer stable gear. I gotta long job for ya to do." He turned back to Deegan. "I guess I owe ya an apology. Ya need anything right now?"

Deegan grinned painfully. "I'd like a clean bucket of water. A pass through to the gate would be good too."

"Somebody else'll be deliverin' the food," Odell declared. "An' I'll make sure it's not a friend of Milligan's."

Deegan took the pail of stew to his bunk, pulled the spoon out through the soggy chunk of bread and began to eat. "So you just sat over there and let me blabber on like a fool, huh?"

The Indian shrugged.

"Well, you talked when it was important. Thanks."

The Indian set the stew pail on the floor and tasted the coffee. "I like much sugar in coffee," he stated, set the cup beside the pail, curled up on the bunk and went to sleep.

CHAPTER THIRTY-TWO

Charlie Deegan finished his stew and coffee and began to pace in his cell. *Well, they're gonna send somebody up here from the prison or the fort to identify me.* He stepped up onto the bunk, grabbed the bars and stretched up to look outside. There was a stable and several wagons including one with barred sides. *That must be the hoosegow wagon. That's probably the one'll take me back to Yuma.* He shuddered, dropped and sat with his face in his hands. He touched his swollen lips, but the pain stopped him. *Damn, that hurts.* He gingerly inspected his teeth. *I guess I'm lucky I didn't get them knocked out.*

The cell-block door opened and the fort doctor, Major Riley, peering over his glasses, noisily dragging a chair behind him, shut the door with his heel and sat down. "This damned altitude gives me terrible headaches early in the morning," he stated. "I've got to get myself transferred to a lower part of the country." He lifted his medical bag unto his lap, brought out a medicine bottle, pulled the cork and had a long swallow. He closed his eyes, smacked his lips, sighed, and sat motionless with the bottle clasped on top of the medical bag. "Ah, it'll be just a short time and I'll be feeling well again."

The doctor opened his eyes, slid the bottle into his bag, clapped his hands, pulled off his glasses and vigorously polished them on the hem of his white coat. "Well, now, you two look like you've both been in one hell of a fight. Not with each other, I hope. You, there," he said, pointing at Deegan. "How are you feeling this morning?"

"Probably about as bad as I think I look."

"I'm told you went out for a bit of drinking last night and got yourself into a bout of fisticuffs at one of the local drinking establishments. Is that true?"

"Do I look like I been to church, Doc?"

"I find it hard to believe you consider your present condition humorous," Major Riley retorted. "I'm also told there is a possibility you may be an escaped convict."

Deegan shrugged.

"Now, let me look at your face," Major Riley said, standing and setting his bag on the chair.

Deegan shrugged and stepped to the barred door. He could smell the whiskey on the doctor's breath.

"I'd be guessing this fight last night wasn't your first," the doctor said, as his fingers moved over Deegan's face.

"That'd be a good guess, Doc."

The doctor swabbed alcohol on Deegan's cuts and stood back. "Time will be the best healer."

Deegan's breath hissed between his teeth. "Damn, Doc, that stings."

The doctor nodded and motioned to the Indian in the next cell. "Let's have a look at you."

The Indian walked to the corner of his cell and stood facing away from the doctor.

"I don't think he understands you, Doc," Deegan said.

"Suit, yourself," Riley said, "I don't like working on you red bastards anyway." He closed his bag, opened the door and pushed the chair out ahead of him.

Deegan began to pace. "You got any plans to escape from this place?"

The Indian stood stoically looking down the row of cells away from Deegan.

"Now, damnit!" Deegan shouted. "I know you understand what I'm saying."

The Indian shook his head.

Deegan kicked the bars. "Damnit, don't ignore me!"

The Indian turned and stared at Deegan. "What yer name?"

"My real name's Charlie Deegan."

"I am Chato," the Indian said, thumbing his chest. "Did you escape from prison?"

Deegan nodded. "Yeah."

"I too escape. I escape from San Carlos guardhouse. I was Army scout. General Crook like Apache scouts because they think like Apache and can find trails hunted Apache move on. My sergeant was Apache Kid. He in charge of us when someone brought in *tiswin,* very strong firewater made from corn and we had party. I was very drunk when fight started. Much shooting. A man named *Taklishim,* Grey One, shot me in the leg and was trying to reload to shoot me again. I stabbed him; he died. I was sent to the guardhouse on San Carlos, Arizona, Reservation. I escaped. Kid and his men found me and beat me. The soldiers beat me again when I tried to escape here."

Deegan looked at the ceiling and wondered at Chato's story. *Are You testing me again? Can this be true?* "Then you've got to escape again," he said, studying Chato's face. "We have to think of a way to escape."

Chato shook his head and turned away

from Deegan.

"Damnit, Chato, you can't just give up!" Deegan shouted. "I can't believe you're gonna give up and let them send you back to San Carlos. Not without a fight! You're not a quitter."

"No more talking," Chato stated without turning.

Deegan stood on his bunk and pulled himself up to look out the barred window. *Even if he ain't gonna try to escape doesn't mean I ain't. I've just gotta watch for the right time.*

First Sergeant Odell came in with the soldier bringing the noon meal. "We got a wire from the prison at Yuma. They're sending a man named Wallace up to identify ya. I'm told yer name is Charlie Deegan. Is that right?"

Deegan looked at him blankly.

"Suit yerself, Deegan, or whoever ya are," Odell said. "He'll be here in about two days. We're gonna send the two of ya to Gallup in the prison wagon. Wallace'll take you an' Chato to Yuma by train. You'll go to the prison an' they'll take him back to San Carlos from there."

If it's the same Wallace, then he's moved up a little. Deegan remembered a tall, thin man with a ferret-like face, who walked around the yard slapping a short wooden bat into the palm of his hand. If a prisoner wasn't doing things fast enough or up to Wallace's standards, he was in trouble. He knew a hard bat slap to the kidneys didn't leave much of a mark and more than one man had peed blood because of Wallace. He was a man who was both feared and hated. Deegan had always managed to give him a wide berth and never been given a taste of his bat.

That evening Captain Bailey came into the cell block. "Private Landom told us your name is Deegan and you're an escapee from the territorial prison down at Yuma. He says you killed a man in a bar fight, got a bad discharge from the army and were locked up. You escaped from an escape-proof prison. They hunted you in the desert for a while and eventually gave you up for dead. He told me that at one time you were the best rifle shot at Fort Yuma, then you turned into a drunk and a brawler."

Deegan looked at him with an expressionless face.

"Have it your way. I'd like to do something to help you for what you did for my dead captain friend, but after your little escapade last night and the fact I've got a soldier claiming you're an escaped prisoner with a reward on his head . . ."

The captain's voice trailed off as if he wanted Charlie to give him an answer.

"You could just let me out the front gate," Deegan suggested.

"You know it was your own actions last night that got you locked up in here. You were a hero yesterday afternoon. You went out last night, got drunk and ended up in a fight with a bunch of soldiers. I'm told you did well in the fight for a while . . ."

"Don't preach to me, Cap'n," Deegan interrupted. "I know what I did. I may not be the best talker, but I ain't an idiot. I've done some stupid things more'n once and I know what my problem is. I'm sure as hell gonna try to make sure I don't do it again."

"That's admirable and I'm sure you'll have a lot of time to think it over when you're locked up again," Captain Bailey said. "To be honest, I'd take you out the gate and let you go. I might be wrong, but you don't seem to me to be a hardened criminal. From what I've seen and been told, I think you're just a drunk who can't control himself around liquor. You did a good thing taking care of my friend's body. Captain Warner and his men."

"I think you're preaching again, Cap'n,

but you're very right. I can't be around booze."

Captain Bailey nodded. "Is there anything inside the law I can do for you now?"

"Would it be too much to ask for a bath and a chance to shave?"

"That, I can arrange," the captain said and smiled.

"How about something to read?"

"I can arrange that also."

Two days later Deegan looked up from his book as the door to the cell block opened and Odell entered, followed by a tall, thin man with a ferret face.

The man looked at Deegan and the ends of his scraggly mustache lifted in a slight smile. "Well, well, if it ain't Charlie Deegan, raised up from the dead," Wallace said, and stepped to the bars. He reached into an inside pocket and handed a piece of paper over his shoulder to First Sergeant Odell.

Odell looked at the paper and nodded. It was a photograph of Charlie Deegan, shaved face and head, complete with the number 1207 on the plaque under his chin. "I guess there's no doubt, you are Charlie Deegan."

"As you said, First Sergeant, this is *indeed* Charlie Deegan," Wallace said, his eyes never leaving Deegan's face. "Escaped under a garbage wagon, he did. The trackers hunted him for a long time and then gave up when a couple of the tracker dogs killed the Apache scout who was leading the search. Never did figure out what happened, but they knew the dogs killed him. They figured the dogs had killed Deegan too and hauled off his body. Prison officials decided it was no use to search for him anymore. They were sure the buzzards were picking his bones somewhere out there in the sand. He must've been a lot smarter than they gave him credit for. Yes, sir, it was a surprise when we got the wire he might be up here in your stockade, alive after all this time."

"We'll have the prison wagon ready to transport Deegan and Chato to Gallup, under armed guard, first thing tomorrow mornin'. Ya can take them to Yuma on the westbound noon train. Take care of the whole thing with one wagon trip," First Sergeant Odell stated. "Let's go do the paperwork."

CHAPTER THIRTY-THREE

A lantern hanging by the door dimly lit the cell block as Deegan sat picking at his evening meal.

Chato appeared to be asleep. His untouched supper plate and cup were on the floor just under the barred door of his cell.

"Chato, you awake?" Deegan called out softly.

"I am awake, Charlie Deegan," Chato answered, without moving.

"You heard what First Sergeant Odell said, didn't you?"

"I heard."

"Are you just gonna lay there until they come to put chains on us in the morning? Ain't you gonna try to do something?"

"What are you going to do?" Chato asked.

Deegan sat thinking and then spoke, "I don't know, but I don't wanna go back to the dark cell at the prison and that's sure as hell where they're gonna put me. They chain you to the floor in a metal cage in a room dug outta solid rock and when they shut the doors there ain't any light. They feed you old bread and stinking water. The guards think it's funny to kick scorpions down through a hole in the roof to spend a little time with you. I'm told they really like it when they find a small sidewinder to drop down in there with you. I just ain't gonna go back for that."

"Charlie Deegan, you talk too much," Chato muttered. "Go to sleep. Time is faster when you sleep."

"I ain't in any rush to have the morning come," Deegan grumbled.

"Then talk in your mind. It will not keep me awake."

Deegan put his plate on the floor, drank the last of his tepid coffee, sighed, laid back and put his arm over his eyes. *Well, Charlie, you've got to make some serious decisions. You ain't gonna escape from Yuma Prison because they're gonna really watch you from now on. You won't do it again, because they ain't gonna let you. You're gonna have to do it on the way to the train or after you get on the train. Probably the easiest when you're on the train. There'll be too many guards on the hoosegow wagon, but it'll be just Chato, you and Wallace on the train. The train's your best bet.* Deegan drifted off to a troubled sleep.

The next morning neither Deegan nor Chato ate their breakfast stew. They drank their coffee and Deegan paced his cell.

"You do not talk much today, Charlie Deegan," Chato noted.

Deegan stopped and hung on the bars looking at Chato sitting cross-legged on his bunk.

"Ain't you afraid of going back to San Carlos?" he asked.

"I do not worry about things I can do nothing about," Chato answered. "You worry about too many things, Charlie Deegan. You worry about men dropping things on you in the dark. It is light now. Worry about the dark when it is dark."

Deegan studied Chato's face. Most of the swelling had gone down around his eyes and the scrapes and cuts were healing well. He knew how his own face was healing because he'd studied it that morning when he had bathed and shaved.

First Sergeant Odell entered the cell block followed by Wallace and a small contingent of armed soldiers. "Deegan, go back over and sit on yer bunk," he ordered. "We're gonna put leg shackles and handcuffs on both of ya, one at a time and then load ya in the prison wagon. Yer leg shackles'll be locked to the floor so there's no way ya can get away. Two soldiers'll ride on the wagon. Mister Wallace and four other soldiers'll be outrider escorts to Gallup."

Deegan and Chato walked out of the jail with short, choppy steps, controlled by the length of the shackle chains.

Chato was marched up the short ladder to sit on a bench on one side of the wagon. The soldiers watched as First Sergeant Odell pulled his shackle chains through a ring in the center of the floor and the corporal in charge of the escort party tried to work a stubborn padlock.

A white, hot flash of pain raced up Deegan's back and he gasped as he fell forward heavily onto the steps of the ladder.

Odell spun to look down at him.

Deegan fought to pull in his breath and uttered a soft moan. He knew Wallace had just given him a demonstration of the power of his short bat.

"What's wrong, Deegan?" Odell asked.

Deegan shook his head and fought to get his breath back. *You bastard! You're gonna regret that, so help me God, you are gonna regret it.*

"I think he must've slipped on that first step," Wallace answered, pointing at the ladder.

Deegan looked through tear-filled eyes over at Wallace. There was no sign of his bat.

"Watch that first step, Deegan," Wallace said, with an evil smile. "It looks like it might be a bit slippery."

Deegan pushed to his feet, wiped at his eyes and managed to take a deep breath. "Yes, sir," he answered. "I'll try to be more careful."

Deegan sat on the bench opposite Chato and watched Odell and the corporal secure his leg shackle chains to the floor ring. He could feel the burning sting on his back where Wallace had slapped him with his bat. *I'm gonna get you for that slap, Wallace. I will get you one way or another.* He looked up and saw Captain Bailey approaching the wagon.

First Sergeant Odell looked at his watch. All of the men were mounted and waiting. "Go ahead and move on out," he commanded, motioning toward the main gate.

About an hour out of Fort Wingate, the driver turned back into the prison wagon and grinned.

Deegan saw it was Private Milligan. "Seems I'm surrounded by friends today," he muttered.

"What you say, Charlie Deegan?" Chato asked.

"Shut up back there!" Milligan shouted over his shoulder. "No talking!"

The guard riding on the seat beside Milligan turned and thrust the barrel of his rifle back through the bars into the wagon.

"It is not dark yet, Charlie Deegan," Chato said, ignoring the glaring guard in front.

Deegan gave Chato a puzzled look.

Chato looked back at Deegan impassively.

He thought he saw a slight trace of a smile on the Indian's mouth. He turned and looked at the guard. "Turn around, boy, this ride's hard enough without you showing us your ugly face."

The guard sputtered and waved the rifle at them.

Chato laughed and spit on the barrel of the weapon.

The guard roared a curse, leaped to his feet, spun and toppled backward out of the wagon. He screamed as the front wheel of the wagon broke his leg.

Milligan fought to control the horses and the soldier cried out again as the back wheel passed over him.

The outriders rushed back to the wagon. The front riders helped Milligan control the horses and the soldiers at the rear dismounted to look at the soldier writhing in pain.

Wallace rode up close beside the wagon, his drawn pistol lying across his saddle horn. "I hope you and the Indian try something, Deegan," he drawled. "I'll have to shoot you in the leg to keep you from escaping."

The other two soldiers dismounted and stood looking down at the man thrashing, screaming and cursing with pain.

The corporal pulled down the ladder at the back of the wagon and unlocked the door. "I'm going to have to put the injured soldier in here. I'll unlock your chains from the floor and move them to the side bars to make room for him in the middle. Deegan, you first," he said, motioning for him to sit back.

One of the soldiers stepped to the bottom of the steps and pointed his rifle up into the wagon. "I got 'em covered, Corporal," he announced. "Go ahead."

As the corporal knelt to unlock Deegan's chain, Chato swung his hands over the man's head and yanked him back with the chains of the handcuffs. He spun the corporal, putting him between himself and the man with the rifle.

"Don't shoot," the corporal managed to croak, waving his arms at the soldier.

Wallace swung his pistol in through the bars; Deegan grabbed his hand, jerked his face hard into the bars and twisted the pistol free with one violent yank. He turned the gun and pressed the barrel against the corporal's nose. "Drop the rifle or I'll blow his damned head off!" he shouted, cocking the pistol.

The soldier laid the rifle on the ground and raised his hands.

Wallace's horse skittered back away from the wagon, dropping his dazed rider to the ground.

The three remaining soldiers looked at each other as if waiting for one of them to take charge.

"Put your hands in the air!" Deegan shouted and glanced over his shoulder at the driver. "Milligan, get down and ground tie the wagon. Then get over with the rest of these heroes. Don't do anything stupid. Nothing here's gonna get you a medal, but being stupid can get you dead. Now *move,* damnit!"

Out of the corner of his eye, Deegan saw one of the soldiers reach for his pistol, his fingers fumbling with the flap on his holster. Deegan fired, the slug kicking up a cloud of dirt near the soldier's feet. "You dumb bastard!" he yelled. "Put your hands up."

The soldier's hands shot up over his head.

"You damned, stupid idiot!" Deegan shouted. "I could've killed you!"

Chato raised his head and shouted something in the Apache tongue.

Deegan looked in amazement as a half dozen Apache warriors materialized from the trees and brush beside the road.

CHAPTER THIRTY-FOUR

The Apache, Chato, laid his head back and laughed. "I told you, Charlie Deegan, do not worry about dark when it is still light. These are my friends. They wait for the right time. Me and you made it the right time." Chato's laughter was joined by the laughter of the other Apaches.

Deegan shook his head and laughed nervously.

Chato pulled his chained hands up over the corporal's head and the man choked and wheezed as he rubbed his throat.

"Gimme the keys, Corporal," Deegan ordered.

The soldier dug out a ring of keys and handed them to Deegan.

Minutes later Deegan and Chato stood beside the wagon looking at the soldiers lying in a line. One of the Apaches stood behind them, a rifle loosely cradled in his arms.

Wallace sat at the bottom of the stairs, carefully holding his head in his hands and staring at the ground to avoid eye contact with Deegan. Dark bruises and scrapes extended down both sides of his face.

The remaining Apaches stood off to one side talking among themselves and gesturing from time to time at the wagon, the horses and the men on the ground.

The man with the broken leg screamed out again. One of the Apaches walked over and kicked him in the head. The soldier went limp.

Deegan looked at Chato questioningly.

"He is not dead, maybe," Chato stated. "He cried like a woman. Apache men do not do that. We do not want to kill any white men. Killing will make them hunt for us harder. I will talk to my friends. We will decide things. You wait, Charlie Deegan."

Deegan stood in front of Wallace, waving his pistol loosely in front of him. "You're pretty handy with that little bat of yours when nobody's looking, ain't you?"

Wallace looked up at him expressionless.

"Gimme that bat," Deegan instructed, holding out his hand. "I wanna take a closer look at it."

Wallace reached inside his coat for the bat and handed it to him.

"Stand up," Deegan ordered. "Gimme your gun belt."

Wallace stood, fear showing in his eyes as he unbuckled the belt and swung it over to Deegan.

"Turn around," Deegan commanded as he holstered the pistol and buckled the rig onto his waist. The bat was a blur as Deegan swung it in a short arc.

Wallace cried out and crumpled back, holding his side as he fell to his knees.

"How'd you like that, Wallace?" Deegan asked, prodding him with his toe. "How many men in the prison have you done that to? I ain't necessarily a spiteful man, but I figure I owed you that."

Wallace gasped a mumbled answer.

Deegan kicked him sharply in the leg. "I can't hear you!"

"You . . . you . . . didn't have any reason to do me like that," Wallace managed to gasp.

Deegan laughed. "You must be dumber'n a rock. There's something in the Bible about an eye for an eye, a tooth for a tooth. Well, I just added something to it about a slap in the kidneys. Let's see if you like peeing blood."

"Deegan," Chato called, motioning him to join the Apaches.

297

Deegan leaned down close to Wallace. "Now we're gonna discuss how those Apaches wanna torture you. I like the anthill. They say sometimes they cut off a man's eyelids and stake him out in the bright sun. You got a favorite?"

Wallace looked up at Deegan with wide, fear-filled eyes. "Please . . . ," he begged.

Deegan snorted, threw the bat off into the bushes and walked to join the Apaches. He could read nothing on their faces as he joined them.

"We are going into the mountains," Chato said, waving at the peaks. "The white soldier will not find us and he will not look long if we do not kill any of these soldiers. We will let the horses loose and they go back to fort. The army will come and find these men quick as soon as the horses are back. What you do, Charlie Deegan?"

"I ain't sure, but if I let the army think I was heading south for Mexico and doubled back to Gallup, I could get on the train heading east a ways and then get off and head north. I got a problem now because Wallace'll tell them I'm still alive and they'll put out new reward posters. That'll make things rough. I gotta stay out of towns for a while. Besides that, I don't have any money."

"Soldiers have money," Chato stated.

"They sure as hell ain't gonna give me any," Deegan declared. "And I don't wanna take it from them. I ain't a thief. Not just yet anyway."

"Indians supposed to steal from soldiers," Chato stated, knowingly. "We get money from soldiers, give to you. They don't know you have their money. Okay?"

Deegan thought and nodded. "Wait a minute, the soldiers don't have that much to begin with. Wallace's probably got some to cover expenses and such. Go take the money from the civilian."

"Good." Chato nodded. "We go steal money for you." He spoke to one of the Indians and the man walked toward the men on the ground.

"Why are you doing this for me, Chato?"

"You escape from prison like me. The soldiers not treat you so good, like me. You talk to me. Too much sometime, when I try to sleep. I like you, Charlie Deegan. I think army try to find you more than they try to find me. To most white man Indian is Indian. All look alike. White man escape from prison worth money. Reward for you. I don't think much reward for me. They look for you hard. Not much for me. I am Indian. You the one they look for."

Deegan studied Chato's face as he spoke.

"You're a damn sight smarter'n people give you credit for," he declared. "And I do believe all you just said is true. They'll sure as hell be looking for me now that they know I ain't dead."

"We can kill man from prison," Chato declared. "He is not soldier so they don't care too much. Then he cannot tell where you are."

"No," Deegan answered. "Go ahead and take his money, but I don't want his death on my conscience. We'll just put the fear of the devil in him before we go."

One of the Apaches returned, handed Chato a large leather wallet and spoke to him in rapid sentences.

Chato answered and handed the wallet back to him. "It will be in burned tree behind you," he told Deegan as the Indian walked off tossing it up into the air and catching it.

"I wanna talk to Wallace for a minute," Deegan said. "I'll be right back."

"I think I talked them outta cutting your eyelids off," he said, looking down at Wallace's ashen face. "It's too bad your clothes are too skinny for me. I need some better clothes to travel in. I won't be able to buy any new duds until I get to the money I got stashed down by Sonoita. Then I'll be able to buy me some mighty fancy new clothes before I cross over into Mexico. Something to impress the *señoritas*. I got enough money to live comfortable for a long while in Mexico. Yessiree, a long while. Well, I gotta go see what they decided to do with you boys."

Deegan had a slight smile on his face as he rejoined the Indians.

"Something funny?" Chato asked.

"No, but I'm sure Wallace'll tell them I'm heading to Mexico."

"I have told my friends about soldier who was a dog to you," Chato said.

"A dog to me? What do you mean . . . ?" Deegan asked. "Oh, you mean when Milligan peed on me the other day."

Chato nodded. "What will you do?"

"Do? I wasn't gonna do anything."

Chato spoke to the Apaches in their tongue. They chattered among themselves. Chato nodded. "You must be honorable and strike back. He made fool of you. We have plan."

Deegan listened intently as Chato laid out his revenge. "It'll be good. Do it."

The Apaches tied each of the soldier's hands and feet where they lay.

When they approached Wallace, he rose to his feet, his face became paler, he began to shake violently and threw up. "Pl . . . pl . . . please," he managed to stutter, wiping his chin with his hand. "Don't let them s . . . stake me on an anthill. Please, Deegan, just shoot me, I beg you, shoot me."

Deegan began to laugh.

Chato translated to the Apaches, standing in a circle around the frightened man, and they began to howl hysterically, pounding on each other and pointing at Wallace.

"What . . . what's so funny?" Wallace demanded.

"They think you should be braver looking at slow death," Deegan answered, frowning. "I think they wanted to beat your kidneys for a while with that little bat of yours. Like you did to all of those cons. Problem is I threw it away. Now they wanna skin you alive."

Wallace wilted to the ground and the chuckling Indians quickly trussed him.

The Apaches lifted Milligan to his feet and held him upright, as Deegan looked him up and down. "The Indians think you really insulted me when you peed on me a couple a days ago. What do you think?"

"It was a joke," Milligan cried, tears running down his face. "I's just tryin' to be funny. I's just trying to get even for the black eye ya gave me."

Deegan looked at the backs of the men lying on the ground. "Well, what you did to me is a great insult to the Apaches. Now I've got to do what they want me to do to save face. We're gonna take you over there in the woods and I'm gonna cut off your peeing gear."

"No," Milligan moaned and struggled against the Indians. "No, please, no."

Chato motioned with his head and they carried the crying soldier, toes digging ruts, into the trees.

Deegan tore a piece of cloth from Milligan's shirt, stuffed it into his mouth and ripped off another one to tie over his mouth. One of them brought a rope from the wagon and bound him securely to a tree.

One of the Indians handed Deegan a heavy bladed knife and he waved it in front of Milligan's tear-filled eyes.

One of the Apaches raised his head and emitted a gut-wrenching scream. The Apaches laughed loudly and gave victory shouts.

Deegan saw the soldiers on the ground trying to turn to see what was happening to Milligan. "If I see any man's eyes looking over here," Deegan shouted, "he gets the same treatment as Milligan and it ain't pleasant!"

One of the Indians screamed another cry of great pain.

The soldiers all straightened and stared at the wheels of the wagon.

Deegan took a strip of the shirt and tied it over Milligan's eyes. "If you move, one of these Apaches is gonna pull your tongue out and cut it off so you drown in your own blood."

Deegan held out his hand and Chato gripped it firmly. "Good-bye, Charlie Deegan. Good luck!" He motioned and he and the Apaches drifted off to disappear into the trees.

Deegan stood with his hands on his hips and looked at the scene around him. *What the hell?* He smiled as he lifted his head and gave a final blood-curdling scream.

CHAPTER THIRTY-FIVE

Charlie Deegan had walked to Gallup, but decided not to go into the town. He found a wooden water tower and knew the train would be stopped there to take on water. It was late in the day when a train stopped at the water tower and the boiler was filled. The brakeman signaled back with his lantern to the conductor standing beside the lone passenger car at the end of the train. Both men swung on board and the engineer blasted a long mournful wail from the whistle. The stack of the engine belched huge clouds of black smoke into the evening air, the wheels started to turn and the train began to crawl down the tracks. It was barely moving when Deegan dashed out of the brush, jumped and pulled himself up into the open door of a cattle car. He turned and hung out the door, looked ahead, back and then ahead again, blinking into the growing wind as the train picked up speed.

"Good-bye!" he shouted, waving a fist at the disappearing landscape. "I'm gone! Good-bye!" He staggered against the rolling motion, flopped into a pile of hay at the end of the car and dug Wallace's wallet and papers out of his shirt. "Charlie, old hoss, now you've escaped for good," he told himself, as he shuffled through the papers and pocketed the money. "There's no way in hell they're ever gonna catch you now. You've learned your lesson, no more booze." He stuck the wallet and the papers out through a space between the slats and let the wind take them away. "It's a new life now," he told himself as he lay back, put his arm over his eyes and drifted off to sleep. The north wind whistling through the slats of the car made Deegan burrow deeper into the hay.

Deegan was awaked from a sound sleep by a loud voice shouting nearby. He realized the train was no longer moving and the clamoring was coming from outside. He pushed up from the hay, crept to the open door and cautiously peered outside. The meager moonlight showed him the train was in a railroad yard with cattle pens spreading out as far as he could see and a line of empty cars on a track nearby. Two men stood on the ground near the end of the car. One of them wore a battered derby hat and a long wool coat. The other wore a shapeless cowboy hat, high boots, spurs and a short leather jacket.

"Ya freeloadin' bums gotta learn ya don't ride on these trains fer free!" the larger man in the derby shouted. In one hand he held a shotgun and in the other a long, steel-shafted buggy whip. Moonlight reflected briefly off a badge on his coat. "Now I'm gonna teach ya a lesson about trying to ride for free on my trains." The whip made a whistling sound as he swung it.

The cowboy sidestepped and the leather lash sliced through the air near his shoulder. He pointed at the other man as he backed away. "You hit me with that whip and I'm gonna take it away from you and shove it up your ass."

The man with the badge laughed. "Ya ain't big enough!" he shouted. "Besides I still got my shotgun here to help me if I need it." He twirled the whip in a circle above his head and snapped it at the cowboy.

The cowboy dodged, but a boot heel twisted in the rocks and he staggered off balance.

The man in the derby charged, cracking

the wobbling man across the back with the whip.

The cowboy fought to regain his balance as the braided leather whistled and slapped across his shoulders and he fell to his knees. He muttered and scrambled across the gravel. The whip came down again across the back of his head, sending his hat flying. The return swing brought it across his forehead, opening a small gash above his eye and a small rivulet of blood ran down his face. He curled his arms over his head for protection. "No more!" he yelled. "Damnit, don't hit me again with that damned whip."

The big man laughed, circling the wounded man, his whip noisily cutting through the air. "Ya ain't gonna forget this beatin', are ya?" he shouted, working the whip above the downed man.

The whip was violently yanked backward, throwing him off balance. "What in . . . ?" He spun to find Charlie Deegan above him in the door of the cattle car, the lash end of the whip gripped tightly in his hand.

"Leave him be," Deegan ordered. "He's learned his lesson. Now let him go. I heard about you railroad yard bulls and how some of you're like damned prison guards. I don't like prison guards and from what I just saw,

I don't like you either." He could feel his holstered pistol had shifted to the small of his back during his sleep. *He can't see a gun so he probably thinks I'm unarmed.* He gave a tug on the whip. *That's gonna make him meaner and probably dumber.*

The yard bull let go of the whip and swung up the barrels of the shotgun. "Ya ain't very smart," he sneered. "Yer interferin' with the duties of a duly appointed officer of the law and I can blow a hole in ya right now if I gotta mind to."

"I don't think there's anything in your duties says you're supposed to whip a man because you caught him riding on a train," Deegan argued.

Behind the guard, the man sat up, wiped fingers through the line of blood on his face and looked at his hand.

The snaps were loud as the yard bull cocked the hammers of his shotgun.

The whip continued to swing from Deegan's right hand. "You gonna shoot us both?" he asked, judging the distance to the man. "Two unarmed men?" *Now he's sure I don't have a gun.*

The guard kept glancing at the man behind him and back at the swinging whip.

Deegan slowly worked his gun belt around with his left hand, knowing the pistol would be coming to him backwards, but at least he'd have a gun.

"Shooting both of ya sounds good," the man answered, waving the shotgun. "The two of ya jumped me and I didn't have a choice. How'd I know in the dark ya didn't have no guns?"

Deegan widened the arc of the swinging whip.

The yard bull stepped back several paces. "Ya ain't gonna hit me with that thing from up there," he stated and grinned. "This here scattergun'll cut ya in half if ya even try."

The cowboy struggled silently to his feet and, with a roar, charged, and slammed his fists down on the yard bull's shoulders.

The man crumpled forward, one barrel of the shotgun belched flame and the buckshot chewed away the wood in the doorway over Deegan's head as he dropped to his knees, struggling to free his pistol.

The cowboy grabbed the barrels of the shotgun, yanked it from the fallen man's hands and pushed the twin muzzles hard against his back. "Now, you bastard!" he shouted. "No man whips me like a damned dog and gets away with it."

"Don't kill him!" Deegan yelled, pointing his pistol at the cowboy.

"You taking his side in this?" the cowboy

asked, wiping his hand at his face. "He was gonna shoot you too."

"No," Deegan answered. "I ain't taking his side, but there's no reason to kill him like that."

The man studied Deegan's face in the weak moonlight. "What's your name?"

"What difference does that make?"

"Because this bastard owes you his life and I think he oughta thank you proper." The cowboy swung the shotgun up into the crook of his arm.

Deegan pulled his holster around and slid the pistol into it. "I'm coming down." He dropped to the ground and stuck out his hand. "Name's Charlie Deegan."

The cowboy gripped his hand. "McCall, Charlie, Creed McCall."

"Well, Creed, he ain't moved," Deegan said, looking down at the downed man. "Maybe he's already dead. You hit him awful damned hard."

McCall shrugged.

Deegan knelt, rolled the guard over and sat back as he groaned and stirred. "He ain't hurt all that bad."

McCall pulled the bandanna from his neck and held it on the cut above his eye as he paced around the downed guard. "Well, Charlie, what're we gonna do now?"

Deegan shrugged. "It's your call, Creed. He was whipping on you, so it's your call. Just don't use that scattergun on him. Okay?"

McCall took the bloody bandanna from over his eye and looked at it. "I guess this cut don't give me the right to blow his head off."

The yard guard moaned and opened his eyes.

McCall dropped the shotgun barrels to rest on the man's nose. "I'm the fella you used the whip on. You want it back so you can take another swing at me, huh?"

The guard rolled his eyes imploringly to Deegan.

Deegan shrugged. "It's over there if you want it back," he said, a slight smile appearing below his mustache. "I'll be more'n glad to get it for you."

"What happened?" the railroad guard whimpered.

McCall lifted the shotgun barrels up to rest on his shoulder. "You're a damned lucky man 'cause Mister Deegan here talked me outta shooting you. You got a gun under that coat?"

The guard nodded.

"Open up real slow and hand it to me."

McCall lowered the shotgun to the man's chest.

"Real slow and easy."

The guard opened his coat, hooked his thumb into the trigger guard of the pistol in his shoulder holster and slowly lifted it free.

McCall snatched the gun from the guard's hand and stuck it into his own belt.

"Let's you and me talk a minute, Creed," Deegan said. "Step back a ways so the bastard can't hear us."

"Don't do anything stupid," McCall warned, waving the shotgun.

"I'm heading east to try to find a job working cattle," Deegan explained. "I don't want more trouble with the law and this whole situation's beginning to stink like trouble with the law."

"This is your lucky night, Charlie, beause I'm heading east to join a cattle drive up to Dakota Territory." McCall chuckled. "I'll put in a word with the trail boss, Joe Burdette, so you can consider yourself hired."

Deegan looked carefully at McCall. "You ain't kidding me, are you?"

"No, I'm the number-two man on the drive. You'll have a job."

"I really appreciate that. I really do." Deegan stuck out his hand. "Thanks, Creed."

McCall gripped his hand firmly, nodded

313

and smiled. "Hell, I owe you."

Deegan returned the smile. "Now what're we gonna do with him, whimpering over there?"

"There's a westbound train coming through here soon," McCall answered. "They back in, take on water, hook onto empty cars, switch and take 'em west. How about we tie him in one of those cars and let him ride a ways? They'll be hooking on empties two tracks over. I've worked cattle through these yards, so I know. It's a cattle train, so they don't take long to get moving again."

"And we stay on this train heading east?"

"Exactly."

CHAPTER THIRTY-SIX

Charlie Deegan stepped back and looked Creed McCall up and down. "If you're gonna join a cattle drive, how come you're riding the train like a bum?"

McCall shrugged and answered. "I got word while we were still in Texas that my father had died, so I left the herd to go back, bury him and take care of necessary family business. I was headed up to catch the herd when my horse came up lame, so I turned him loose and hopped the train. I sure as hell wasn't gonna carry a saddle and the rest of my gear all the way to Dodge City."

"That where you're meeting the herd?"

"Yep, they should be there about now. Joe Burdette's ramrodding a herd north for Mister Charles Goodnight. Taking 'em up to some French prince or count or royal something or another. Anyway, this Frenchman's starting an operation up there where he fattens and slaughters the cattle at his place and sends the meat back east in cars full of ice."

"Cars full of ice?"

"Some newfangled idea this Frenchman's got."

"How come you ain't got a gun and let that yard bull get the jump on you? Where's all that gear you didn't wanna carry?"

"It's up in that car two back from us. It was easy enough to get in there when the train was slowed down for a grade a good ways back. When it stopped here, I jumped down to stretch my legs and take a pee. That bull must've seen me hop off and figured I's a bum. Hell, I could pay for a ride, I got over fifty dollars cash on me . . ." McCall's voice trailed off as he realized he didn't know anything about the man he was talking to and it'd been stupid to mention money.

Deegan sensed what McCall was thinking. "Stand easy, Creed. I ain't gonna try to steal your money. Hell, I'll pay you for a job. I got a few dollars on me." He smiled and dug his hand into a pocket. "How much do *you* want?"

McCall chuckled and pointed at the man on the ground. "You paid for the job when you took the damned whip away from him."

"You sure?"

McCall nodded, dabbed the bandanna at the cut over his eye, saw that it had stopped bleeding and draped the bandanna over his shoulder. "Looks like I'll live. What say we take this bull's badge and papers 'fore we put him on the train? Maybe some mean, bastard yard bull'll find him and give him the same treatment he gave me."

Deegan smiled. "I like that idea, Creed. We'll tie him so he can get loose in a while and hope he meets an ornery yard bull down the line. Find a car with lots of cow shit on the floor. I saw some rope over there on the fence."

He returned with the rope and McCall prodded the man to his feet with the shotgun. "Let's go, mister, I found a special car for you to ride in over there."

Deegan pulled himself up into an empty car, looked around, grinned and motioned for the guard to join him.

McCall prodded the man. "Git your rotten ass up into that car."

"What're ya gonna do?" the cowering man asked.

"We decided you're gonna take a ride," Deegan answered. "My friend wanted to tie you under the train and let you drag a ways, but I like you, so I convinced him to tie you inside instead. C'mon, get up here."

Deegan tied the guard's hands behind his back and McCall climbed up to join them.

"Ya can't git away with this," the guard muttered.

"Ha, looks like we're doing a pretty damned good job so far," Deegan answered. "We better gag him so he can't holler and be found before he's outta here." He found a wadded handkerchief in the man's pocket and tore it in two. The man fought as he tried to shove half of it into his mouth.

McCall gave him a sharp rap on the top of his head with the shotgun. "Behave."

Deegan tied the remainder of the cloth around the man's face to hold the wad in and the man gagged.

"If you puke now, you're gonna drown in it," Deegan warned, as he rolled the man over and tied his feet to a wall slat. He pulled the badge off the guard's coat and rummaged in his pockets until he found his wallet.

Satisfied with their work, Deegan and Mc-Call jumped to the ground.

"The cut on my head ain't bleeding anymore, so I guess it ain't that bad. But my eye is sure as hell almost swelled shut," Mc-Call said, tentatively touching a finger to the cut.

Deegan nodded. "I'm sure you'll live to

get to your cattle drive, but your eye's starting to look like a damned plum."

McCall chuckled. "I'll get some shit from the boys about it. They don't have much mercy when it comes to other men's injuries."

A distant train whistle floated mournfully through the night air.

"Better hurry, I hear the westbound train coming. Soon as it gets water and hooks on these empties, it heads on out," McCall said. "The eastbound's ready to roll when the track's clear. I'll go over and wash the blood off my face before the train pulls out."

Deegan worked the handle up and down and a trickle of water quickly turned into a deluge.

McCall put a hand into the water and splashed some on his face. "Damn, that's cold!"

"Put your head under it," Deegan instructed, smiling.

"There ain't so much blood that I gotta put my head under the water," McCall argued, dunked his bandanna and wiped his face. "How's that?"

Deegan stepped close and examined the wound. "You got most of the blood. You probably got worse cuts from bobbed wire and I don't think you're even gonna get a good scar outta that one. Your eye'll be back to normal in a few days. Let's go and say good-bye to our friend before his train leaves."

"I'll find his derby and toss it in with him," McCall volunteered. "We don't want his head to get cold down the line."

"Hey, Yard Bull!" Deegan shouted into the car.

The guard lifted his head and glared at the two men standing at the door of the car.

Deegan pulled the man's badge from his pocket and flashed it at him. "Your badge is out there somewhere," he shouted and the silver shield flew off into the darkness. "Your wallet and all your official lawman papers'll be in that water trough over yonder. They'll be a little soggy, but that's where they'll be."

The guard struggled against the ropes and muttered obscenities through his gag.

"Have a good trip, you bastard!" McCall shouted, as he slid the door shut.

"Sounds like the eastbound engine's getting fired up to move," Deegan noted as he walked over to the trough and dropped the yard bull's wallet into the water.

"Soon as the westbound passes, we'll be moving. Get your gear and toss it in my personal car back there," McCall instructed with a grin as he picked up his hat and wedged it on his head. "I got plenty of extra room."

"Everything I own is right here," Deegan answered, spreading his arms.

McCall shook his head. "You mean to tell me you don't even have a hat?"

"Lost it a while back and ain't been to a town to get a new one. I'll buy one in Dodge City."

"You can have the yard bull's derby, if you want it. We can go get it for you."

"Thanks, but I ain't the derby kind. I'll just wait."

"Why am I beginning to feel like I just adopted an orphan?" McCall asked, with a sigh. "C'mon, Charlie, I gotta bottle of some passable drinking whiskey back in my saddlebags."

Deegan shook his head. "I ain't a drinking man, Creed. Thanks, just the same. I'll get a drink of water from the pump before we leave."

"I'll be damned, Charlie," McCall muttered. "I'd a sworn you was a drinking man."

"Yeah," Deegan answered. "Let's just say that at one time I was a drinking man."

CHAPTER THIRTY-SEVEN

The train whistled a signal as it began to slow and Charlie Deegan and Creed Mc-Call hung from the car door watching the stockyards of Dodge City grow larger in the early morning light.

"Tell me when you think we should drop off," Deegan shouted.

"Hell, we'll ride her all the way in," Mc-Call answered. "No yard bull's gonna give us any trouble." He tapped the gun hanging from his belt. "Besides that, I been told if you give them a dollar they'll pretend they never saw you get off the train."

"Now, why in the hell didn't you do that back there? It would've saved you a lot of trouble, wouldn't it?"

"He never gave me a chance to say anything before he started swinging his whip. Once he'd hit me there was no way in hell I was gonna offer him anything but a few busted teeth."

"Well, it appeared to me he had the upper hand when I stepped in."

"I'll admit he had me between a rock and a hard place," McCall answered, with a nod. "You planning on holding that over my head for a long time? Hell, I'm getting you a job."

Deegan smiled. "No, I ain't holding that over your head, and I appreciate the job."

"Speaking of jobs, how much experience've you got with cattle?"

"It's about time for us to be getting ready to get off this train, ain't it?" Deegan asked.

"You didn't answer my question. How much experience you got with cows?" McCall demanded.

Deegan pursed his lips and grimaced. "Ah . . . I figure this cattle drive'll gimme a little."

"You mean to tell me you've never worked cows?" McCall asked, incredulously.

Deegan nodded.

McCall began to chuckle.

Deegan studied him, began to laugh and then stopped. "What'n the hell's so funny about something like that?"

"If you've never worked cattle, and I get you on the drive crew, you'll be starting out as Little Suzie," McCall answered, rubbing a finger across his mustache.

"As little *what*?"

"You'll be starting out working the chuck wagon with War Wagon. They always need a man to help him with the chuck. Sometimes they rotate the cowboys through the job on a day-to-day basis. Other times they do it as a form of punishment. Anyway, a cook's assistant is called Little Suzie," McCall explained.

"I'm sorry, but I ain't working as a cook's assistant. I'm hiring on to be a cowboy," Deegan stated. "And I sure as hell ain't gonna be no *Little Suzie*!"

"If you want a job, with no cattle experience, you'll be starting on the chuck wagon, helping War Wagon and doing a little cowboy work when you can. You do good and maybe you'll be a cowboy. Until then, if you want a job, you'll be an assistant cook," McCall said, curtly. "Hell, you can ride a horse can't you?"

"Can I ride a horse?" Deegan asked. "No, hell, no, I been walking all this time because I can't ride a horse. Be serious! Yes, I can ride a damned horse!"

"Okay, that's a start," McCall said, trying to keep a straight face. "Get ready to jump. The train's slowing down and the stockyards are just up ahead. We'll get off now so we don't have to tangle with any yard bulls."

"You told me a bit ago we didn't have to

worry about the bulls."

"There's always one you don't wanna tangle with and I figure with your luck that'll be the one in this yard."

"Hold on a damned minute!" Deegan shouted over the wail of the train whistle. "I wasn't the one being beat on with a buggy whip a few hours back down the track."

"Granted, but it could've been turned around if you was the one jumped down to take a pee," McCall reasoned.

"What in the hell does that have to do with anything?" Deegan demanded.

McCall shrugged.

"Let's just get off the damned train."

"Okay," McCall answered, as he gathered up his gear, made sure it was all secured to his saddle, leaned out the door and threw it off to smash through a large bush. "Cushions it a bit that way. Let's go!" He swung his lanky frame out of the door and hit the ground running.

Deegan leaped from the car, crashed forward and tumbled to a dusty stop. He heard McCall laughing as he sat up spitting and shaking his head.

"You were a thing of grace and beauty, Charlie," McCall said as he hunkered down beside him. "I'd imagine that's about how a blind goose lands on a rock-filled lake."

McCall offered his hand to Deegan, who slapped it away and managed to get to his feet.

He glared at McCall. "I got down here myself, I can get up by myself."

McCall shrugged. "Suit yourself."

"Let's go get your stuff and see how it landed," Deegan said. "Maybe that bottle of passable whiskey got broke crashing through those bushes back there. Of course, there probably ain't too much left anyway. You were working on that bottle like some kind of a starving calf on a teat whenever you thought I was asleep or wasn't looking."

"You know, Charlie, there ain't nothing worse'n a man who's quit drinking and then tries to make all of his drinking buddies as miserable as he is. I didn't wanna drink in front of you 'cause I didn't wanna tempt you."

"I appreciate that and I don't care if you drink, Creed. It'll take you a few years to catch up with all the liquor I poured over these teeth of mine anyway." Deegan turned and started limping along the tracks.

"You get hurt, Charlie?"

"Nothing I can't live with," Deegan answered.

McCall skidded down into a little hollow, gave his gear a quick once-over, swung it up onto his shoulder and worked his way back up to Deegan.

"It appears everything's in pretty good shape," McCall announced and dropped the saddle at his feet.

"Where're you supposed to meet your people?" Deegan asked.

"There's a bar up across from the sales ring called the Running Iron. If they're in town, that's where they'll be. Joe Burdette's got him a whore works outta there. At least she was there the last two times we came through. He keeps trying to get her to leave there and go live with him on the ranch," McCall said. "Name's Angelina. He calls her his 'special angel.' "

"She a good-looking woman?"

"Good looking and about half of Joe's age. Dark skin, raven-black hair, dark dancing eyes and nice teeth. She's got a damn-well-curved body too. Only thing wrong with her is that wooden leg," McCall said, glancing at Deegan out of the corner of his eye.

"A whore with a wooden leg?"

"Yep," McCall answered and grinned.

"What happened to her?"

"Ah . . . well, it's a long story. Seems she got it cut off in a sawmill accident."

"You're lying to me ain't you, Creed? You're stringing me along, ain't you?" Deegan stepped in front of McCall. "You must think I'm some sorta country bumpkin just fell off the manure wagon or something. Sawmill accident, my ass!"

"As God is my witness, she's got a wooden leg. She walks good on it though. There's times she don't even limp. I've seen her dance like a leaf in the wind and then times she drags it around like a fence post and can't even get up to go to the bar and fetch drinks," McCall said, looking directly into Deegan's eyes.

Deegan put a finger on his chest. "Now I know you're lying to me. How come is it one time she doesn't even limp and then she drags it around behind her?"

McCall shrugged. "I ain't a doctor, Charlie. Wait until we get there and see for yourself." He swung his saddle up onto his shoulder, pushed past Deegan and started walking. "Let's go, we still gotta ways to walk to town," he shouted back over his shoulder. "And don't let Burdette catch you staring at her wooden leg. He's mighty sensitive about it."

Deegan watched him and yelled, "I thought we'd wait for the next train, so I could see if your railroad bull idea worked."

McCall hung his saddle over the top rail of a pen at the stockyards, unbuckled his saddlebag, pulled out a bottle of whiskey and held it up to look at it. "There's a bit left, but I ain't offering any to you," he stated, pulled the cork, turned it up to his mouth until it was empty, smacked his lips and set it on a fence post. "So you were a hard-drinking man at one time?"

Deegan nodded.

"You get religion or something?"

Deegan shook his head.

"You got awful quiet," McCall stated. "You sure you didn't get religion?"

"No, I didn't get religion. It seems I always tend to get in trouble when I drink . . ."

"Sorry," McCall apologized. "I didn't mean to rile you."

"That's all right. There's been recent times I wasn't sure about things."

"Meaning?"

"Nothing," Deegan answered, looked out across the stockyards and turned back to McCall. "Creed, there's been a time or two lately that I had luck I couldn't explain. I was so low I knew I couldn't get any lower and then . . ." Deegan looked down at his boots as if embarrassed to continue.

"Well, what happened?" McCall demanded.

Deegan's mind flew across his escape from

Yuma Territorial Prison; Mangas and the dogs; Angus McKenna's caves; *El Loco Lobo,* the little Mexican village and the gold left on the altar; Pine Spring and Sheriff Baca stealing all his canned peaches; the Indian battle, Fort Wingate, First Sergeant Odell, Private Landom, Chato and his last escape. He shook his head. "Oh, never mind, it wasn't anything I want to talk about. Forget it." He rubbed at his stubbled chin. "Something I'm gonna do as soon as I get a chance is take a bath, and get a shave and a haircut by a real barber. I can use a little cleaning up."

"We were talking about your not drinking," McCall reminded him.

Deegan nodded.

"Why'd you really quit drinking Charlie?"

Deegan sighed. "Like I said, it got me in trouble one too many times and so I decided it was time to quit."

"All right," McCall said. "Well, I ain't quit and I just got started again." He lifted his saddle up onto his shoulder. "Let's go down to the Running Iron and see if Joe Burdette and some of the boys are in there."

Deegan nodded. "Lead the way."

"Were you a fighter when you was a drinking man, Charlie?" McCall asked, as they walked between the pens.

"You think all this is natural beauty?" Deegan asked, pushing his nose flat with his thumb.

"That's what gave me the inkling you was a drinking man. You ever been in jail, Charlie?"

"Creed, why in the hell are you all of a sudden getting so nosey?" Deegan demanded.

"I'm going to recommend you to Joe Burdette for a job and he's gonna wanna know a few things about you," McCall answered. "You ever been in jail?"

"Ah . . . yes, I've been in jail. In my drinking days I was locked up a time or two," Deegan replied. "Hell, anybody drank as much as I have and been in as many fights as I have has got to have been in jail a time or two. I ain't qualified for sainthood."

"But, you aren't drinking anymore?"

"Damnit, I told you I wasn't. Let it lay. I'm a man of my word, Creed."

"All right, Charlie," Creed said, sounding satisfied with the answer. "I'm gonna take you for your word and I'm gonna hold you to it. You ain't drinking anymore."

McCall lengthened his stride and began whistling tunelessly.

Deegan stopped and studied McCall's back. "That's fine. I ain't drinking and I

ain't gonna be no damned Little Suzie!"
Deegan yelled. "I'm gonna be the *assistant
cook!*"

McCall nodded and waved his hand for
Deegan to catch up.

CHAPTER THIRTY-EIGHT

Charlie Deegan and Creed McCall walked until they located the stockyards offices.

"I'll go in and see if Joe's stopped by yet," McCall said. "I'll leave my saddle there so I don't have to tote it around."

"I'll be out here," Deegan stated and began to study the street crowded with horses and riders, wagons and people picking their way through the drying mud.

McCall returned shortly. "Joe and a few of the boys came through here earlier." He pointed at a false-front building across the street. "That's the Running Iron and that's where they'll be."

The two men dodged across the street and McCall stopped and patted the flank of a horse tied to a hitch rail. "See this *JA* brand? That's Charles Goodnight's mark. The boys are inside."

They clumped across the board sidewalk

and McCall pushed through the swinging doors.

Deegan stood just inside the door and took in all of the familiar sounds and smells. *You gotta be strong now, Charlie, you gotta be strong.*

"There's Joe and some of the boys over there!" McCall said and waved his arm at a group sitting around a large table. He nudged Deegan's arm. "C'mon, let's go over and I'll introduce you."

Several of the men returned his wave and shouted greetings.

"Ah . . . maybe I should go buy me a new hat and a few of the other things I'm gonna be needing," Deegan said, weakly.

"No way, Charlie!" McCall said, pushing Deegan ahead of him toward the table. "You can get that stuff later, before we go back to the corrals. C'mon."

Deegan carefully studied the group at the table as he and McCall approached.

An older cowboy sat with his arm around a dark-skinned, young woman perched on his lap. His hat was back and a pale line of wrinkled forehead showed above his gray eyebrows. He concentrated on the face of the woman, with eyes of a schoolboy in love for the first time. He nodded with every word she spoke to him. Several of the men told him of the approach of McCall and he waved their words away with the flip of his free hand.

"Didn't take Joe long to get hooked up with Angelina again," McCall noted.

The other five men at the table stood and McCall made introductions.

The first man was a tall black man. "Bose, this here's Charlie." They shook hands.

"Pleased to meet ya, sir," Bose Ikard said, with a toothy grin.

Deegan returned the smile.

McCall said, pointing to the man with the sad, hound-dog face. "This here's Reb."

Deegan shook his hand.

"Glad to meet you, Charlie," J. J. "Reb" Quarles said, with a slight smile. "Nasty-lookin' eye, there, Creed."

McCall grunted and nodded.

The next man with the long corn-silk mustache stuck out his hand. "The name's Cameron McShane," he said, with a slight Irish accent. "If you're going to be riding with us and you should be needing any-thing, I'm the man who can get it for you."

"For a price," Reb added, and the others laughed.

Deegan smiled and nodded. "I'll remember that."

"I'm Al Penny," the next man, with a thin

face, square jaw and piercing gray eyes, announced and held out his hand. "I think I know ya from someplace."

Deegan's handshake hesitated. *Where'n the hell does he know me from?* He gave the man's hand a final shake. "Can't say it's mutual, sorry."

"Oh, I'll think of it," Penny said, nodding. "I never forget a face."

McCall stepped up to the next man, with a shaved head, a sweeping black mustache and a large, pronounced scar down his cheek, standing ramrod straight, hand thrust forward. "Ah . . . you must be a new man," McCall said, looking him up and down and grasping his proffered hand. He was surprised when the man dropped his hand, snapped his heels together, made a stiff bow and quickly straightened.

"My name is Herman Fenzel," he stated, with a heavy Germanic accent. "I haf chust been hired on by Mister Burdette."

"Name's Creed McCall. I'm usually the number-two man right under Mister Burdette. Glad to meet you. This is Charlie Deegan," he said, hooking a thumb over his shoulder.

Fenzel gripped Deegan's hand and repeated the bowing routine. "It is my pleasure, chentlemen," Fenzel said.

336

"He was an officer in some foreign army," Reb announced.

"I vas a major in da Prussian army," Fenzel proclaimed.

"He's a hell of a horseman," McShane added. "A damned fine rider."

Fenzel looked at McShane and nodded. "I haf great training und experience in horsemanship. I vas a member of da Kaiser's personal guard."

"Good to know that," McCall said and motioned for everybody to sit down. "Soon as Burdette comes up for air, I'll introduce you to him."

Burdette raised his hand from the girl's back and waved.

"He knows we're here," McCall said.

McCall whistled and motioned at the woman talking to a cowboy at the end of the bar. "Hey, darling, bring us a round of drinks. Mister Burdette's buying."

She sauntered over to the table and looked at each of them in turn. "I know what they're drinking. What'll you boys have?"

"Beer," McCall answered.

"Beer," Deegan echoed and nodded.

McCall took a quick look at Deegan out of the corner of his eye, but said nothing.

The woman brought the drinks to the table, scooped up money from the pile in front of Joe Burdette and returned to her conversation at the bar.

"To Charles Goodnight," McCall shouted, raising his glass.

The others raised their glasses, chanted "Mister Goodnight" and took a drink.

Deegan lifted his glass in toast and set it back on the table. He let his eyes wander around the saloon, taking in all the familiar sights and sounds.

Fenzel leaned toward Deegan. "You do not drink to Mister Goodnight?"

"I don't drink," Deegan explained.

"If you do not drink, zen vhy did you order dat beer?"

"It's a test."

"Vat do you mean, a test?"

"You wouldn't understand," Deegan replied, softly.

"If Mister Burdette vas good enough to buy you a drink, zen you'd better be good enough to drink it," Fenzel stated, through clenched teeth. "He paid gute money for zat beer."

Deegan dug a coin out of a vest pocket and tossed it onto the pile in front of Burdette.

"That'll more'n cover it. Somebody else can drink it."

Fenzel finished his beer, wiped his mus-

338

tache, set the mug on the table and pushed to his feet. "Maybe you did not hear me."

Deegan slowly rose to his feet. "I heard and I paid Mister Burdette for the beer. Let it lay."

The big Prussian squared his shoulders and pushed out his chest. "Maybe you need to be taught zome manners."

Deegan became aware that everyone at the table was listening and watching them. He saw McCall shake his head slightly.

"I don't know exactly what you're trying to prove, but you're picking on the wrong man. If you wanna be the big he coon a this outfit, you best take on somebody that'll make a difference," Deegan said, his narrowed eyes looking directly into Fenzel's. "I ain't even working for this brand yet. You and me fight, no matter who wins, nobody cares. Why'd you wanna get your ass whipped by somebody who doesn't matter one way or another? Back off!"

Creed McCall stood and stepped between the two men. "Fenzel, I don't know much about you, but you're beginning to irritate me and I'm not a man you wanna irritate," he said, in a hard voice. "Now, why don't you just sit down and I'll buy you and the boys another beer."

Fenzel glared at both of them and slowly

sat down.

"You don't have to protect me, Creed," Deegan protested. "I can take care of myself."

"You sit down and cool off, too," McCall said, pointing at an empty chair. "Matter a fact, let's you and me go get those supplies you needed."

McCall threw a five-dollar gold piece on the table. "Drink this up, boys. It's gonna be a long dry spell on the trail."

Deegan looked across the table and saw Joe Burdette was no longer totally engrossed in the girl on his lap.

"War Wagon's down the street getting stocked up on the necessary supplies. You can follow him out to the herd. We're gonna be here for another two days before we head out. Getting more cattle from a ranch east of here, resting up the herd and I've got a few things to settle before we leave. We'll be out about dark," Burdette said, and smiled. "Welcome back, Creed. You forget to duck under a low branch?"

McCall chose to ignore the comment. "Joe, this's Charlie Deegan," he said, hooking a thumb at Deegan. "He did me a big favor and I told him I'd get him a job on this cow parade."

Deegan leaned across the table and held

out his hand.

Burdette took his hand off the girl's waist, reached out and shook it. "You didn't give him that swollen eye did you?"

Deegan shook his head.

"Well, Charlie, I got a full crew, but if Creed said he'd . . ."

"I told him he'd start out working for War Wagon," McCall interrupted.

"I'm willing to start anyplace, Mister Burdette," Deegan pleaded.

"I was afraid I was gonna have to rotate the boys to take turns being Little Suzie, but if Charlie here wants the job, it's his," Burdette stated. "Like I said, Creed, welcome back. I'm looking forward to your story about that eye."

McCall touched his finger to the brim of his hat. "Don't hold your breath," he muttered and smiled at Burdette. "We'll see you at the herd, Joe." He drained his mug and set it back on the table. "You boys be sure and tip the lady with some of that money now, you hear? Let's go, Charlie."

The two men walked out of the saloon and clumped down the board sidewalk.

Deegan spoke, "You didn't have to do that for me, Creed."

"I heard you the first time," McCall replied. "Joe ain't gonna hire a bar brawler

341

and you were about to show us all how bad an *hombre* you really are. I think you and that Cossack'll make an interesting fight when it does happen, and I'm sure it's just a matter of time."

"I wonder what that shiny-headed bastard's problem was?" Deegan asked. "He's definitely on the prod and we both know it's a matter of time before we lock horns again."

"Some men are just like that, Charlie. Give him a wide path. He doesn't strike me as the kind that'll let what happened in the saloon today go by easy. No sense in pushing it, but be watching out for him."

"You don't have to tell me that."

"Why'd you order that beer? You said it was a kinda test?"

"Yeah."

"I hope you proved something to yourself and passed the test," McCall stated. "I guess we'll ride out to the herd with War Wagon. Joe must've taken it for granted we had horses."

"Hey." Deegan put a hand on McCall's shoulder. "Was that gal sitting on Burdette's lap the one that's supposed to have the wooden leg?"

"Yeah, that's her," McCall answered, fighting to keep a straight face.

"You are a lying sumbitch, Creed! That gal didn't have a wooden leg."

"How do you know that?"

"Because, I saw her kicking her legs in the air and I took a close look at them, both of them, when I was shaking hands with Burdette."

"Can't a woman kick a wooden leg in the air? Well, can't she?" McCall demanded, as Deegan stomped off ahead of him. "I told you there was days you couldn't tell. This is one of those days. 'Sides that, she's wearing stockings. She has to cover that knot hole in her ankle." McCall struggled to regain his composure and ran to catch up with Deegan.

"Whoa, there, Charlie. Slow down a bit," he said, putting a hand on his shoulder.

Deegan shrugged off McCall's hand. "It doesn't matter, but I know you're lying. I ain't got any way to prove it right now, so forget it. I ain't the country bumpkin you think I am. Knot hole in her ankle, my ass!"

CHAPTER THIRTY-NINE

Creed McCall shrugged as he matched Charlie Deegan's pace. "That's War Wagon up there," he said pointing to a small man leaning against the wheel of a wagon down the street.

"How come you call him War Wagon?"

McCall laughed. "His real name's Rud Evans. He was a hell of a cowboy until his horse dumped him into a canyon and busted him up bad. When he was healed up, he couldn't sit a horse anymore. Mister Goodnight was good enough to keep him around the ranch and put him to work in the cookhouse. He turned into a pretty decent cook and Joe decided to take him on a cattle drive as the hasher.

"Well, Rud started laying down rules. No riding or tying horses close to the chuck wagon because of dust, horse apples and flies. Anybody bitched about the food had to wash dishes. If a cowboy found wood, he had to bring it to the chuck wagon because he didn't like cooking with dry cow pies. Nobody took food or anything else from the wagon without asking him first. There was a few more rules I can't recollect right now. Anyway, somebody said, chuck wagon hell, sounds more like he's the boss of a damned war wagon and the name War Wagon stuck. Most all the chuck bosses got the same rules, but he got that nickname anyway."

McCall and Deegan stopped and looked down at the little man leaning on the wagon wheel.

War Wagon wore a beat-up, crusty derby hat perched squarely on a halo of thick white hair that matched his mustache and beard. He looked up at the two men over the top of his wire-rimmed glasses and spit a stream of tobacco juice out of the corner of his mouth.

"Well, yer timin' is perfect, Creed," he said, unhooking his glasses and polishing them on his flour-sack apron. "I busted my ass gettin' this here wagon loaded with supplies, by myself I might add, and you show up about the time I's finished. Ya probably stood down the street and watched for a while, didn't ya, huh, didn't ya?"

"No, War Wagon, I didn't. If I'd a seen

you loading this wagon by yourself, I'd a gotten a whip and made sure you did it faster."

A strapping young man, with a sack of flour on each shoulder, pushed out of the door behind McCall and Deegan. "You want me to put these where I put all the other stuff, Mister Evans?"

"That'll be fine, son," War Wagon answered quietly, looking down at his shoes.

"Why, you old reprobate!" McCall declared.

War Wagon hooked his glasses back onto his ears, dug into a vest pocket and flipped a coin to the young man. "Here ya are, son."

He deftly caught the coin and smiled. "Thanks, Mister Evans, it's always a pleasure to help you load your wagon."

"Yeah, yeah," War Wagon muttered and waved a hand as if dismissing the boy.

McCall and Deegan stepped down into the street.

"War Wagon, this is Charlie Deegan. He's gonna be helping you for a while."

Deegan and War Wagon shook hands.

"So yer gonna be my Little Suzie, huh?" War Wagon asked, looking him up and down.

"I'm gonna be helping you until . . ." Deegan let the words trail off and nodded. "I'll be helping you, but I don't take to being called Little Suzie. You can call me Charlie, or hey, you, or anything else, but I ain't gonna be putting up with Little Suzie."

"Suit yerself . . . , Charlie," War Wagon answered, nodded and grinned.

"We'll be riding out to the herd with you, War Wagon," McCall stated. "Charlie needs a few things and I've got to pick up my saddle and gear over at the stockyards office before we head out. Why don't you trot on down to the Running Iron and have Mister Burdette buy you a beer? Tell him I sent you. We'll keep an eye on the wagon."

"Sounds like a good deal to me!" War Wagon cackled as he wiped his hands on his apron. "Looks to me like ya already kept an eye on somebody's wagon, or their fist." He slapped his leg and cackled at his humor. "By jingee, I'll tell Mister Burdette ya sent me down to have him buy me a beer. Yessiree, I will!" He untied his flour-sack apron and threw it up on the seat of the wagon. "Yessiree, I will!"

"Tell him I said to buy you a *couple* of beers," McCall added.

War Wagon grinned, cocked his derby forward and hobbled off up the boardwalk in search of his free beers.

The two men watched him until he

pushed through the doors of the saloon and disappeared.

"You were right about the boys and your eye, Creed."

"I've been around cowboys long enough to know if something's hurt you, but hasn't killed you or bunged you up permanent, they'll make a smart remark about it if they have a chance."

"I'll remember that."

"This is usually the soogan wagon or the hoodlum wagon where the boys keep their bedrolls and other personal belongings," McCall explained. "We use it to get supplies. With a two-mule team, it's smaller and easier to get around in town and it saves moving the chuck wagon any more than necessary. This is the wagon you'll be driving. You can drive a two-mule hitch, can't you?"

"Gees," Deegan muttered. "First you stick me with a girl's name and now you're beginning to treat me like I got ruffles on my drawers."

"You're getting a little defensive. I still don't know much about you, so I got to ask."

"Okay," Deegan agreed. "Let's go find a barbershop and then go in here and get the stuff I need 'fore War Wagon gets back."

McCall laughed. "There's no reason to hurry. With Burdette buying War Wagon beer, we got lots of time. I'll go over and get my saddle and gear."

CHAPTER FORTY

The two men sat on the tailgate of the hoodlum wagon, McCall twirling a stick of candy in his mouth and Deegan studying the crown of the new black hat resting on the knee of his new tan canvas pants. A new blue cotton shirt and tan canvas vest completed the outfit.

"I can't leave it like this," Deegan stated. "It looks too damned much like a new hat. Hell, I don't even remember the last time I had one of these."

"I can toss it into the street and jump on it a few times," McCall volunteered. "That'll give it that well-used, trail-drive look."

Deegan glanced at him and shook his head. "I just wanna give it a little character. Get rid of that new hat look."

"Suit yourself. Can I ask you a question?"

"Go ahead," Deegan answered, turning the hat and carefully putting a pinch in the crown.

"I counted six toothbrushes in that pile of stuff you bought in there."

"That's right."

"Why in the hell'd you buy six tooth-brushes?"

"So I don't end up looking like War Wagon someday."

"You mean his teeth?"

"What teeth?" Deegan asked. "He doesn't have any teeth."

"Sure he does," McCall answered. "He keeps them in his vest pocket until he needs them."

Deegan gave a snort of disgust. "You just answered your own question and, speak of the devil, here he comes now."

Peering over his glasses, War Wagon sauntered down the boardwalk, a stubby pipe bobbing in his smile. He pulled the pipe free, gave a toothy grin, tipped his beat-up derby and made an exaggerated bow to a woman he met. Then he fought to regain his balance.

"Looks like he managed to down a fair share in a short period of time," McCall noted. "He always manages to do that when somebody else's buying."

"Yeah, and now he's turned into a real dashing ladies' man," Deegan agreed. "I see he's got his teeth in. I hope he doesn't fall and hurt himself doing all that fancy foot-work."

Both men laughed at the antics of the little cook as he clomped toward them.

War Wagon stopped, stared warily and then grinned at McCall and Deegan. "Ya boys get all the stuff ya wanted?" he asked, in a slurred voice. "If ya need more time, I be happy to go back and kill a little more time while ya get the rest of it."

"No, we're ready to head back to the herd," McCall answered. "Why don't you crawl up in back and take a nap? I'll drive. The herd in the usual place north of town?"

War Wagon smiled at them drunkenly, nodded and stepped down to hang on a hitching rail.

The two men helped him crawl up among the supplies and closed the tailgate. War Wagon put his stubby pipe into a vest pocket, popped his teeth out, wiped them on his sleeve and carefully put them in another pocket. He wiggled into a comfort-able spot and pulled his derby down over his face. "Sorry to hear about yer eye, Creed," he muttered, sighed and immedi-ately began to snore.

"I wonder what he heard about my eye?" McCall asked, climbing up onto the driver's seat.

"Probably some pretty good stories going around already."

"Yeah, I'm sure."

"You want me to drive, Creed, to prove I can drive a team of mules?" Deegan asked.

"No, I know where the herd is and I kinda enjoy driving a team once in a while. You'll get your chance soon enough."

Half an hour later, they crested a hill and looked down at a mass of grazing cattle.

"They look mighty tame and content down there, don't they?" McCall asked.

"Look peaceful enough to me," Deegan agreed.

"Well, the first time you go through a stampede of those bastards, you'll appreciate a quiet grazing herd like that one."

"How many head do you figure there are down there?" Deegan asked.

"Oh, I'd guess about twelve to thirteen hundred head," McCall answered. "That's about the size herd Mister Goodnight likes to start with on long drives. We give some to the Indians as a toll for crossing their land, we eat a few and we lose some along the way. We should get up to Dakota Territory with somewhere between eleven hundred and eleven hundred and fifty head to sell. Hell, I remember one drive we ended up with more cattle than we started with."

"You do some rustling along the way?"

McCall laughed. "No, we just kept finding a few head of unbranded cattle here and there and first thing you know we had more than we started with. Figured they'd been calves drifted off other herds before somebody put an iron to them."

War Wagon grunted as he sat up, pushed his pipe stub into his mouth and pointed to the chuck wagon at the edge of a small grove of trees. A tent fly stretched out onto poles behind the wagon gave a certain feeling of permanence and stability to War Wagon's kitchen kingdom.

"Well, git us on down there. I gotta start supper for the boys. I had my nap, now I gotta git to work. You two unload this wagon," War Wagon ordered. "Then, I'll get Charlie here doing a few a his chores."

"Yes, boss," McCall answered and slapped the lines on the mules. "Hyap, hyap. Let's go, mules!" he shouted.

As they neared the chuck wagon, McCall brought the mules to a slow walk. "Don't wanna be raising any dust with the boss sitting behind me."

Both men laughed.

"What'n the hell's so funny about that?" War Wagon demanded, jabbing the stem of his pipe into McCall's back. "Ya know my

354

rules about dust."

"And horse apples bringin' in flies," McCall added and started to laugh again. "War Wagon, I got all your rules written in my tally book and I review them on a regular basis."

"Ya better be watching out I don't slip ya a horse-apple biscuit one of these days," War Wagon snorted.

A tall, thin cowboy stepped over the chuck-wagon tongue and waved as they approached.

"Ho . . . ho . . . howdy, C . . . Creed," he called, taking the halter of one of the mules and pulling the team to a stop. "Ev . . . ev . . . everything's j . . . ju . . . just fine, W . . . War Wa . . . Wagon," he announced. "I . . . I go . . . got that critter skin . . . skinned out and hung up, jis . . . jist like ya to . . . told me before you le . . . left."

"Charlie, this is Reno Hartman," McCall said. "Reno, this is Charlie Deegan."

Deegan jumped down and shook Hartman's proffered hand. "Glad to meet you, Reno."

"Li . . . like . . . ah . . . same here," Hartman replied and smiled weakly.

"Charlie's gonna be the full-time Little Suzie for a while," War Wagon proclaimed. "Soon as we get these supplies moved over

355

to the chuck wagon, ya can head back out to the herd, Reno, and send someone else in to eat."

"Tha . . . that's goo . . . good news to me!" Reno exclaimed as he moved around to the rear of the wagon and dropped the tailgate. "Wa . . . watch yourself, Charlie, he . . . he's a bas . . . bastard to wo . . . work for." Reno ran laughing and ducked under the wooden spoon War Wagon threw.

War Wagon muttered to himself as he tied on his apron, retrieved the spoon, wiped it on the apron and tossed it back onto the table folded down from the chuck box.

Deegan pulled the first bag of flour onto his shoulder and looked questioningly at War Wagon, who pointed at the main box of the chuck wagon.

War Wagon took a dipper of water from the barrel beside the wagon and sparingly washed his hands. Satisfied, he wiped them on his apron and began to bang pots, pans and other cooking utensils around on the table. "Charlie, you git the fire built up and then start peeling spuds from that bag by the front wheel. I washed them before, so all you gotta do is peel, quarter and put them in that big pot. Put enough water in to cover 'em and hang the pot on a hook over the fire."

"Yes, boss," Deegan answered, selecting a knife from the chuck box.

"The wranglers on the herd'll be straggling in for supper and the boys coming back from town'll be drunk and hungry, so I best git something on the fire for all of them. Gotta cut off good steaks and stew meat from that carcass . . . I got biscuits and pies to make . . ." War Wagon's voice trailed off as he walked off to concentrate on his butchering.

"I'll take care of the fire, Charlie," Creed said, as he gathered wood. "You go ahead and start peeling those taters."

Reno walked to the hitch line strung between several trees, saddled a horse and rode off.

McCall sat and leaned back on his elbows to watch Deegan peel potatoes. "Well, Charlie," he said. "You'll be happy to know that your hat's taken on a little character. Actually, it's not character, it's more like a nice coating of flour."

Deegan pulled off and examined his hat. "Well, at least it don't look new anymore," he agreed as he pushed it back onto his head.

CHAPTER FORTY-ONE

A black cowboy, singing softly to himself, rode up, dismounted, tied his horse to the hitch line, loosened the cinch and raised his voice as he approached the camp.

"That's Roosevelt Jones and he's a singing fool," McCall commented. "He knows more damn songs than any man I ever met. He's got a guitar and he plays at night. On Sundays he gets to singing hymns and spirituals and you can hear him for a mile."

". . . good-bye, Old Paint, I'm leavin' Cheyenne . . ." The last notes of Roosevelt's song dwindled and he broke into a toothy grin.

"Well, howdy, there, Mister Creed, how ya doin'? Good to see ya back. I's 'fraid that ya wasn't gonna be with us on this drive."

"Good to see you again, Roosevelt," McCall said as he stood and shook the black man's hand. "I'd like you to meet Charlie Deegan."

Deegan stood, wiped his hands on his pants and shook Roosevelt Jones's hand. "Glad to meet you, Roosevelt."

"Same here, Mister Charlie," Roosevelt answered. "You the Little Suzie now?"

"No, I'm helping War Wagon with the cooking," Deegan stated. "Why in the hell does everybody have to call me Little Suzie?"

"Easy does it, Charlie," McCall responded. "That name was around a long time before you were. There's nothing personal about it. It's just a name."

"Yeah, okay," Deegan agreed. "Anyway, nice to meet you, Roosevelt. I wasn't getting on you personally about the name. I's just blowing it out of my system. Creed tells me you're quite a singer and I'm looking forward to hearing you."

A mass of white teeth flashed under Roosevelt's mustache. "I figured that Mister Charlie, so I didn't take no offense. Nice to meet ya. I gotta git me something to eat and go back out to the herd. I be glad to be singing for ya later."

The next man to ride in was a tall, handsome Mexican cowboy, dressed in traditional *vaquero* clothing, a wide-brimmed *sombrero* and straddling a large-horned Mexican saddle. He swung down from his horse, tied it on the hitch line and sauntered casually into the camp. His heavy silver spurs rang noisily as he walked.

"Javier, how are you?" McCall asked, thrusting out his hand.

"*Señor* McCall, I am *muy bueno.* And how are you doing *mi amigo?*" Javier asked, shaking McCall's hand.

"I am also *muy bueno,* my friend," Mc-Call answered. "How does the herd look?"

"The cattle I have brought from my father's ranch are well fed," Javier answered. "Many of Mister Goodnight's are in need of good grass."

McCall studied Javier's face for a moment and then laughed. "Since those cows of yours are well fed, they'll probably be the first ones we'll eat on the trail. No sense in wasting good, fat beef when it comes to feeding the men."

Javier laughed. "Then I will be watching for that, *Señor* McCall."

"Javier, I'd like you to meet Charlie Deegan," McCall said, waving his hand at Deegan.

Javier and Deegan shook hands.

"Javier's father has been sending a small herd of about two hundred cattle along on the last three of Mister Goodnight's drives so Javier can learn the cattle trail drive business," McCall explained. "His father owns a ranch down in Mexico that runs over a hundred thousand head."

Deegan whistled. "Damn, that must be a good-sized place you've got down there."

"Yes, it is very large, *Señor* Deegan," Javier agreed. "It is a pleasure to meet you."

Javier touched his fingers to the brim of his *sombrero.* "If you will excuse me now, *señores,* I must eat and get back out so the others can come in and be fed before it gets dark."

"It was good to meet you, Javier," Deegan said.

The tall Mexican turned and walked to where War Wagon was cutting pies.

"Pull that pot of spuds off the fire, dump the water and mash 'em, there's a masher hanging around here someplace," War Wagon ordered and spit a stream of tobacco juice in the general direction of the fire. "And give that pot a beans a stir while yer over there."

"Yes, boss," Deegan muttered.

McCall chuckled. "I'm gonna ride out and take a look at the herd before it gets dark and the boys get back from town," he announced, pulling his saddle from the hoodlum wagon and starting to the hitch line to choose a horse. "The boys are usually a little rambunctious when they get back from an afternoon at the Running Iron."

"Hey, Charlie!" War Wagon shouted. "Don't be standing around! Food don't fix itself!" He wiped his hands on his apron, dug out his plug of tobacco and gummed off a fresh chew. "Git with it now. Them boys gotta be fed."

The next cowboy to ride into camp was a small man, wearing a hat that was so big it rested on his ears. A leather string from the hat looped loosely under his chin. An elbow stuck out through a hole in the sleeve of his baggy shirt and his chaps were scuffed and patched. He swung down, tied his horse, loosened the cinch and walked to the camp.

Deegan stepped forward and held out his hand.

"Name's Charlie Deegan," he announced to the little man. "I'm helping War Wagon with the cooking for a while."

"Well, howdy, Charlie," the little man answered. "Name's Sam. Sam Spooner. Glad to make yer acquaintance, Charlie. I could smell them pies way out. Guess I won't have to be Little Suzie tomorrow, since you got the job now, huh?"

"Yeah, Sam, I'll be handling that job for a while. Go get yourself something to eat," Deegan said, pointing at the chuck wagon.

"War Wagon's put together a good feed."

Deegan noticed that Sam only wore one spur.

A cowboy with long black braids flying out behind his tall black hat came whooping toward the camp and gave it wide circle at a full gallop before pulling his horse up and walking it slowly to the hitch line.

"Damn red savage does that jist because he knows it pisses me off!" War Wagon bellowed and shook a butcher knife at him. He sliced off a thick steak and waved it at the Indian. "I'll be takin' a chunk this size outta yer red ass, ya savage!"

The cowboy laughed and waved the ends of his braids at the old cook.

"I'll be taking what little hair you've got left one of these days, old man!" he called back and laughed.

McCall had told Deegan about Willie Red Horse on the ride out to the camp. "Willie's a Kiowa Indian, who'd been educated at the Carlisle Indian School until he decided to run away and become a cowboy. He's got long, black braids down to the middle of his chest and he wears a tall, black reservation hat with an eagle feather stuck in the side of it, a beaded vest and beaded bands on his shirtsleeves. His only real concession to being a white-man cowboy is his chaps, high-heeled boots and silver spurs. Willie and ol' War Wagon got a constant pissing contest going on, but the old man really likes him."

Willie sidled around the wagon until he was at the chuck box and began rummaging in a drawer.

"Git away from there, ya red heathen!" War Wagon shrieked. "How many times I gotta tell ya that I's the only one digs in my chuck box?"

Willie shrugged, raised his hands and stepped back. "I know you've got to have some candy sticks in there somewhere."

"Well, if I do, and I ain't saying I do, ya'll get one when I'm damned good and ready to give it to ya, and not before," War Wagon shouted, waving the steak he had just cut.

"That old man really likes me," Willie said, as they watched War Wagon arrange the steak on the grill.

"Yeah," Deegan agreed. "It really sounds like it. Name's Charlie Deegan," he said, offering his hand to Willie.

"I'm Willie Red Horse," Willie answered, giving his hand a firm shake. "You just sign on?"

"Uh-huh, for the time being I'm helping War Wagon with the cooking," Deegan answered and held up his hand. "Don't say anything about Little Suzie."

Willie looked at him, smiled and shrugged. "That's a white man's term. I don't use it."

Deegan studied Willie's face trying to decide if he was making fun of him.

"Hey, old man, don't overcook that steak!" Willie shouted. "Remember, us savages like our meat raw."

Willie turned to Deegan. "He still thinks I prefer dog," he whispered.

"Well then, come and get it ya long-haired devil," War Wagon called, lifting the steak with a long-handled fork. "I burned the hair off it, jist like ya do with a dog."

Willie grabbed a knife and fork and pulled a metal plate from the stack on the table. "See you around, Charlie Deegan."

CHAPTER FORTY-TWO

Charlie Deegan watched the next cowboy to ride in sitting ramrod straight in his saddle, his eyes hidden in the shadow of his hat brim. He reined his horse in the trees and sat there, hands crossed on the saddle horn.

McCall rode in, pulled his horse up and spoke to him. Both men swung down from their saddles, loosened their cinches and walked to the camp engaged in deep conversation.

"Charlie," McCall began. "This is Clive Palmer. Clive, this is Charlie Deegan, the man I was telling you about."

Deegan and Palmer shook hands.

Palmer studied Deegan up and down, nodded and smiled, showing a gap of two missing teeth under his mustache.

"So, you wanna be a cowboy," Palmer stated, with a true Texas accent. "In my case, it wasn't a matter of choice. It was the best way out of the territory. Probably the only way out of the territory." Palmer turned his whole upper body when he turned to face McCall. "You see, Creed here cut me down from a tree where I'd been left hanging by two irate brothers after I'd shot their other brother in a fair duel three days before. They'd jumped me, beat me and tossed me over the saddle of my horse to haul me a long way from their home territory and hang me." Palmer loosened his bandanna and revealed a scar that circled back under his ears. "My neck was broken, but I guess I was too skinny to have enough weight to choke to death. Creed ran them two off right after they'd whipped my horse out from under me and I was starting to swing."

"I'd heard some commotion over a hill when I was looking for strays," McCall continued. "I came riding around to investigate just as they ran his horse off. I fired a shot and spurred my horse to catch Clive on his second swing. The shot scared them off, but then they must've decided to come back and finish their work. I had him cut free and was laying him on the ground when they came riding back into that grove, hell-bent for leather, screaming and firing their guns. I was a small target because I was on my knees and they were on running horses and it's damned tough to hit anything from a horse at a dead run. Anyway, I shot both of them dead. I went back and got the hoodlum wagon and hauled Clive to a town a day away."

"The doctor there put a splint on my back and tied my head to it so I couldn't move. I laid like a trussed hog for almost a month," Palmer added. "The doctor said I's lucky Creed found me when he did and the neck wasn't broken any worse. I don't have any movement of my neck, but it's a hell of a lot better than being dead."

"A couple of the boys went back and buried the brothers in unmarked graves," McCall said. "Hell, they wanted to get away from their home territory so nobody'd know about their lynching Clive and now nobody'll find them anyway."

"I found Creed at the Goodnight ranch a year later and been with this bunch ever since."

"You better come get this steak, Clive!" War Wagon shouted. "I got apple pie and fresh biscuits, too. So you better come and git them before I throws them out."

"I best go before War Wagon comes over and takes me by the ear," Palmer said with a laugh. "I know he won't throw it away, but he'll let it get cold to prove he has the cook's power. Nice to meet you, Charlie," Palmer said. "We'll talk more later."

"Those missing front teeth are from the beating he took from those brothers before they lynched him," McCall said, quietly. "He's got money saved to get a set of store-boughts to fill in that gap one of these days."

"Hey, Clive," McCall shouted. "Hold up and I'll come along and get a cup a coffee."

Deegan saw another cowboy ride into the shade of the grove, dismount, loosen his saddle, hang his hat on the horn of his saddle and walk toward the camp.

"Hello again, Javier," Deegan called. "Come back in for seconds?"

The tall Mexican stopped, crossed his arms on his chest and glared at Deegan. "I am not Javier, *señor,*" he said.

Deegan laughed and nodded. "Okay, Javier, whatever you say."

The Mexican stepped up to Deegan and looked directly into his eyes. "My name is Ramon."

"Okay, Javier, you're Ramon. Hell, you can bc Poncho or Carmclita for all I carc," Deegan joked and became aware of a long-bladed dagger in the Mexican's hand.

"Are you making fun with me, *señor*?" he asked, bringing the knife higher.

"Whoa, there fella. I ain't making fun of you," Deegan stated, raising his hands and taking a step back. "Put that sticker away. You can be anybody you wanna be. Makes no never mind to me." He heard muffled laughter behind him and he turned to see McCall and War Wagon leaning on the wagon laughing.

Deegan turned to see the Mexican grinning and cleaning his fingernails with the tip of the knife blade. "What in hell's going on?" he demanded.

"Charlie, this is Javier's twin brother, Ramon," McCall announced.

"Works every time," War Wagon cackled.

"Very funny," Deegan stated.

"I am Ramon Gutierrez, *Señor* Deegan," Ramon said, extending his hand. "Javier told me you were the new man on the crew. It is a little joke we play when we can."

Deegan shook Ramon's hand. "You got me on that one," he conceded. "It *was* funny, I guess."

"Come on, Ramon," War Wagon called. "I got a steak on the grill for ya right now."

Deegan poured himself a cup of coffee, sat on a keg beside the fire and looked up at McCall. "This's been one helluva day."

"We'll pull out day after tomorrow," McCall said. "We'll start bringing the cattle in

370

and get them bunched into a herd tomorrow morning. First light the boys'll load their soogans on your wagon and you and War Wagon'll move out after you get everything cleaned up and packed. You'll go on ahead and set up for dinner. The boys'll take biscuits and dry meat with them to eat while they're riding. They call them greasy sack riders. You'll get the hang of it quick enough. There's another flour-sack apron in one of those drawers. Better put it on."

"Yes, boss."

With a series of whoops, hollers and shouts, Joe Burdette and the rest of the crew returned from town.

War Wagon threw steaks on the grill and busied himself filling plates with potatoes, biscuits and slices of fresh pie.

Deegan did little tasks as directed by War Wagon and tried to keep out of the way of the cowboys while they were getting their food and eating.

"Hey, Leettle Soosie," a voice behind Deegan growled.

Deegan knew who was talking to him.

"Ven onc uf da cowboys talks to you, Leettle Soosie, you vill pay attention."

Deegan tried to ignore the voice until his new hat was yanked from his head and he turned in time to see Fenzel send it flying

371

across the camp in the direction of the fire. He stood trying to maintain his composure as one of the other men caught it and sailed it across to another cowboy, who waved it, slapped it in the dirt and skimmed it over the top of the kitchen fly.

Just maintain yourself. It's their idea of a game with the new man. They're trying to see how far they can push you before you blow up and take a swing at somebody. Stay calm. Deegan forced himself to smile and laughed as his hat sailed by, just out of his reach.

"Leettle Soosie, I need a cup of coffee."

Deegan turned to Fenzel standing close behind him. *Just punch the bastard.* He let his eyes wander over the men watching and knew it was not the time.

"The pot's there on a hook over the fire. Help yourself to all you want," Deegan said with a tight smile. "Go ahead and help yourself."

"Leettle Soosie, you are da cook's helper. Dat means you are da cowboy's helper und I am a cowboy," Fenzel stated. "Dat means you vill help me by getting me a cup uf coffee."

Someone stepped up behind Deegan and pushed his hat onto his head. *Easy, Charlie,* he told himself as he pulled his hat tight, grabbed a cup from the wagon table and walked to the fire. He poured a cup of steaming coffee and returned to Fenzel. "You want me to help you drink it?" he asked, through clenched teeth.

"No, Leettle Soosie, I can do dat myzelf. I vill let you know vhen I need anuder cup."

The other men witnessing the scene chuckled nervously.

McCall stepped away from the others and approached the two men.

"Fenzel, you're pushing your luck with Deegan again. I don't know what your problem is with him, but it'd be wise for you to let it lie for a while," McCall warned. "You're beginning to bother me a little too. Now, just let it lie."

Fenzel took the coffee from Deegan and shrugged. "Vat efer you say, Mister Mc-Call."

"You didn't have to do that for me, Creed," Deegan muttered.

"What'd you say?"

"I said you didn't have to do that for me," Deegan answered. "That's the second time you've stepped into something I could handle by myself."

"I was doing that for him," McCall stated, with a wry smile. "I figured you were about ready to throw that cup of hot coffee on his face and then pound it in."

Deegan raised his hands and smiled weakly. "Sometimes you're smarter'n I give you credit for. Those were my exact thoughts, my exact thoughts."

"Well, I don't know what the burr under his tail is, but it seems he's gonna keep prodding you. I'll say from now on he'll make sure I'm not around when he does it."

"I told you I don't need your protection. I can take care of myself okay."

"Hey, don't get up on your hind legs with me," McCall said. "I know when the time comes you're gonna give him a firm ass whipping. Just don't do it around Burdette. I told you before he won't hire you if he thinks you're some kind of a damned bar fighter. He's got a thing about men like that. I don't know what it is, but I learned a long time ago he doesn't like brawlers."

"That doesn't make any difference to me. I'll be okay."

"Good! Nice apron. Now get *me* a cup of coffee." McCall laughed and sidestepped the mock punch Deegan threw at him.

"Hey, Charlie!" War Wagon yelled. "I need more flour and ya can grease a couple a those Dutch ovens for more biscuits."

"Yes, boss!" Deegan shouted. "See you later, Creed, I got work to do."

Deegan stood at the chuck box table wiping bacon grease into a Dutch oven when he looked up to find Al Penny studying him from across the table.

"Penny, isn't it?" Deegan asked. "I don't remember your first name."

"Albert, Al Penny," Penny prompted. "I remember where I know you from, Deegan."

"You don't know me from anyplace," Deegan argued, shaking his head. "I've never seen you before in my life."

Penny moved around the table and stood beside Deegan.

"You're mistaking me for somebody else."

"You were wearing a striped suit," Penny said quietly. "A wide-striped gray-and-white suit."

Deegan's hand snaked out and grabbed Penny's forearm.

"I told you, you don't know me," Deegan hissed.

"Your secret's safe with me," Penny said softly and twisted his arm free.

Deegan began to tremble as he glared at Penny through narrowed eyes. His hand swept across the table and clutched the handle of a butcher knife.

"I said you don't know me."

"I'm not telling anybody about your past

life. That's your business, none of mine," Penny stated quietly, looking down at Deegan's hand holding the knife. "I was in there doing a short stretch for shooting an ear off the man who'd stolen my wife. I know now I should've shot her. I got out about the time you escaped. Last I heard the prison people were sure you'd died in the desert. As far as I'm concerned, the coyotes gnawed your bones clean."

Deegan relaxed a little as he studied the man standing beside him.

"I'll give you a little advice, Deegan," Penny said. "If you're going to stay in this part of the country, you'd better take up a new name. Charlie Deegan's an easy name to remember. You look different now in those clothes, but you got an unusual name. Change it. See you around." Penny turned and walked off toward the horses.

Deegan watched Penny as he disappeared into the growing shadows of the trees. *Do I trust him? I guess right now I don't have much choice. Change my name? Hell, everybody here knows it and we're heading north . . . Changing my name is the least of my problems.*

CHAPTER FORTY-THREE

One by one, the men began to ride out to change places with the others watching over the herd. The sun slid behind the hills and the men on the far side of the grove built up their fire and gathered around it. The men found it better to sleep a distance from the chuck wagon because of the noise of War Wagon's work and the riders coming in to change shifts, drink coffee and talk.

War Wagon lit two lanterns, hung them inside the kitchen tent fly and began working on biscuit dough. "Grease up them other two Dutch ovens," he called around the pipe clutched in his gums.

"I did them when you told me the last time."

War Wagon looked at them and nodded. "Then grind up some coffee beans. That jar screwed on the bottom of the grinder holds what you'll need for a good strong pot. The boys appreciate strong coffee when they come in later. Use water from the barrel on the wagon. When ya git that done, take those two pans a dishes down to the crick and wash them."

"Yes, boss."

A half hour later War Wagon and Deegan were the only two men still awake. The others had burrowed into their bedrolls to get a little sleep before their turn to ride night herd.

War Wagon picked up the alarm clock from a shelf in the chuck box. "It's nigh unto ten o'clock," he announced and blew out one of the lanterns. "I'm gonna climb up in the wagon and sleep until about four while that dough rises and then I'll start the morning biscuits. The boys on night herd'll want one a them supper biscuits with their coffee and that's all right. There's a jar a honey if they wanna sweeten them up a bit. Stoke the fire under coffee and turn in when ya wanna. They can take care a themselves."

"I'll wait up a while. I ain't really tired yet."

"Suit yerself," War Wagon said as he climbed up a wheel and disappeared into the chuck wagon.

Reb Quarles rode in, tied off his horse and limped in to join Deegan.

"What'd you do to your leg?" Deegan

asked, as Reb poured a cup of coffee.

"I took a minié ball at Gettysburg," Reb stated.

"Ah . . . you wanna biscuit? Here's honey for them." Deegan pushed the jar toward the pan of biscuits.

Reb nodded, tore one open, poured honey on it and sipped his coffee. He finished, remounted and rode off into the darkness.

"Nice talking to you," Deegan called, sarcastically.

Deegan heard another rider come in and tie off his horse. He stepped to the fire, filled a cup with steaming coffee and set it on the table as he waited for the rider to come into the circle of light.

"Vell, Leettle Soosie, it seems dat ve haff now met midout yer guardian angel to keep us apart," Fenzel said softly from the shadows behind Deegan.

Surprised, he spun to face the Prussian.

"I don't need any guardian angel," Deegan said, softly. "I don't know what's got into you, but I can whip your ass any day of the week. Now don't start anything here because Burdette doesn't like men fighting and I wanna keep my job. Have some coffee and a biscuit and go back out to the herd. I'll meet you someplace away from here and we can settle this once and for all."

Fenzel stepped into the ring of light and stood grinning at Deegan. The light from the lantern exaggerated the size of the scar on his cheek. "Leettle Soosie, you haff made me look foolish in front of da udders," Fenzel stated. "No man makes me look foolish in front of udder men."

Deegan slid the cup toward Fenzel. "Here's coffee. If you wanna biscuit, help yourself. There's honey in that jar."

"Do you zee zis scar on my face, Leetle Soosie?" Fenzel asked, running a finger down the ditch in his skin.

Deegan nodded.

"In my country a scar like zis is a ting of honor. Do you know how ve git zees scars? Ve duel mit sabers for dem," Fenzel continued to run his finger up and down the scar. "Ven ve git cut, dey put pepper in de cut to make a scar dat looks like dis. In my country men look at me mit respect because uf dis scar. You haf made a fool of me in front of ze men in dis camp. Dey had respect for me because of my horsemanship. Now dey no longer respect me because uf you."

"You got it wrong, Fenzel," Deegan argued and looked over the quiet camp. "The men in this camp don't care about you and me arguing. They might like to see us fight, just for the sake of seeing a fight, but I doubt if they care who wins or loses. I'm not gonna fight you here in camp. Someday we'll settle this, but not now. Have some coffee. I got work to do."

Fenzel stepped up and put his hand on Deegan's chest. "I vus not done speaking to you, Leettle Soosie."

"You shouldn't a done that," Deegan muttered and buried his left fist in Fenzel's gut.

The air swooshed out of the Prussian, he doubled over and vomited.

Deegan brought his right fist across and caught Fenzel with a solid punch beside his left eye. The power of the blow turned Fenzel in a half circle; he staggered off into the shadow of the wagon and fell to his knees.

Deegan stepped over and cocked his fist to slam it into the dazed man's face. He shook his head, backed off and dropped his hands to his sides. He flexed his fist and muttered to himself, "You've beat him, Charlie. Let it go." He leaned in close to Fenzel. "Now listen, you stupid bastard," he whispered. "I want you to get on your horse and get out to the herd. This is over for now. Understand?"

Fenzel looked up, his eyes blinking rapidly and nodded.

Deegan stepped back. "Now git," he said, pointing out into the darkness.

Fenzel slowly got to his feet, holding his hand over his swollen eye and wiping his mouth with his shirtsleeve. "I vill kill you for dis," he snarled. "I *vill* kill you."

"You won't be the first to try. Now git the hell back to the herd!"

Fenzel turned and slunk off into the darkness.

Deegan heard the saddle leather creak and the sound of the hooves fade as he rode away. He took a deep breath and let it out slowly as he calmed down. "That was not good," he told himself, flexing and shaking his aching hand as he slowly walked toward the sleeping cowboys to see if anybody was awake and had heard his run-in with Fenzel. Several of them were snoring and someone was talking gibberish in his sleep. No one was moving. *That's one good thing anyway. . . .* He walked slowly back to the chuck wagon table and looked for something to make himself busy. "He'll be back, just like Mangas." He sniffed the air. *Ugh, I better get a shovel and cover up Fenzel's mess before anybody else comes in and smells it.* He chuckled to himself as he picked up the shovel under the wagon. *They might think it's from War Wagon's cooking.*

Satisfied, he tossed the shovel back where he'd found it. His mind raced as he ran water over his hands from the spigot on the barrel and wiped them on his apron. He pulled one of the Dutch ovens over and ran his hands inside it to make sure it was well greased. Satisfied, he repeated the process with the second one. He could hear War Wagon snoring in the wagon.

Deegan sensed someone was in the shadows behind him. He spun, holding up the Dutch oven, just as Fenzel thrust a knife at him. The blade glanced off the side of the oven and Deegan spun it to crash down on the back of Fenzel's knife hand.

Fenzel grunted in pain, dropped the knife and cried out, "You bastard, Leettle Soosie, you vill die!" He glanced down at the knife, up at Deegan, still holding the oven in front of him, and, fists flailing, charged.

Deegan grasped the oven with both hands and pushed it to meet Fenzel's assault.

Fenzel's fist crashed into the cast-iron pot; he moaned and stood bent over, clutching his injured hand to his chest as it swelled and began to turn color.

Deegan stepped up and lifted the oven high above Fenzel's head. "Don't do it," he muttered to himself and dropped the oven by his feet. He glanced at the injured man, bent down, picked up the knife, walked around the tailgate table and slid it out of sight. He pushed his trembling hands down on the table. *You almost killed him,* he told himself as he looked up to see the others running into the circle of light to see what the commotion was about.

They found Fenzel bending over, holding his injured hand. His left eye was swollen shut; small tears of pain ran down his cheeks and along his scar as he muttered words that no one understood.

"What the hell happened?" Joe Burdette demanded, yawning and stretching.

"He pushed me as far as I's gonna be pushed. He shouldn't a put his hand on me," Deegan answered simply.

"Fenzel's been prodding Charlie since the first time he met him, Joe," McCall interrupted. "I've warned Fenzel to back off and separated them a couple of times before."

Herman Fenzel glared with his one good eye at the group of men standing around him. He straightened, wiped at his face, unbuttoned his shirt and stuck his swollen hand inside. "I vill be going now," he stated, squaring his shoulders and holding his head high.

"You," he said pointing at Deegan. "You vill be seeing me again. You can count on dat. Ven my hand iz healed, I vill find you again."

384

Fenzel turned and strode off to where his horse was tied in the darkness.

All of the men stood silently waiting for Joe Burdette to speak.

Burdette stood with his arms crossed on his chest, looking at Deegan and then Mc-Call. "You all go back to sleep," he ordered. "There's cattle to work tomorrow, so you'd best get rest when you can. Creed, come over so I can talk to you."

McCall put a hand on Deegan's shoulder. "Well, Charlie, you sure keep things in my life interesting. I'll go see what Burdette's got to say about all this."

War Wagon's cackle startled Deegan. "By jingee, I's sure ya was gonna kill him with that pot, Charlie. I saw it all from up in the wagon. Why didn't ya tell 'em about his knife?"

"Doesn't matter now."

"Where'd ya put it?"

Deegan just shook his head. "Go back to sleep."

McCall returned into the circle of light, got a cup, filled it from the pot over the fire and walked to where Deegan was leaning on the tailgate table. "Well, Charlie . . ."

"It's a good thing I don't have much to pack," Deegan interrupted.

"Why?"

"Didn't Burdette fire me?"

"No, but it took a lot of talking on my part."

CHAPTER FORTY-FOUR

The cowboys lined up for breakfast all glanced at Charlie Deegan as he scooped eggs and bacon unto their plates. "Help yourself to the biscuits and honey," he instructed.

Creed McCall was the last man in line. "I had another talk with Burdette before he rode out this morning," he said as Deegan slid the food onto his plate. "He rides out first thing every morning to scout the trail, check for water and find a campsite for the night. We're gonna send someone into town with Fenzel's bedroll and other gear. We figure one of the doctors in town'll know where he is or where he's been. If they can't find him, they'll just leave it at the sheriff's office." McCall sprinkled salt on his eggs, wiped the fork on his shirtsleeve and started to eat. "You did a helluva job on Fenzel last night."

"I can only be pushed so far. He shouldn't

a put his hand on me. You want coffee?"

McCall nodded as he chewed on a slice of bacon.

Deegan filled a metal mug with steaming coffee and set it in front of him.

"War Wagon tells me Fenzel had a knife."

"Yeah."

"Why didn't you say anything last night?"

"It was over, so it didn't make any difference."

"He coulda killed you with that knife."

"Yeah."

"War Wagon said you coulda killed him with that pot."

"That old fool talks too damned much."

McCall sipped his coffee and smiled. "Helluva way for a Prussian army officer to die; having his head smashed in by a Dutch oven."

"Being stuck with a knife ain't much better. You're still dead."

"Well, we're short one man now so we've come up with a little test to see if you qualify to be a cowboy," McCall said, sliding his empty mug in across the tailgate table.

Deegan poured him more coffee. "What's the test?"

"We got a bell mare named Booger Red that leads the remuda on these drives. I convinced Burdette before he left this morning that if you can ride Booger Red, he should let you try your hand at being a cowboy."

"You wouldn't lie to me again, would you?"

"What do you mean, lie to you *again*?"

"You know damned good and well that story about Burdette's girlfriend's wooden leg was a lie! Admit it! It was a lie!"

McCall sipped his coffee, smiled and slid his plate forward. "Can I have some more eggs?"

"Sure," Deegan answered and scooped eggs onto the proffered plate. "Now about your lying to me . . ."

"Good eggs," McCall said, around a mouthful. "We don't get these very often once we hit the trail. Only when we get close to a town." He seemed to relish what he was chewing. "Got a chicken coop at the ranch so we've always got fresh eggs. Ol' War Wagon can sure make some good scrambled eggs!"

"Damnit, get on with what you were telling me!"

"Oh, yeah, if you can ride Booger Red for a full minute, you'll be starting out as a night rider and doing some drag riding."

"Drag riding?"

"Riding drag. All new men start out riding drag. That's a dirty, dusty job, riding at the back of the herd keeping the cattle moving. Also watching out for animals that stray off or fall behind. You'll appreciate that bandanna of yours when you can pull it up over your nose to keep out most of the dust. You'll keep driving the hoodlum wagon and helping War Wagon, but you'll be learning the cattle business from the bottom up or I should say, from the back forward."

"It's a start, I guess. Better'n being fired . . ."

McCall nodded and took a sip of coffee. "A couple of the boys'll get mounted up and have their ropes ready just in case Booger gets away from you. Ordinarily, at the ranch, we'd do this in the breaking corral, but out here we'll make do with a couple of chase and pickup men. You help War Wagon git cleaned up and packed. We'll get Booger Red and bring her in for your ride when the time is right."

Deegan grinned and began to clean off the table. *This doesn't sound all that bad. Hell, riding a horse for a minute shouldn't be too hard. Then again, there's something he ain't telling me. It just sounds too easy.*

Reno Hartman, Al Penny and Willie Red Horse walked their horses around the edge of the campsite and, one by one, shook loops into their ropes. They looked knowingly at each other as they waited for Palmer to bring in the big mare.

War Wagon leaned against the chuck box, wiping his glasses on his apron, his stubby pipe bobbing in his mouth as he muttered to himself.

McCall joined him, dumping a saddle and blanket by their feet. He dropped a roll of leather on top of the saddle. "Here's a spare pair of chaps been in the hoodlum wagon for a while. He'll need them eventually."

"You boys ain't being very nice to that new man," War Wagon said, sliding his glasses back on his nose and peering over them at McCall. He cackled and gave a great, toothless grin as he slid his pipe in a vest pocket and brought out a plug of tobacco. He wiped the plug on a shirtsleeve and offered it to McCall.

McCall rolled his eyes and shook his head. "War Wagon, I'd be a complete fool to eat anything came out of one of your pockets. It's bad enough I have to eat your damned cooking."

War Wagon shrugged, put the plug into his mouth and proceeded to wiggle off a chunk. "I always see ya coming back for seconds."

"It's one hell of a hard choice between your cooking and starvation," McCall retorted. "So I find myself taking the lesser of the two evils. And there's times I find it a damned tough decision."

War wagon snorted and spit a stream of brown juice, narrowly missing McCall's boots.

Deegan returned from the creek with a large pan full of freshly washed dishes and set them on the table. "Dishes're done, boss."

"This is your saddle now," McCall said, pointing to the saddle by his feet. "It was my spare. It's a good saddle and I'll figure out what you owe me for it later. Those chaps don't belong to anybody, so now they're yours too."

Palmer came walking from the rope horse corrals leading a large bay mare with a heavy horsehair lead rope attached to a hackamore.

"She's a good-looking horse, ain't she?" McCall asked, smiling at Deegan.

Deegan looked at him through narrowed eyes. *You ain't telling me something, Creed.*

"Git her out a ways from my kitchen so she don't git dirt in it," War Wagon stated to McCall, who glared at him. War Wagon shrugged, turned and disappeared around the end of the wagon, cackling softly to himself.

"I told the boys you knew how to saddle a horse, Charlie, so you best go out there and put this rig on her," McCall instructed. "You won't need those chaps for a while."

Deegan looked at the three cowboys slowly circling the edge of the camp and then at the big bay mare standing patiently, her tail switching at flies. *She looks gentle enough. I wonder why I gotta ride this particular horse. There's something they ain't telling me about her. Damn you, Creed!* "Here goes," he said as he lifted the saddle and blanket and walked out to the waiting horse. He could feel his heart begin to beat faster as he tossed the blanket up onto the big mare and adjusted it. "What about a bridle?"

"She's never been broken to a bit," McCall answered. "She works just fine with a hackamore. Go ahead and saddle her up. Cinch it tight, now. Wouldn't want you to roll off to the side because of a loose saddle."

Booger Red turned her head and looked at the blanket when Deegan laid it on her back, then she looked straight ahead at some of the cowboys. He swung the saddle up into place, did the cinch work and stepped back. He thought he sensed the mare beginning to tighten up and he saw the muscles along her back roll and tremble. *That ain't a good sign.*

"Just climb aboard and I'll hand you the lead rope," McCall directed. "She's yours then. All you gotta do is stay on for a minute. Take her for a short run around the camp, but stay away from War Wagon's area. We all know how he can be about dust."

Deegan hesitated, then reached up and grabbed the saddle horn. "How many times this horse been ridden?"

"The kids at the ranch ride her all the time," McCall said. "Hell, I've seen as many as four kids on her at once. Just get on up there and let's get this over with."

Deegan looked from McCall to Booger Red. "This ain't gonna be as simple as it seems, is it?"

McCall shrugged. "It shouldn't be any big problem for a man with all your horse experience to race her for a few runs around the camp."

Deegan turned the stirrup, put his boot in it, swung up and settled himself into the saddle. "If she's such a gentle horse, how come those boys are hanging open loops?" he asked, pointing a thumb at the nearby riders. *You sumbitch, Creed, you lied to me again, I know it,* he thought, glaring at Mc-Call.

McCall flipped the rope up to Deegan and retreated. "Keep a tight rein on her, Charlie."

Deegan nodded, pulled the rope tight and gripped it so hard his hand hurt.

The big bay mare turned her head and studied the man on her back with one eye. She gently blew her breath out making her lips ripple.

Deegan tensed up when he felt her back muscles quiver.

CHAPTER FORTY-FIVE

Booger Red rolled her head, looked back at the rider again and slowly lowered her head down as if looking at her front feet. Her head shot up, she snorted and began to spin in a tight circle.

Deegan leaned out away from the spin, found his balance and dug his knees into the sides of the horse hoping and praying he could stay on for the ride. She stopped abruptly and he was pitched straight up in the saddle.

"You got her now!" McCall shouted.

Booger Red's shoulder muscles trembled, but she didn't move.

Deegan looked questioningly at the other men. "Is she done . . . ?"

Without warning, the mare's hind legs kicked straight up and she rolled hard to the right.

Deegan tried to bring himself into balance, but the mare's hind feet hit the dirt and she rolled her shoulders hard to the left. He let out a holler and felt himself being catapulted over the mare's head. He looked up, saw his toes pointing into the sky, and knew he was in for a hard landing. His brief flight ended when he reached the end of the rope wrapped tightly around his wrist and slammed hard into the ground. A cloud of dust settled over Deegan and stars danced before his blinking eyes as he fought for breath.

McCall stood over him clucking his tongue like a mother hen. "You can't learn the cowboy business on your back, Charlie. You best get back up there and give it another try. Here, lemme give you a hand."

"Get away from me!" Deegan gasped, still struggling for air and trying to decide if he was maddest at the mare, McCall or himself. He decided he was damned mad at all three.

"You was way short a yer minute," War Wagon cackled from the distance.

Deegan eventually managed to get to his feet, shaking his head and rubbing his aching back. "I thought you said kids ride that damned horse," he sputtered.

"That's the truth," McCall assured him. "The kids at the ranch play on and around her all the time. But, there's never been a man stayed on her. She's a hell of a fine bell mare. The *remuda* follows and stays with her. She just doesn't like men."

"Not on her back anyway," Palmer added and laughed.

The circling cowboys joined in the laugh and War Wagon cackled.

Deegan picked up his hat, slapped it against his leg and pulled it down on his head.

"Don't wrap that rope around your wrist this time," McCall cautioned. "You can break an arm that way."

Deegan nodded, flexed his fingers and looked down at the red, raw, stinging burn mark on his wrist. "Now you tell me," he muttered as he looked at the big horse standing off a short distance.

Booger Red watched Deegan limp back to her, grab the lead rope, guide his boot into the stirrup, take a deep breath and swing back into the saddle.

The big mare leaped straight up with all four of her feet leaving the ground. She landed and did four quick crow-hops. When her front feet hit the ground on the last hop, her back legs kicked hard to the right, hit the ground and immediately kicked hard to the left.

Deegan found himself flying through the

air again. He landed hard on his shoulder, rolled forward and lay in the settling dust, coughing and watching stars dance across his eyes. He slowly sat up, spitting and blowing dirt from his nose. He could taste blood in his mouth as he struggled unsteadily to his feet and glared at Booger Red calmly studying him.

"He plowed a bit of dirt with his nose that time," one of the cowboys howled.

"From the way he plows, I think he wants to be a farmer, not a cowboy," another called.

"Looked like a big bird," someone added, grabbing his ribs and letting out a guffaw.

"Kinda ugly flyin' through the air though."

McCall walked up, handed Deegan his hat and put a reassuring hand on his shoulder. "That's enough, Charlie. You'll ride night herd tonight. You gave it your best shot. I think we all agree you got the sand in your craw to be a cowboy."

Deegan shook off McCall's hand and struggled back to the big bay mare.

"You beat me so far, but I ain't giving up yet," Deegan told the horse as he grabbed the rope and struggled back up into the saddle.

Booger Red turned her head, gave Deegan a one-eyed look, put her head down and pulled up a bunch of grass. She chewed slowly as if trying to decide what to do.

"You ain't gonna fool me this time," Deegan mumbled as he prepared for the worst. "I'm on to your damned tricks now. Go ahead and spin, I'm ready."

She threw her front feet high in the air, spun tightly to the left, planted her feet, and ducked tightly back to the right. Deegan fought to get his balance as she brought her front feet up again and twisted back to the left, planted her front feet, kicked her hind feet up and sunfished.

Deegan didn't remember much after that. But later, he sat up sputtering and spitting a long-forgotten taste from his mouth. He continued to spit, trying to get rid of the taste of whiskey.

"Who . . . who . . . who'n the hell gave me whiskey?" he stuttered as he blinked and wiped dirt from his eyes. He tried to blow his nose clear, gingerly touched it, rubbed his mustache and looked at the blood on his fingers.

"It was purely for medicinal purposes," McCall assured him.

Deegan shook his head and continued air spitting.

"You took a pretty good dive that time," McCall said. "Looked like you plowed up a small garden plot with your face when you landed. I told War Wagon to pour some whiskey in your mouth. I'm sorry."

War Wagon pressed a wad of cloth to his forehead. "Hold this where it is," he ordered.

Deegan held the cloth to his head, spat and tried to stop his world from spinning. He struggled to his feet, dry spitting and rubbing the back of his hand across his mouth. His mind flew on the memories the taste of whiskey brought and he tentatively ran his tongue over his front teeth. *At least they're okay.*

"You and Booger Red ain't gonna try each other any more today," McCall stated. "You'll be riding nighthawk tonight. Now go get cleaned up and help War Wagon. You ain't a full-time cowboy yet."

CHAPTER FORTY-SIX

The sun was going down behind the low hills when Charlie Deegan saddled up to go out for his first swing of night herding. He had scabs on his nose and forehead, one eye was swollen and he had aches in places that hadn't ached since his hard drinking and fighting days.

McCall approached him as he was about to pull himself up into the saddle. "You look like hell, Charlie."

"I've felt worse, I think. I've got a question for you."

"Ask."

Deegan looked around to see if anyone was close enough to overhear him. "What am I supposed to do out there with the herd tonight?"

McCall chuckled. "You really don't know about any of this, do you?"

Deegan shook his head. "I guess everyone figured I knew what to do, so I was gonna go out there and ask the man about it. Hell, that'd really brand me as a greenhorn, wouldn't it?"

McCall grew serious. "Most of the cattle will be laying down. That's one of the reasons we keep them moving all day at the beginning of a drive. They're tired at night and not so likely to be up and restless. There'll be four of you on the first four-hour shift. All the night riders do is ride slowly around the herd in opposite directions. You can talk soft, sing or even hum to them. Gives the herd a certain feeling of security, I guess, and they'll lay quiet. Watch for anything that might spook them and remember it's a bad sign if they start snorting. If you hear horns clicking, it means they're up and milling around. That ain't good either. You'll catch on fast enough. Nighthawk ain't all that hard, just boring. Most of the time. But like I said, keep a sharp eye out for anything unusual."

"I can do that."

"I figured you could. Here." McCall stretched out his hand holding a lone spur.

"What's this for?"

"You'll need something more'n a boot heel to get that horse moving fast in case of a stampede."

Deegan held the single spur out at arm's

length and looked at it questioningly. "How in the hell's this thing gonna help me?"

"I learned a long time ago, from Sam Spooner, if you kick that spur into one side of your horse the other side'll go with it," McCall said, with a laugh. "When I figure you're a real cowboy, I'll buy you a damned fine pair of silver spurs."

Deegan sat on the ground, flipped up a leg of his chaps, pulled on the solitary spur and buckled it tight. He stood up, wiggled his foot, listened to the ring of the jingle bobs and smiled.

"I want to thank you, Creed." Deegan stuck out his hand. "You've done a lot for me and I owe you. I won't forget any of this."

McCall shook his hand. "Now get out there and show Burdette what you can do. I'll see you in the morning."

Deegan swung up into the saddle, touched his fingers to the brim of his hat and slowly rode out of camp. He called back, "I don't want War Wagon to get after me for raising dust."

Charlie Deegan reined his horse on a low hill overlooking the herd laying quietly in the moonlit meadow. He could see the other three riders moving slowly around the cattle. He swung his leg up around his saddle horn and admired his lone spur. He slowly turned the rowel with a fingertip and tapped the jingle bobs to hear them ring softly. He looked up at the sky feeling proud of himself and rather grateful. "I owe You a lot, too," he said, softly. "And like I told McCall, I don't forget. Thank You. Thank You."

He paused and finger spun the rowel of his spur again. "But, I'll tell You again, and I said it before, I'm never gonna be a preacher man."

Charlie Deegan was awakened by a tap on the bottom of his boot. He raised his hat from his face to see War Wagon standing over him.

"Get up, Charlie, sun's a cracking on the horizon an' there's work to be done."

When Deegan grunted, War Wagon shuffled off toward the fire glowing by the chuck wagon.

Damn, I just got to sleep, Deegan thought as he sat up, jammed his hat down on his head and kicked free of his bedroll. He pulled his boots on, stood, scratched himself in several places, slowly stretched and shivered in the cool morning air. *None of the aches have gone away, that's for damned sure.*

War Wagon looked up from the biscuit dough he was kneading to see Deegan standing across the tailgate table, working a toothbrush up and down across his teeth.

"Charlie, what'n the hell're ya doin'?"

"What in the hell does it look like I'm doing? I'm brushing my teeth," Deegan stated around the toothbrush.

"What'n the hell're ya doin' that fer?"

"So I won't have to carry my teeth around in a vest pocket someday like you do."

War Wagon snorted and shook a flour-covered finger at Deegan. "There's work to be done."

"You said that when you woke me up. What do you want me to do?"

"Start cutting bacon off that slab and spread it in the big pan on the grate over the fire."

Deegan spit several times before rapping the toothbrush on the bottom of the tailgate table and pushing it down into a vest pocket. "How thick a cut?"

"Best cut it heavy. After they eat it with breakfast the boys are gonna take some with a couple of biscuits in their greasy sacks for noon eats. Once they git the herd moving, they don't stop to eat until we set up camp for the night. That'll go on for the first couple of weeks or until the herd is used to traveling together. There's some natural leaders, and they'll move up to the front for the rest of the drive. Kinda like Booger Red is with the horse *remuda*. When Burdette thinks the herd is traveling okay, we'll be stopping from time to time to make hot lunch for the boys."

Deegan found a large knife and began to cut at the bacon. Satisfied, he dropped a pile of pieces in the pan and spread them with a wooden fork as they began to instantly sizzle, snap and smoke.

"Morning, Charlie."

Deegan glanced up to see Joe Burdette sipping from a steaming mug. "Morning, Mister Burdette."

"How's your first night with the herd?"

"The sleep part was damned short, but I ain't complaining, mind you."

"You'll get used to it."

War Wagon cupped his hands around his mouth. "Bacon's in the pan, coffee's in the pot," he shouted. "Come and git it, boys, git it while it's hot."

Several of the other wranglers, steaming cups in hand, joined Burdette.

"Morning, Charlie," McCall greeted. "Looks like you made it through your first night okay. War Wagon sure puts you to work early. Didn't get much sleep, huh?"

Deegan shook his head, yawned and pushed the wooden fork at the noisy meat in the pan.

War Wagon wedged a large Dutch oven into the side of the fire and scooped a shovel full of hot coals around and onto the top of it. "They be ready in a few minutes, boys," he announced, wiping his hands on his apron. "Ya better stand around close an' git ready to catch 'em when I take the lid off the oven. They gonna be so light, they'll just float up into the air an' if ya don't catch 'em the birds'll git 'em." He cackled at his humor as he looked around the circle of men. "I can always tell the first day on a drive because I never have to call breakfast. Ya'll want eggs again?" he asked, holding up a handful. "Eggs don't last long on the trail, but we always got 'em when we start out."

The men clamored their approval and War Wagon began cracking eggs into a large crockery bowl and throwing the shells into the fire. "Scrambled with the works, boys," he said, pointing at a pile of chopped onions and peppers. "With the works!"

"Reb, you and Clive eat, then go out and send two of the nighthawks in," Burdette ordered. "Creed, you rotate the boys out ready to start pushing the herd. War Wagon,

I'll eat, git saddled up and be back in a few minutes for my traveling food."

The men finished eating, threw their bedrolls into the hoodlum wagon, tied their greasy cotton sacks of food onto their saddles, mounted up and headed out to start moving the herd north.

"When we finish gitting cleaned up and packed, Little Suzie, we'll be driving the wagons until we pass the herd and git to the place Burdette picks for tonight's camp," War Wagon said as he returned items to their assigned spots in the chuck box. "Then we'll start putting together our night meal."

"We've got to have an early understanding here, War Wagon, about something I thought we'd ironed out last night," Deegan said, softly. "I'll work for you and I'll work with you because this is the way I get to learn the cattle business. You can call me the cheap help, you can call me a stupid sumbitch, you can call me Charlie, but if you call me Little Suzie one more time . . ." He made a fist and rapped his knuckles on the tailgate table. "Just don't call me that anymore, understand?"

War Wagon took his glasses from his nose, wiped them on his flour-sack apron, slid them back into place, rubbed his chin and slowly turned to face Deegan. He squinted over the tops of his glasses and the corners of his mouth turned up into a large toothless grin. "Charlie it is," he said. "Hell, there's no need to git sore because I was just pushin' to see how far I could go with ya. So far, yer a damned good worker. C'mon, let's you and me finish getting loaded, harness up them mules and start rolling . . . , Charlie."

Once Deegan and War Wagon came to an understanding, things were good as the herd moved steadily north. Each day Deegan helped with the cooking, feeding and cleanup, hooked the mules up to the hoodlum wagon and pulled it in behind the chuck wagon driven by War Wagon. The two wagons would drive off to the upwind side of the herd, eventually pass the moving cattle, find the spot Burdette had picked for the night camp, set up and prepare for supper. If there was time, Deegan would saddle a horse and ride back to help with the dusty job of riding drag. It gave him personal satisfaction as he learned to work with and understand cattle.

After supper cleanup, he'd pull the first four hours of night herding and soon became adept at catching short naps on the seat of the wagon as it rolled slowly across the countryside.

On the fifth day of the drive, McCall approached Deegan as he untied one of the spare horses from the rope line tied between trees at the edge of the camp. He held out a coiled riata. "Here, take this, Charlie, I'm gonna show you how to throw a rope so you can start catching your own horses. Burdette told me to help you pick four out of the *remuda* to be your permanent string so you won't have to be taking different horses from the spares. It's best for a man to know what he can expect from his horses. You partial to any of those you been riding?"

"I been riding the same two every time because they worked good for me."

"Makes it easy to pick out the first two. One more thing, Charlie, Burdette likes the way you work, so keep it up. I don't think you'll be working for War Wagon all that much longer."

A week later Burdette rode up to Deegan as he finished saddling for the first shift of the night. "Well, Charlie, looks to me like you picked some decent horseflesh for your personal string."

Deegan patted the neck of the horse he had saddled. "I picked the two that I liked and had some good advice from McCall on the other pair."

"I've been watching you on drag and night

411

herd and you do good work. You handle a horse well and seem to picking up some cow sense. You even throw a fairly good rope. So, if you want it, I'm making you a full-time wrangler."

"You're damned right I want it, Mister Burdette!" Deegan answered, a grin breaking up under his mustache. He thrust out his hand. "Thank, you, sir!"

Burdette shook Deegan's hand. "All right, you got the job. Sam'll drive the hoodlum wagon and help with the chuck chores like he was doing before you were hired. He's been working cattle for a long time and doesn't sit a horse all that good anymore. He and War Wagon understand each other and get along good. They make quite a pair, don't they? Sam says pay's the same and he'd rather do that anyway. We'll keep greasy sacking the noon meal for a while and you can help with the big meal at supper, if you're needed."

"I can do that, Mister Burdette!" Deegan couldn't stop grinning.

"Now that you're a regular wrangler, Charlie, I prefer to be called Joe."

Deegan pumped Burdette's hand again. "Joe, it is . . . , Joe."

Both men laughed.

CHAPTER FORTY-SEVEN

Charlie Deegan quickly fell into the routines of the cattle drive. Being the new man he still rode nighthawk and drag most of the time. Midway through the third week he pulled down his bandanna, trotted up to the front of the herd and pulled his horse in next to McCall's.

"You lost, Charlie?"

Deegan shook his head, wiped a sleeve across his mouth, spit and smiled. "Creed, I'd like you and a couple of the others to gimme a little help with something after we eat supper tonight."

"Doing what?"

"I'm gonna take another shot at Booger Red."

"You ask Burdette about that?"

Deegan shook his head. "Not yet."

"I don't think he wants anybody messing with his bell mare," McCall stated. "Besides, she can't be *rode* and you can be *throwed*."

413

McCall chuckled at his own humor. "The fact you been riding drag and managed to stay in the saddle don't necessarily make you a bronc buster. That big horse throwed a lotta good cowboys and you know she ain't never been rode for a full minute."

"That might change tonight," Deegan said, as he pulled up his bandanna and reined his horse away from McCall. "I'll talk to Burdette at camp."

McCall turned to watch him ride away. "I'll give you credit for guts," he called to the rider galloping toward the rear of the herd. "Not a lotta brains, but a lotta guts."

The men finished eating and those still in camp stood around making small talk and glancing at Burdette as he sat on the tongue of the hoodlum wagon making notes in his logbook. The right decision by him could add a little excitement to the camp tonight. The word had spread quickly about Deegan's desire to try to ride the big mare again and they all knew it was now up to Burdette's approval.

Burdette put his pencil stub into a vest pocket, snapped the little book shut and slid it into a shirt pocket. He looked up at the men as if wondering why they were pretending not to be paying attention to him. He stood, stretched, casually walked to the chuck wagon, got an enamel cup and filled it with steaming coffee. He faced away from the men and thought, *I wonder how long it'll be before one of them talks. Patience is something these boys won't have at a time like this. Especially now that they know there might be a little action to break up the monotony of night camp.*

"Well, Mister Burdette, do I get another chance?" Deegan asked, nervously twisting a coiled rope between his hands. "Joe, I mean."

Burdette turned. "What'll it prove, Charlie?"

Deegan thought carefully for the correct answer.

"I ain't really sure, but it's something I gotta do. Mostly for myself, I guess."

"Booger Red's sure as hell gonna throw you again," Burdette stated. "Better bronc stompers than you've tried her and spent time in the air."

Deegan looked down at the rope in his hands. "I ain't saying I'm gonna ride that big mare for a full minute." He looked up at Burdette and squared his shoulders. "It's a matter of proving to myself I ain't afraid to try her again. The time I'll spend on her ain't that important. It's the fact I'm getting back on."

"I can understand, Charlie. I'll let you try again, but if you get throwed and break a leg or an arm or maybe your damned fool neck, I'm telling the boys to leave you where you land and you can try to figure out if it was worth it. Now if you still think you gotta do this, then go ahead. I ain't sayin' another damned word."

Deegan shook a loop into his rope. "Thanks, Joe. I'll go fetch Booger Red right now."

Deegan soon returned to camp followed almost lazily by the big bell mare. The rope hung loosely around her neck and she turned her head from time to time to look at the men watching her entrance.

"Now wait just a damned minute!" War Wagon shouted, waving his hands over his head as he ran toward Deegan and the big mare. "You ain't gonna raise dust here where I do the cooking!"

Burdette hooked a thumb away from the wagons. "Let's go out a ways, boys."

"Calm ain't she?" McCall commented, frowning at the big mare. "Here, I'll hold the rope while you get her saddled."

Deegan tightened the latigo, dropped the stirrup into place and pulled on the horn to see if the saddle was tight. He put a hacka-more over the horse's nose, pulled the bands up over her ears, buckled the strap under her jaw and let the heavy horsehair reins hang to the ground.

Booger Red turned her head and looked the man standing beside her up and down as he stepped back and checked his work.

I wonder what the hell she's thinking? Deegan asked himself nervously as he slid the rope from around her neck.

All of the men in the camp watched Deegan and the big mare prepare to battle each other again. Willie Red Horse and Clive Palmer were mounted, holding their ropes ready. Al Penny and Reb Quarles whispered to each other and shook hands to seal their bet.

"How long you gonna ride her, Charlie?" McCall asked.

Deegan pulled his hat down tight and gathered his reins. "Until I feel like getting off," he answered, trying to show an air of self-assurance.

Everyone laughed.

"That mean you're gonna land on your feet?" Palmer asked.

"You guessed right, Clive. Land on my feet . . . not my face. That means I finished the ride on my terms, not hers." He put a foot in the stirrup, squared his shoulders, took a deep breath, grabbed the horn and swung up into the saddle.

Booger Red turned her head, looked at the man and slowly lowered her mouth to a tuft of grass. She pulled the grass free, chewed it, stepped forward and ripped up another mouthful.

"I know what you're gonna try," Deegan told the big horse as he tensed and waited.

"You got her so cowed by your new cowboy abilities," Penny yelled, "that she ain't gonna buck. She's just gonna graze!"

The men in the camp hooted.

Booger Red took another step and another mouthful of grass.

"Well, he might git that full minute ride real easy," War Wagon said, with a cackle, to Burdette, who was waiting for something to happen.

"C'mon, damnit!" Deegan shouted, dug in his lone spur and yanked on the reins.

The big horse's head shot up and swung back, teeth bared and snapping toward the man in the saddle.

Startled, Deegan jerked back from the bared teeth and Booger Red instantly threw her hind legs high in the air and swung them to the left. The rider was totally off balance and he toppled heavily from the right side of his saddle, landing on his back in a small cloud of dust.

Booger Red ran off, hind legs kicking high in the air and whinnying.

To Deegan it sounded like mocking laughter.

The men began to laugh and cheer as the downed man sat up with a sheepish look on his face. Silently he retrieved his hat and pulled it down tightly.

". . . don't think that was a full minute."

". . . didn't exactly land on his feet."

". . . gimme my money!"

". . . damned mean horse, ain't she?"

"You want the boys to get your saddle back, Charlie?" Burdette called.

Deegan brushed himself off and scowled at each of them in turn. "Just bring the damned horse back here!" he shouted at the mounted riders following the runaway. "I ain't done yet, not by a long ways!"

Clive Palmer returned, leading Booger Red. She was fighting the rope around her neck and dancing.

Deegan walked slowly out to meet them. *She ain't gonna start slow this time.*

"You sure you wanna do this again?" McCall asked as he grabbed Palmer's rope and managed to get a grip on the hackamore.

Booger Red reared up and pawed at McCall, who jumped aside and put all his weight on the hackamore, pulling her off

419

balance. He threw his arm over the horse's neck, grabbed an ear and bit down on it hard! The horse immediately stood still, trembling. McCall shouted something indiscernible to Deegan.

"He wants you to get back on her," Burdette shouted. "Before he bites her ear off. Damnit, McCall, don't you go damaging my bell mare!"

Deegan grabbed the dangling reins, shoved a foot in the stirrup, swung himself back up onto the saddle and locked a grip with both hands onto the saddle horn.

McCall spit out the horse's ear and threw himself clear of the animal.

Booger Red immediately sunfished, reared, kicked and swung around to try to bite Deegan.

Deegan pulled one hand free of the horn, slapped the horse's nose, shouted something at her and grabbed back onto the horn. He flopped around in the saddle like a rag doll, but, to everyone's amazement, kept his seat.

He threw his hands in the air, kicked free of the stirrups and, laughing, leaped from the back of the bucking animal. He landed hard on his feet and staggered forward, almost falling, but butterflying his arms to regain his balance and running to a stop. Laughing, he pulled off his hat, threw it into the air and shouted, "Yahooooo, I did it! Damn it, I did it!"

The cowboys began to clap and cheer the grinning Deegan.

Booger Red ran off toward the grazing *remuda,* hind legs kicking high and whinnying.

McCall handed Deegan his hat and stuck out his hand. "Well, Charlie, you did it your way, like you said you would. Nice going, my friend, nice going!"

Deegan pumped McCall's hand and grinned at him like a fool. "Damn, that felt good!"

Palmer rode up and reached down to clap Deegan on the shoulder. "I'll go get your saddle."

"Hold on there, Clive. If you don't mind, I'll ride out behind you and get my own damned saddle. I gotta get back here and mount up because I'm riding the first shift of nighthawk."

Palmer kicked a foot free of a stirrup for Deegan and hung down an arm for him to grab and pull himself up behind the saddle.

"Nice riding, Charlie!" Burdette shouted. "I guess you showed us that you can handle the work, . . . cowboy!"

Deegan touched his fingertips to the brim of his hat and his grin grew wider. "Thanks,

Joe! Those're probably the best words I ever heard! Now, excuse me, I got work to do. We all got work to do. There's cattle to move and it's a damned long way to Dakota Territory."

ABOUT THE AUTHOR

Mike Thompson is a prize-winning author and photographer. He retired from the government where he tested explosives and was curator of a military museum. He was a medic in Vietnam (1966–1967), with a military career spanning forty-two years (1960–2002), including Air Force, Army, National Guard and Reserves. Mike, his wife, Ruthie, and cats, Daisy and Molly, live on the Laughing Horse Ranch, Land and Cattle Company, San Angelo, Texas. He has owned several businesses, raised horses, and worked as an actor, carpenter, bartender, oil landman, and an explosives project engineer and done many other things while trying to decide what he's going to be if he grows up. Today he writes and collects western art, books and cowboy gear.

The employees of Thorndike Press hope you have enjoyed this Large Print book. All our Thorndike, Wheeler, and Kennebec Large Print titles are designed for easy reading, and all our books are made to last. Other Thorndike Press Large Print books are available at your library, through selected bookstores, or directly from us.

For information about titles, please call:
  (800) 223-1244

or visit our Web site at:
  http://gale.cengage.com/thorndike

To share your comments, please write:
  Publisher
  Thorndike Press
  10 Water St., Suite 310
  Waterville, ME 04901